Stinky Tofu

A Comedic Novel

ROSS NODELL

Published by: Swamp Soup Corp.
111 W. 67th Street, Suite 42E
New York, NY 10023

First paperback edition January 2019

Book Cover Art designed by Kelly Pang

Published in conjunction with CreateSpace and KDP

Manufactured in the United States of America

ISBN 978-0-9600043-1-7 (paperback)
ISBN 978-0-9600043-0-0 (ebook)

DEDICATION

I dedicate this book to my live-in in-law oppressed brethren. May you all find solace in the possibility (albeit a longshot) that one day you'll live under your own roof in quiet solitude. Unfortunately for me, membership in that illusive club is pure fantasy.

AUTHOR DISCLAIMER

While this is a novel, it is *based on a true story.* The locales where the action takes place are real, and most of the events actually happened to one degree or another—and may or may not have been altered for dramatic or comedic effect. Of course, names have been changed to protect the innocent...the idiots...and the author.

PROLOGUE

I was stumbling through my dark kitchen at 2 AM, in search of a snack, when my forearm came into contact with metal, followed by a loud *CRASH-SPLASH!* I opened the fridge for some light and exclaimed in horror, "Oh my freakin' God!" I knew I'd knocked over my Taiwanese wife's pot of "Swamp Soup" that had been brewing for over a week—but what I wasn't prepared for were the ingredients, I was just now noticing, splayed across the floor. I swear some of them were either crawling or vibrating. Others were hues I cannot describe; except to say they were something outside of the color spectrum. If my live-in in-laws were to write a Chinese cookbook, it could be called *50 Shades of Gravy*.

"Damn," I shook my head. "I'm gonna need a hazmat suit to clean this up." I began reflecting on how I got myself into this ludicrous situation...

HELLO!

My name is Samuel Lowe; shortened through several Jewish generations from Lowenstein. My friends call me Sam. I've been married for over 30 years to a woman from Taiwan. During that time, I discovered, with no choice in the matter, that I was also married to her large Chinese family—five sisters, one brother, and the hub of the clan, a dominant and strong-willed mother. The father met a most unfortunate demise in a Chinese fireworks factory. But that story later.

While there are similarities between people of the Jewish faith and the Asian community, these are grossly outweighed by the differences—especially when it comes to food, customs and daily life. After more than a quarter century living between both cultures, I felt the need for therapy. A shrink would've probably been the smart move, but I decided on scribble therapy and penned my story instead...warts and all.

SECTION ONE
The Eligible Bachelor

1. Catch and Release

Life often throws you a curve. Sometimes it devastates; but on rare occasions it opens a window offering opportunities you never could've envisioned.

In 1987 I was single, 26, and living in Chicago. I had a graduate business degree from U. of Chicago and was working in the corporate finance department of First Chicago, a large money center bank. First in my group to arrive in the morning; last one to leave. No brown nosing, if that's what you were thinking; it's just me. With my heavy workload the stress level was high, but the salary and annual bonus made up for it, somewhat. I had a moderately comfortable lifestyle that included a cozy two-bedroom condo in Lincoln Park close to the affluent Gold Coast.

Easy walking distance to the famous Second City comedy club, an elevated train to work and my favorite restaurant, The Weiner Circle on Clark Street, a tiny nothing shack where I'd pop in periodically for a mouthwatering Chicago hot dog or Italian beef sandwich. This type of cheap gastronomic heaven is ubiquitous throughout The Windy City, making it probably the artery-clogging capital of the U.S.

At first, I used public transportation to get around; fine for my daily commute, but not the best conveyance to assist me in the competitive dating circuit. First impressions can make or break at the onset of a relationship. I desperately needed a car; and it had to be something snazzy to elevate my status as a desirable bachelor. After visiting the local auto dealers, I was convinced that something new, cool and speedy was also going to put a fast drain on my bank account, already heavily burdened by my addition of a sizeable monthly mortgage payment.

I turned to the *Chicago Tribune* classifieds for a hot deal and spotted a “slightly used” Nissan 280 Z Turbo 2-door convertible. The header for the ad proclaimed: “DIVORCE SALE”.

I called the number and a man answered: The beleaguered ex-husband, eager to provide me all the details. The feuding couple occupied a townhouse in Wicker Park, just a short train ride from my office.

"The car is kept in our garage and is triple mint," he swore.

The following afternoon I left work early with my checkbook in tow, just in case the car was exactly as described. I didn't want to take the chance of losing it to some other Johnny-on-the-spot.

The house was a beautiful old limestone Victorian complete with a carved gable overhang and decorative hand cut keystones above each window.

I walked up the severely cracked stone steps where a collection of work permits was taped to the door. I noted that both sides of the building were enveloped in rickety, long idle scaffolding, making it evident that the divorcing couple had stalled out in the process of restoring the old mansion.

I rang the bell and waited a couple minutes before hearing the squeaking sound of heavy footsteps descending an old wooden staircase. The door opened, and I found myself face-to-face with a handsome man, possibly in his early thirties, who would've definitely fit the bill of Hollywood actor or male model. Given his good looks and chiseled physique, my first thought: *The new bride caught him cheating and is raking him over the coals for his indiscretions*.

Pleasantries were exchanged, and I followed him down to the garage to see the car. He raised the overhead door then removed a black cloth car cover, explaining, "I bought it to protect the paint job from any dust that might filter into the space."

The car was the latest model Z, painted an exquisite deep metallic blue, only 10,000 miles on the odometer, and was half the price of a new one. A quick test drive around the neighborhood, then I made him a lowball offer which he accepted without hesitation.

He was either extremely desperate, giving me the signed vehicle title certificate for a personal check, or possibly just not too bright. Lucky for him I was a standup guy.

The man had never laid eyes on me before, but apparently, he needed to vent, unloading, along with the car, his life story: "We've been married less than two years. After seeing *Pacific Heights*, starring Matthew Modine and Melanie Griffith, I came up with the bright idea of buying and restoring this dilapidated prewar." He shook his head sadly. "I sweet-talked my *lovely* bride into it. But because of the district's new landmark status, the goddamn renovation is costing us way more than we'd budgeted and will take us twice as long to complete. Daily arguments ensued and life together in the half-finished house has become a nightmare."

If you asked me, I'd bet the shit hit the fan when he unilaterally decided to go out and buy himself a new sports car. As he handed me the keys, the look in his eyes was nothing but bitterness and despair. It felt like I was taking away a toddler's favorite toy.

Tough luck for him and a steal for me! I thought, shaking off the pity, having no doubt this sweet ride would ratchet up my popularity several notches with the babes.

I did my best to mix in a little pleasure with my arduous work schedule. I had dinner out with friends a couple days during the work week, and on weekends we'd meet up at clubs or bars for drinks. When weather cooperated, I'd squeeze in an early Saturday round of golf. Even with the concerted attempts to make time for social activities, my friends still labeled me a workaholic...with good reason. They all knew my breakneck routine and often caught me at the office on Saturday and/or Sunday.

Monday through Friday I woke at 5:00 AM to the smell of a rich dark French roast brewing in my Mr. Coffee machine. A quick shower, two large cups of joe, then I headed out to the East

Bank Club for my morning workout. By 7:30 I was parked at my desk with a third cup of coffee and a vending machine breakfast sandwich digging into whatever work was necessary to keep myself and my group on schedule to meet the current project deadline. This was my Sisyphean ritual and I rarely deviated from the pattern.

At 6' 3", 215 lbs., with a lean athletic body from four years of college wrestling, combined with my regular early morning workouts, I cast an imposing presence in the office. Most of my colleagues were taller than average, and I wondered if perhaps there was a height requirement to work here.

When meeting with clients, a larger build often provided a slight advantage in making that very important first impression. Of course, once you opened your mouth, depending on what came out, that advantage could instantly dissolve.

I've noticed that a lot of larger than average men have made it to powerful positions in the world of high finance. But there are exceptions to every rule, for example, the nation's top finance job, Secretary of the Treasury: Hank Paulson 6' 5" vs. Timothy Geithner 5' 9". It's interesting that both men graduated from Dartmouth. Paulson was an All-American offensive lineman on the Big Green football team, which ties in perfectly with the stereotype. Geithner instead focused his energy on Asian Studies, traveling to Beijing to learn Mandarin. As you'll soon see, I started out like Paulson but gravitated to Geithner.

During the week I operated with a laser-like focus, usually finishing up and back to my apartment by 8:00 PM. A soothing hot shower, throw on something casual, then head out to a restaurant for dinner with friends. Occasionally I'd go out on a date, but nothing long-term ever came of it. Almost all my college buddies had tied the knot; some already had a litter of kids. Without exception, their outlook on life—*Sow your oats as long as you can*—changed the minute they said, "I do". And I became their cause: the lonely single sad man who needed saving.

I'd gone out with quite a few girls during my undergraduate years at the University of Illinois, Urbana-Champaign. For some reason it seemed much easier meeting them at college. Probably because every male and female alike was finally out from under parental rule and hungrily looking to get laid.

The available pool of propitious single males was somewhat vetted by the university admission process. This was one of the best schools in the Midwest. Just being there meant you made the "no lowlifes allowed" cut. In addition to being on a sports team, I also attended the prestigious UIUC College of Business.

Showcasing both muscles and brain, I never had a problem with the ladies. But somehow, once out in the real world, I found myself to be a little shy and uncomfortable approaching and asking out single women. This was true even when I was socializing with friends at one of our neighborhood haunts. I always preferred being introduced. Usually inquiries came through a friend's wife or a relative. Prior to any commitment, I'd request a general bio on the girl and a photo. If I agreed to meet her, it had to be in a fairly relaxed setting such as at a friend's home, a birthday party, a dinner gathering, or with a small group at a local club.

Since moving into my new apartment, nine months earlier, I'd already been introduced in this manner to at least twenty women, making my dating-to-relationship stats 0 for 20. If I was a professional baseball player, I'd have been sent down to the minors!

I had mostly Jewish friends, therefore the setups were primarily with Jewish women. They were all college graduates, and all in their early to mid-twenties (two of my prerequisites). However, I was not particularly looking for a soul mate of the same faith. My parents were both conservative Jews, though ambivalent to the theological side of the movement. They went to temple only twice a year and didn't keep a kosher house which, growing up, was beneficial to my sister and me. We were both more addicted to bacon than a junkie to heroine.

The older I grew the more my interest in religion waned, and I became something of a skeptic. Without scientific proof I could never be sold on an all- powerful, all-knowing super being, based purely on faith. At the same time, I also didn't wholly disbelieve—which I guess classified me agnostic. My parents wanted me to marry within their religion, and being the good son, I wanted nothing more than to please them; so my search for "a nice Jewish girl" continued on and on.

Getting back to my fix-ups, most of them turned out to be real “go-getters”. Translation: "Go get a husband who can provide a luxurious lifestyle." The standard wish list included a mansion in the suburbs, private country club membership, two or more fancy cars, winter vacations in the Caribbean or French Riviera, jewel-studded birthday and/or anniversary gifts...the whole upper-class shtick. The more of these girls I dated, the clearer became the picture of their desperation. Me? I was looking for something else.

Now, I don’t mean to cast aspersions on Jewish women. Many of my buddies are still happily married to them. Side Note (to cover my ass): And most of my Jewish female friends are awesome!

Maybe it was just a string of bad luck? Maybe I wasn't ready for the "till death do us part" pledge? Maybe it was the pressure of eventually having to fulfill the cumbersome requirements of the wish list?

My friends’ wives would call me the day after the date for feedback, and to let me know that the girl was very impressed and interested. But with only a couple exceptions, I just couldn't pull the trigger on a second date.

If you'd ask any of my friends back then to classify me, they'd all say the same thing: “Sam’s a nice guy.” I was always on time, polite and engaging, even when I knew from the start, for whatever reason, that the date would be a one-off. I was often told by my many matchmakers that the girl in question was disappointed when there was no follow-through. Sometimes a date would call me, put me on the spot, forcing me to offer up an excuse as to why I was not available. I had several in my repertoire including "business trip, project deadline, friend in from out of town, sick parent / sister / cousin / aunt / uncle;" or I'd whisper hoarsely into the phone, "I think (*cough-cough*) I'm coming down (*cough-cough*) with something."

Believe me, I didn't enjoy deceiving the girls, but I also didn't have the heart to fire off, point-blank, the blunt truth: "Sorry, but I just can't be your golden ticket to the Jewish-American Dream." For the most part these were all very smart young women who quickly got the message. And lucky for me, I never experienced a repeat of *Fatal Attraction*.

Then there was the time I made the foolish mistake of asking out a girl who lived in my complex. Alice Schneider, without question, was the most attractive of all the girls I'd dated. She also had a very nice demeanor. I took her out a couple times before the inevitable occurred. On the third and last date, we went to a comedy club to see Howie Mandel. Our seats were fantastic, front row, center stage. Howie came out and started his routine. Of course, he was hilarious.

I felt incredibly lucky to be sitting there with such a beautiful, sweet girl who was both intellectually stimulating and well-read. I thought to myself, *This could be The One!* And then…she laughed.

It started out as the high-pitched screeching of a crow and escalated into the braying of a donkey, with a few pig snorts at the end. It was by far the most wicked sounding laugh I'd ever heard. Everyone, including Howie, suddenly froze, then all eyes zeroed in on our table. For the rest of the evening, each time a joke emanated from Mr. Mandel's lips, that obnoxious noise reverberated throughout the room. I made a futile attempt to conceal myself from the irate stares by slumping deeper and deeper into my chair. We were heckled by Mandel all evening. He was somewhat thrown off his game by the odious noise coming from my date. I spent the next excruciating hour and a half rechecking my watch to see when the torture would finally end.

I still vividly remember the first time we met. I could not believe my luck. *How can such an attractive girl still be on the market?* I wondered. She was three years younger than me, had a great job, and came from a very affluent family. What I can't quite remember is, unlike my nature, I must not have cracked any jokes on our first two dates.

I never asked her out again. You're probably thinking, *Not a nice guy*. But if you heard that otherworldly sound, I guarantee you'd run in the opposite direction—arms flailing, screaming in horror.

So now I had to sneak in and out of my building, fingers crossed I wouldn't run into her. The few times I did, Alice didn't say a word; just shot me a scathing glare that communicated her feelings: *Asshole!* If there was a God, her lease would end tomorrow and she'd be moving away to another city or, if I was lucky, downtown Mongolia.

I was also concerned that she was blabbing her story to some of the other building residents. Maybe I was being a bit paranoid, but after I dumped Alice, whenever I passed a woman entering or exiting my condo, I felt the sensation of being scrutinized.

By the way, in case you still think I'm not a nice guy, 30 years later, when she was 55, I visited Alice's Facebook page and found out she never married. I marveled at her current picture; still a looker. I know what you must be thinking: *Just like that* Seinfeld *episode*. Bingo!

So, after Alice, I took a sabbatical from dating. Besides, I couldn't very well risk bringing someone back to my place and running into her. Who knows what emasculating comment she might blurt out? I decided to just delve deeper into my work—if such a thing were possible—to quell my libido, which was firing on all cylinders.

Periodically I traveled out of town to meet a client. It was usually a trip to a large city like New York, LA, Boston or Miami. On occasion, the bank sent me to business seminars to expand my knowledge base by listening to seasoned banking veterans lecture on services offered by my department. The seminars covered alluring topics such as "Divestitures & Corporate Restructuring", "Business Valuation Models", "Dynamic Contracting", "Financial Structure and Ownership Control" and "Investment Risk and the Cost of Capital". Some held my interest; most required a steady stream of coffee to keep me from nodding off. Little did I know that the next one, while by far the most boring, would provide that curveball opportunity—a chance meeting that would change the trajectory of my life.

2. So-called Lunch at the Berghoff

Tuesday, September 8, 1987, I woke up at the usual 5:00 AM, showered, had my double shot of joe and headed to the East Bank Club. I was excited about work that day. At the end of the previous week, the group I headed had just completed a six-month project for a major client. My boss was over-the-top happy with my performance and asked me to meet him noontime at The Berghoff, a famous German restaurant one block from our office. Two years at the bank, working slave hours and successfully handling every project I was given, I was expecting some type of good news: promotion, salary bump, bonus, stock options—maybe even a generous combination of any two.

I walked up the elevated train stairs on Wellington Avenue. The weather was a sunny picture perfect 80 degrees with a light breeze coming off Lake Michigan. The train pulled up right when I made it to the platform; didn't have to break my stride. Twenty-five minutes later I was at the club doing my workout.

For those who exercise on a regular basis, it's common knowledge that some days your workout feels worse than others. There could be many reasons why including: lack of sleep, not enough protein in your diet, stress at home or work, the early onset of a cold, etc. But that day it was fantastic. My weight routine was strong with a new high on bench press. I remained solid through the rest of my muscle training, continuously pushing hard all the way to the end of a final five-mile treadmill run. Fifteen minutes in the sauna, a cool-down shower, and I was ready for work, chomping at the bit to receive my fat reward. I went to my private locker, put on my dress-to-impress black label Hugo Boss business suit and red power tie, then left the club for the 20-minute 8-block walk to my office. *Zip-a-Dee-Do-Dah...plenty of sunshine headin' my way.*

When I arrived at my desk, I found a large envelope and a note left by my boss, Jack Elliott. He'd been the department head of the Corporate Finance Group for almost 10 years. I had great respect for the man. He was very firm and expected a lot from his employees but was always available if you needed guidance on any issue related to your assigned project. I perceived Jack to be a straight shooter with no hidden agendas. Corporate politics was something he seemed intent on avoiding. Instead he focused his efforts on the needs of the department's client base by supporting his staff and burying himself in work. I truly believed that his way was the best way and did my utmost to follow in the path of my fearless mentor.

The note reminded me to meet him at Berghoff's at noon and "do not open" the package until after we talked. I turned it over. It was sealed shut. What could the contents be? A huge bonus check? An all-expense paid vacation to Tahiti? A lifetime supply of Turtle Wax for my 280Z? The anticipation was killing me, but I'd follow Jack's request and wait to be rewarded with the prize inside.

I still had a few items to clean up from my previous project; mostly related to cataloguing miscellaneous files for the department's archives. Storing originals and copies of all work-related materials was standard procedure at the completion of a client project. The bank auditors required a detailed record for any potential litigation or future IRS audit of the bank or the client. In other words, work that is as boring as it is necessary.

I finished up everything by 10:00 AM and decided to scan through today's copy of *The Wall Street Journal*. In my line of work, it was imperative that an employee be up on all the latest financial news prior to a meeting with a superior. At 11:45 I beat a hasty path to The Berghoff.

I arrived five minutes early and checked in with the hostess. To my surprise, she told me that Mr. Elliott had already arrived and directed me to follow her. Jack was sitting by himself at a table in a back corner of the restaurant. When he saw me, he immediately stood up and waived me over. Jack was also a tall man, about my height give or take a half inch. He was in great shape for his age (60), but Jack did have a starter belly that pushed out slightly, forming a narrow ring that perched on the top edge of his black Gucci belt.

As a department head, Jack was often required to wine and dine some of the bank's biggest clients. All those fancy and rich tasting menus with wine pairings catch up to you, especially once you reach middle age. After 50, it gets harder and harder to drag yourself to the gym for the intense workouts needed to burn off those caloric excesses.

Jack had a full head of dark brown hair with not a trace of grey or silver. I was only 26 and already noticing stray white strands popping out in my sideburns. I assumed Jack dyed his hair, but he never said anything, and I'd never ask.

We got along very well, likely because I was devoted to my job and worked my ass off. It may also have been related to our similar backgrounds. We both started with bupkis and worked our way through college and grad school. Like me, he played sports in college (basketball), and was a health nut, exercising (semi-regularly in his case) at the East Bank Club. He lived a short three-mile jaunt from me in a luxury high-rise on the Gold Coast. Sometimes, after work, we'd take the train together. During those brief commutes, we normally discussed work-related topics only. If we did talk about other matters, they were always financial in nature, such as a shake-up article we'd both read in *The Wall Street Journal* or *Forbes*.

In the office, Jack Elliott was always there to support me and my team on anything work related, but he made it a point not to socialize with the help. That was a line I never saw him cross. Our train conversations never lasted long since his stop, Chicago Avenue, was but 12 minutes from the office. My ride continued another 10 minutes to the Diversey Street station.

While I mentioned we had somewhat similar backgrounds, we also had some very distinct differences. Though he was currently single, he'd been married twice before; his last divorce taking place two years earlier. Elliott was an exceedingly private person. I overheard him on the phone with his divorce attorney, otherwise I would've never known. He seemed to live a somewhat lonely existence with little or no social life, whereas I truly loved meeting up with friends. Just like Jack I was devoted to my job, but I separated myself from work the first step out the front door. (Okay, I confess, I often received calls from the bank on the weekends when an emergency popped up. And yes, I dropped everything and rocketed to the office to deal with whatever "cannot possibly wait until Monday!")

Now for the more trivial differences, although many a corporate climber would tell you that these should be classified as "most important". His expansive three-bedroom condo had a panoramic view of the city, Chicago River and Lake Michigan. My tiny two bedroom flat featured a brick wall view. He drove a new, spacious Mercedes S500 sedan. I drove a used, cramped Japanese car. He spent his vacations at his second home outside Avignon in the south of France. My vacations were usually shared with my parents at my grandmother's summer cottage in South Haven, Michigan. The list could go on and on, but I think you get the drift. He was plantation-owner rich, and I was struggling like a field worker to get there.

We shook hands and I sat down on the opposite side of the table that was set up for four diners. During lunchtime The Berghoff was a beehive. The reservation must've been made well in advance. An ordinary patron would never be given a four-top under a two-person reservation at the height of the lunch rush. The bank was a big customer and had clout. I noticed that Jack had several folders piled up on the side which I assumed were related to our meeting. I snuck a quick glance at the front cover of the top folder. In large capital letters: "COMMERCIAL BANKING SERVICES PROFITABILITY – SKELLER". Now I was seriously concerned. *Why would Jack have a file from Rob Skeller's group?* There was no direct connection between Corporate Finance and Commercial Banking Services. I was totally confused but very curious what this was all about.

Jack looked me straight in the eye and broke the bad news: Rob Skeller, head of Commercial Banking Services and an old college friend of Jack's, was log-jammed in the middle of a major project to complete a cost and profitability analysis of all the products currently offered by his department. This included building computer software to track and improve the flow of services. Rob's second in command, who was heading up the study, had decided to jump ship in the middle of the project, taking a better "position" (Translation: "better paying") at a competing bank. This was not an unusual occurrence, but a replacement (Translation: "unsuspecting pushover") with the skill set required to pick up the pieces needed to be found ASAP or the project would be further delayed and someone top ladder would have to pay the consequences. Skeller's group was under the main Commercial Banking division—the most profitable part of the bank. It was run by Paul Schmitt, a mean-spirited individual known to easily lose his temper, which often led to people perfunctorily given the boot.

After working many years in the corporate culture I've discovered there are two common types of leaders. Type A (The Inspirer) leads by example, using the tools of intellect, experience, support and guidance to get the most from each employee. In my estimate, Jack Elliott fit the definition of a Type A leader. Paul Schmitt was a Type B Leader (The Prick). He managed his people through mostly in-your-face confrontation and fear tactics. His employees came to work each day fretting it could be their last. If they screwed something up the repercussion would be severe and swift: ordered to "Pack up your shit," followed by a walk-of-shame security guard escort out the front door.

Jack saw the confusion on my face and said, “Sam, with your Master’s in Finance and strong quantitative background, you’re the only person in-house who's capable of helping Rob pick up the pieces and finish the project. With you on board, it shouldn't take more than six months to complete the work.”

I could read between the lines. This maneuver would save his college buddy’s ass and give Jack points with the higher-ups, at the same time improving the bank’s profitability. A win-win for everyone...except me. He was sacrificing one of his own employees to help another department complete a task that (from what I later learned) was a pet project of the recently appointed bank president. This slick move would make Jack look like a hero in front of the new powers that be. Heretofore, I thought I had a good handle on things. *How naive could I be? Jack doesn't play politics? Well he sure played the hell out of me!*

Jack mentioned nothing about a salary bump, bonus, stock options, or promotion. Not even a lousy can of Turtle Wax. I felt like I was being used as his personal foot stool to reach the next rung up the corporate ladder. I'd just completed six months of working late nights and weekends, and now I was being served up like a piece of meat to another department exec for the sole purpose of getting Jack a pat on the back. I felt used and betrayed by the man, who just a moment ago, I considered *my hero*.

From this experience, I discovered that there's a third type of leader. Type C (The Stealthanator). These power-hungry executives operate like an Al-Qaeda cell, lurking in the shadows for long periods of time, fooling everyone around them. When the moment of opportunity arises, they strike, taking whatever action is necessary, including sacrificing one of their own, to achieve their goal of career advancement.

Jack concluded with, "Based on a recent meeting of department heads, Corporate Finance looks like it's going to experience a slowdown in its project workload over the next six months." Jack actually smiled at me when he concluded, "I'm just being efficient...keeping one of my prize stallions busy during the lull."

I shit you not. He literally used the phrase "prize stallion". *What a crock of bull! I'm being used as a tool to kiss the ass of someone farther up the food chain.* But reality smacked me in the face. *What choice do I have?* It was time for me to swallow my pride and hope he'd one day acknowledge my sacrifice by bringing me up through the ranks with him.

Following the blindsiding, Jack announced, "Rob thought it'd be a good idea if you took a refresher course in Bank Profitability Analysis." Another Cheshire Cat smile. "And by coincidence, there's an upcoming seminar covering the exact material you'll need to bone up on."

Oh, they had me pegged; knew for a fact I wouldn't put up a fight. The bank had already registered me for the four-day course in New York City scheduled to begin in just two days. They'd reserved a room for me at the Marriott Hotel in Midtown near the theatre district. This whole thing was clearly discussed and set up weeks if not months ago.

Maybe Rob Skeller never lost a key employee to a competing bank, I mulled. *He or she could have screwed up or been fired.* It was also possible that Skeller or his staff didn't have the collective brains to bring this project to fruition. They now needed someone with the financial skill set and willingness to put in a super human effort to pull it all together. Enter Sam Lowe, aka the patsy.

Jack pushed the stack of files to my side of the table. "Here you go—something to start working on, *sucker!*" Okay, not really; that's just what I heard in my head.

Just as I was contemplating, *What's my worst-case scenario?* I got my answer. The man sitting across from me at the table, the man I respected and looked up to as a mentor, the one who allegedly was going to help me build an upwardly mobile future at the bank, the man who I expected that day to be promoting, bonusing or lavishing stock options for all my hard work, smiled a *charming* third time and said, "Sorry Sam, I have a client meeting me here in five minutes for lunch. See you back at the office." He tapped on the top of the file pile.

"If you have any questions, I'm sure they'll be answered when you meet with Rob Skeller. Please stop by his office tomorrow at 7:30 AM. I spoke to him this morning. The meeting is confirmed."

And that was it. A big fat *nothing*. Not a hearty handshake. Not even a free lunch. I was thrown a paltry bone...oh goody, he called me his prize stallion. Well, I remember reading somewhere that stallions must first be broken. So it shall be written; so it shall be done. I walked out of The Berghoff a broken man.

When I got back to my office, I dumped the files on my desk, collapsed in the chair and put my spinning head down. I was frustrated, angry, sad, exhausted and despondent all at the same time. After that alleged lunch meeting, where no lunch was served, it was a sure bet that more white hairs had sprouted from my head.

A minute later, curiosity drove me to sit up and open the sealed envelope. Inside was a roundtrip ticket to New York, an information package and an ID card with my picture on it for access to the seminar. I eyeballed the tickets. The flight was booked out of O'Hare on Delta Airlines, leaving Friday, September 11 at 9:15 AM. Also included was the ticket receipt, which I assume the bank's travel group forgot to detach. The coach class ticket was purchased on August 7, over one month earlier. Now there was no doubt in my mind. They were using me as a pawn in their underhanded game of corporate politics. *Drop pants, grab ankles, get ready to shout, "Sir, may I have another, Sir?"*

3. A Soldier of Corporate Misfortune

For the remainder of the day, I sucked it up and spent my time mulling over the files Jack had given me. I read through all the material and had a much better understanding of the situation, but there were still gaps, some large enough to drive a Brinks truck through, that needed to be filled.

I first discovered that the employee, who allegedly left the bank to take another job, had the same last name as our new bank president, Ronald Simms, who was hired just six weeks earlier. Our previous president had suffered an undisclosed health issue and opted to step down and retire. The board concluded there was no one internally who could fill his Ferragamos. Therefore, they quietly brought someone in from the outside to take over the top spot. Ronald Simms was hired away from a large Wall Street investment firm. Those NYC investment houses are notorious for paying out big salaries and huge bonuses. The board must have offered him an exceptionally sweet compensation package. *Maybe that's where my well-deserved bonus and stock options went?* I sulked inwardly.

I tapped into the bank's grapevine and learned that the person who supposedly left the bank, a Mr. Howard Simms, was in fact Ronald's son. And not only that, he didn't leave, he was promoted, after only six weeks, to vice president then transferred to the Commercial Lending Division. Puzzle pieces were snapping into place. I'd bet the farm that Howard Simm's daddy, our new president, must've included hiring his son as part of the deal to bring him to the bank. He then placed greenhorn Howard in Commercial Banking Services and asked the group leader, Ron Skeller, to put him in charge of an important project to help catapult his career. But six weeks into the project, Rob saw a disaster in the making and complained to the division head, one Mr. Schmitt, who then spoke to the president. His pappy stepped in and instead of firing him, like a normal boss would have, he promoted widdle Howie, then moved him to the most profitable section of the bank where, naturally, the employees are paid the highest salaries.

The head of that division, Paul Schmitt (alias The Prick) was a very difficult person to work for. However, he also was a master at corporate politics, a true ass-smoocher, and would never do anything to upset the bank president. "*Some are born great, some achieve greatness, and some have greatness thrust upon them, fail miserably, and still get promoted.*" I borrowed that from Will Shakespeare along with my little twist. Game over—The incompetent Howard Simms would get the gravy train ride to the top of the mountain...and I'd be stuck working even more obscene hours over the next six months cleaning up his sorry mess.

The following morning, at 7:15 AM, I went up to the top floor to meet with Rob Skeller. His office was located in a separate wing next to the Bank's Commercial Lending Area. Of the bank building's 20 stories, this was the only division to occupy an entire floor. At a towering 24 feet, it had by far the highest ceilings in the building. The sheer magnitude of the mostly wide-open layout, coupled with the cavernous interior, 16-foot tall massive windows dressed in silk curtains, and walls paneled in a rich dark walnut, made for a breathtaking sight. When a big commercial client walked off the elevator, they'd be hard pressed not to feel a sense of awe and recognize the power wafting in the air.

Somebody made a smart move putting the most profitable division in the bank on this floor. No doubt this space was designed and selected to give the bankers a true home court advantage when meeting clients. This idea was probably borrowed from Washington, D.C. where the early architects blueprinted an impressive center mall surrounded by the various grand halls of government. Visiting diplomats' and dignitaries' first impression was that of a great and powerful nation. It’s often said that Washington, D.C. gives the U.S. government the *world’s greatest* home field advantage.

I traversed this voluminous chamber of capitalism, then entered the Commercial Banking Services department through a set of massive bronze paneled doors. The receptionist at the main desk, sipping a cup of coffee, didn't pick up on my presence. When I cleared my throat, I startled her and, jumping up from her seat, she splashed coffee on her dove-white blouse. Instead of being angry or annoyed she seemed a bit embarrassed.

"I’m so sorry," she said, ineffectually fanning her blouse with her French manicure fingernails. "Can I help you?"

I asked, "Are you okay?" And professional that she was, waved her hand like no biggie, and got back to business as usual.

"I have a 7:30 meeting with Mr. Skeller," I announced, still a little shell-shocked. She turned on her computer and we both waited a couple minutes for it to boot up. Commercial Bankers usually roll in a little later, and it appeared obvious she was not expecting me—or anyone for that matter—at this hour. I was betting my appointment wouldn't show up on the computer. This was probably a confidential meeting cooked up behind the scenes between a few senior executives who were playing the junior staffers like a chess master toys with an inferior opponent.

A minute later my assumption was corroborated. She was unable to find the appointment and asked, "Are you sure you have the right day and *time*?"

I put on my dead serious face and replied, "My department head spoke directly with Mr. Skeller and the meeting was definitely confirmed for today at 7:30."

With that disaffected voice all corporate receptionists have mastered, she informed me, "Mr. Skeller has not arrived yet. Please take a seat." She then marched to the ladies' room to try and remove the coffee stains which had already dried a few shades darker on a very ample, button-stretched section of her top.

There were several daily publications on a table in the seating area including *The NY Times, Chicago Tribune, Wall Street Journal* and not surprisingly the last quarter's bank lending rate sheet. I'd already read the files and seminar info pack Jack had given me several times and didn't need any more review, so I picked up *The Journal* and made myself comfortable. Two hours later, at 9:32, Ron Skeller strolled in and walked right past me without any acknowledgment. I was steaming, but I knew my place and waited patiently. Ten minutes later the receptionist's phone rang, and she sent me in.

Ron's frickin' office was bigger than my apartment. It was also paneled in rich dark mahogany, had two large windows looking out onto Adams Street, plus its own private bathroom with shower. This *farkakte* guy sashayed into work well after 9:00 AM, while I was parked at my tiny cubicle every morning by 7:15. I doubt he stayed as late as me and I'd bet his weekends were sacred. I hoped he'd find the heart to extend those same luxurious work hours to me while I helped pull his fat ass out of the fire. *Dream on, Lowe.*

Skeller was sitting in a large, leather wrapped armchair behind an enormous solid mahogany desk. The surface of his highly polished wood work space was clean. Instead of piles and piles of files, like I have on my tiny desktop, excepting a phone, his only had a tray loaded with his morning meal. It looked like he ordered in the Denny's Grand Slam breakfast. From my vantage point I inventoried two sunny-side eggs, three pancakes, six slices of bacon, a toasted bagel schmeared with cream cheese plus two layers of lox, three Danish pastries, and an X-large cup of coffee. If he was concerned about his weight, he'd need to spend an entire day at the East Bank Club to work off all the calories and carbs. Based on his large gut and triple chin, I assumed he couldn’t care less.

Skeller wiped his mouth with a napkin, gestured to the low chair fronting his desk (so visitors would have to look up at him) and said, "Sit down, son." A swallow of coffee, then, "Sorry for the late arrival."

That was it, no excuses were provided. Given that I was the person being brought in to save the day, I already felt like lint between his toes.

"Sam," he roared, "you're going to help me tweak the numbers and put the finishing touches on our project. This department needs to roll out the new product price list to our customers by the end of the year."

Yeah right, I mused, having analyzed the files' data. I knew that "tweaking" was not what this project needed. A better description would be a complete overhaul. I thought it'd be best for all involved if I was up front with him from the get-go. "I spent most of yesterday looking through all the files. Some of the data and initial analysis might be useful, but I'd be confident of a much better outcome if I started from scratch. Sometimes it’s better to cut your losses and begin again."

I laid out my strategy and pinpointed many of the errors that were made by my predecessor, Howie, who clearly didn’t know an asset from his a-hole. Ron knew Jack Elliott was extremely sharp and trusted him to the letter. Since Jack had given me a glowing recommendation, he decided to put himself in my hands and let me take the reins. The only caveats were that I had to report to him weekly (hopefully those meetings would be set up after 9:00 AM) and it was imperative that the project be completed by the end of November, allowing just enough time to print out and mail the new product price list to all the bank's commercial clients. It was obvious that, prior to our little meeting, Ron already knew the project was a dismal failure. I'd become the bank's new Golden Boy if I could pull this off.

While I had a strong quantitative background, this still was a gargantuan challenge for me. I had to learn about all the department's products, their associated processes, costs, and the banking systems that monitor and support them. Hopefully some of the team members, who worked on the project with Howard, would be able to assist me in this endeavor, but I couldn't count on that. I could deal with the numbers, but given such a short timeframe, taking this project from the depths of Howie's incompetence to the pinnacle of Skeller's expectations might be a feat too great for even the Wunderkind. What then? Crash and burn?

Chapter 3½
The Death Chapter
[Deleted for Fear of the Number 4]

For those of you not familiar with the term Tetraphobia, or the fear of the number four, a brief explanation is due. In Mandarin, the word for death "si3" sounds very similar to the word for the number 4 "si4". (Later on, I will explain the transliteration, using letters and numbers to sound out the Chinese characters.) Just in case there is any dark voodoo buried deep inside that “evil” integer, whether in an address, a purchase price, a closing date on a house, a license plate, or a building floor, Asian people, whenever humanly possible, will avoid it like the plague.

While I don't believe the rationale behind it, my personal philosophy is: Why mess with something you don’t understand? Some may think Chinese people are crazy superstitious, but before you have yourself a chuckle, just remember that we Caucasians foster a similar hang-up with the number 13.

5. Bank Profitability & Internal Controlz-z-z-z-z

I didn’t have to arrive at the airport until 8:15 AM to catch my Delta flight to JFK.

So what the heck...I set my alarm for 6:00, giving myself the luxury of an extra hour of sleep.

But not so fast...getting up at 5:00 AM every weekday for the past two years, my body’s interior clock was on overdrive, and I rolled out of bed an hour before the alarm went off anyway.

On the plus side...I forgot to adjust the clock on my coffee machine. By the time I put on my robe and walked to the kitchen, that wonderful rich aroma had already wafted its way into every corner of the apartment. I downed my obligatory two cups, then grabbed a small carry-on bag and packed light.

The seminar ran a four-day weekend. I'd be back in Chicago the following Tuesday morning. It was becoming more apparent by the minute just how raw a deal I'd been dealt. NYC is an exciting place to visit, but I was given no touristy time. The seminar went from 7:30 AM to 7:30 PM daily. Endeavoring to stay focused throughout a series of ultra-boring topics would leave me exhausted by the end of each day. Afterwards I'd have just enough time to grab a quick dinner, stop by the hotel bar for a couple of drinks, then head to my room to review the day’s notes before lights out.

My upcoming killer weekend was shot. Instead of golf with my buddies on Saturday followed by dinner and drinks with friends, and a relaxing Sunday watching da Bears play (and hopefully beat) the Packers with my old college roommate, I'd be working like a damn dog.

On top of that, upon my return home, I'd no doubt get stuck at the bank several more weekends in a row to get a jump on the godforsaken project. All work and zero play; it looked like Sam was going to be a dull boy.

But here's the final kick in the ass: I had tickets to see Bruce Springsteen on Friday with a good friend of mine from the old neighborhood. The saying is, "Easy come, easy go"—but not in this case. I stood in line for 8 hours to get fourth row, center stage at Rosemont Horizon Stadium. A few days earlier I would've gladly given them to Jack Elliott, who's a big Springsteen fan. *Fat chance now, Jacko!* He was responsible for screwing up my weekend and for all the misery I expected to endure over the next 4-6 months. I would've rather given my tickets to Howie Simms. Getting on *his* good side might rack up some future benefit. The way things were going, if Howie screwed up in Commercial Lending, he'd likely get promoted to Chairman of the Board!

I ended up giving my tickets to an old high school buddy who promised to reciprocate by taking me to a Bulls playoff game. His dad had season tickets and was often out of town on business. At that time, Michael Jordan was on the team, so making the playoffs was practically a slam dunk—good trade!

I left my apartment at 7:30 and caught a taxi to the Delta terminal at O'Hare International. My ride was a small embracer jet, and I was traveling coach. I knew the travel agent at the bank and dialed her the same day Jack informed me I'd be flying to New York for the seminar. She was able to snag me an exit row. With my skyscraper frame the extra five inches made an appreciable difference.

We landed in New York; I carried my light bag and laptop out of the main terminal, hopped a cab and told the driver, "Marriott Marquis." The hotel was located in the heart of Times Square.

It was 12:00 noon, and with the traffic light, it took only 38 minutes to go the 14 miles from JFK to the midtown tunnel. Once we entered Manhattan, it was a different story. The last mile took almost 45 minutes. Mind you, I'm not complaining. The bank was paying the fare, and I was able to take in the sights. It was a hot day in NYC, and there were plenty of scantily dressed young women strolling the streets. I just sat back and enjoyed the view.

I checked in to the Marriott, unpacked, grabbed my files and my laptop, then headed down to the main restaurant for a beer and sandwich. Today only, the introductory session started at 4:00 PM and ended at 6:00. This was my sixth seminar in two years. I'd check in, get my lanyard and badge holder, and attend;

but I knew from experience the first day was always a titanic waste of time. Many of the participants were coming in from out of town. Therefore, the meeting would start late and stop early, giving harried stragglers time to arrive and settle in.

The conference host was the only speaker today. He or she would open with a hearty welcome to everyone from fabulous New York City, thank us for attending, finish with an overview of the material to be covered, and a brief rundown on the six presenters, all of whom were likely kicking back at The Plaza...or getting a lap dance in Times Square. Tomorrow, Friday, the seminar started at the usual 7:30 AM and ended between 7:30 PM and whenever the final speaker ran out of gas.

The whole seminar was not worth my time. I breezed through the information packets, and the complexity of the material was well below my pay grade. If one of the speakers took ill, I could easily step up and give a comprehensive lecture on any of the topics. It didn’t escape my purview that Jack and Ron had insisted I go. It’s possible they needed me out of the way for a few days while they buried certain pages of the paper trail that might tie them to the current fiasco. I was totally disillusioned by the way those two ladder climbing Stealthanators had manipulated me. Then again, it was a relief to get away from the greedy stench at the bank for a few days. Back at the office I imagined Ron and Jack were back patting and calling this "Sam's well-deserved vacation." I wouldn't be surprised if my time away from work was somehow credited against my allocated sick pay or counted as part of my annual two weeks paid leave.

I finished lunch and figured I'd first find the location of the room where the seminar would be held, then proceed directly to the hotel bar and check out the action. Earlier, when I arrived at reception, they told me the hotel was almost full, with several business conferences already underway. Most of the symposiums I'd attended were a bore-fest. The best and often only escape was the hotel bar where you could kick back with fellow attendees; drinking, networking, and drinking, and drinking. If you hung out there late enough, chances were good you'd end up in the sack with a boozy dame.

My laptop was a heavy piece of equipment, compared to today's ultra-light models; instead of lugging it around the hotel, I detoured to my room, opting for a refresher nap before the conference started. In 1987 minicomputers were a recent accoutrement. In order to get the most bang for their buck out of me, the bank purchased a state-of-the-art NEC Multispeed notebook, weighing in at 12 lbs.; three inches thick, tiny liquid crystal display, 640K Ram, and two 3.5" floppy drives. A behemoth compared to the current models, and at over $2,500, quite a lavish outlay. I was boyishly excited when they placed it on my desk, wondering why the bank was willing to pay top dollar for the latest and greatest in laptop computers. It took me but one minute to realize that this big-ticket piece of technology now made it a snap for me to take my work home.

At almost the exact moment that thought ran through my head, Jack strolled over to my desk to see the new toy, then informed me, "The Cadlink, Inc. valuation analysis needs to be completed by Monday," followed by, "With your new NEC you can finish it at home over the weekend." Funny, I always thought technology was supposed to make your life easier.

Back in my room I was unable to sleep a wink. All the events from the past two days were swirling around in my head. An hour later I put on a pair of designer jeans, polo shirt, and a pair of dark brown loafers, then headed down to find the conference room.

I walked off the elevator into the lobby and saw a sign posting the various symposiums and their designated rooms. This was a huge hotel, and there were over 20 events listed. I scrolled down and found mine smack in the middle: "Bank Profitability and Internal Controls—Marquis Ballroom, 8th floor".

A few minutes later I was standing in front of a long black metal sideboard outside the conference room looking for my name card and assigned table. There it was: "Samuel Lowe, First Chicago Bank, table 98". Since I arrived early, most of the cards had yet to be taken. The numbers went up to 209. With five people per table this conference room could potentially accommodate over 1000.

Wow, that's a shitload of severely apathetic or depressed individuals crammed into one room, I reflected.

The companies that host these events are aware of this issue and try to balance the scales by providing coffee dispensers on both sides of the room. These industrial-size stainless steel vessels constantly needed refilling as seminar attendees go back and forth all day long continually feeding their body with the customary drug of choice. For these meetings, decaf would be laughed out of the room.

I entered the humongous Marquis Ballroom. Most people associate the word ballroom with a grand space finished with decorated plaster ceilings, spectacular crystal chandeliers, large mahogany wainscoting, a rich hardwood herringbone floor partially covered by an antique oriental rug and hand painted frescos on the walls. This was a corporate ballroom...no frescos, only flat off-white paint. The other elegant refinements were substituted with basic flat moldings, a dropped tile ceiling, recessed fluorescent down lighting and a dun polyester coffee-stain resistant carpet. The room had about as much charisma as the typical speakers I'd have to listen to over the next few days. Please take note, when I started at the bank, I was full of enthusiasm and anticipation, but recent events had turned me into a cynic.

Table 98 was perfectly situated in the middle of the room, close enough to clearly see any information put up on the projector screen, but far enough from the presenters not to be noticed if you nodded off or were talking a little too loud to a colleague.

At one seminar I was seated at a table directly in front of the podium. It was a cutting-edge topic on Commercial Jet Sale and Lease Backs. The young speaker, however, had the flattest monotone voice I'd ever heard. Two hours of that dreary, dull babble was enough to cure the world's worst case of insomnia. The poor guy was abysmally nervous standing in front of a large group. He decided to look at my table, and me in particular, throughout the entire lecture to avoid the general audience. He was sweating profusely. I felt sorry for the newbie and held eye contact the entire time. When he finished, I was exhausted, as if I'd run a marathon. The next day I made a point to arrive late, grabbing a chair in the farthest corner of the room.

When I reached table 98, I was surprised to find a buxom young lady with long reddish blonde hair sitting alone.

"Julie Solomon." She smiled and extended a hand. Even though she was sitting down, I could tell the lovely lass was tall and thin.

Oh, did Julie love to talk! Within five minutes I knew everything about her: Jewish, 25 years old, single, grew up on Long Island and currently lives in a shoebox sized studio in Hell's Kitchen. She hated her job as an analyst at Mellon Bank in NYC working in IPA (Internal Profitability Analysis); and was on the hunt for a successful husband who'd rescue her away from her humdrum life. (Okay, I guessed on the last one.)

But Julie was cute and sweet, and it'd be nice to a have some female company. Back in the late 80s there weren't many women in banking. At all the other seminars I'd ended up sitting with a group of gung-ho males; and just as that thought crossed my mind, two hyper-energetic guys showed up at our table. They were very young, perhaps more aptly described as boys. Both formally dressed in standard suit and tie banking attire, I instantly surmised: *Rookies in the business world.* A seasoned seminar attendee like myself was clothed for comfort. I guessed they were both in their early 20s and this was their first seminar. Pleasantries were exchanged, and my hunch was confirmed.

John Riley, 21, just started two months earlier at Irving Trust; an analyst in the bank's profitability group. He was taller than me by at least two inches but skinny as a straw. Short hair except for the front bangs. I assumed he let them grow long to hide what looked to be a severe case of acne lurking underneath. It's also possible the bangs were the cause of the numerous skin inflammations (blackheads, pockmarks and zits). His suit looked cheap and his shoes were a little beat up; undoubtedly, he was not from money.

George Millstein, 22, short and slightly rotund, was just accepted into the Commercial Bank training program at Citibank. He looked more like a teenager. No doubt he was carded whenever he ordered anything alcoholic.

"Tomorrow," I counseled them, "ditch the suits. Wear something comfortable." You never know what a pair of extreme-green dudes will do, so I added, "But no sandals, shorts or T-shirts." However, I doubt they even heard me. Both were fixated on Julie’s cleavage.

She knew they were staring but paid no attention. Julie, who'd already started flirting with me, offhandedly asked, "Any plans for dinner?" Then seamlessly segued to, "From looking at the website, the hotel rooms seem very luxurious. Suppose I could take a peek at yours?" Julie might just as well have said, “Buy me a nice dinner tonight and I'll gladly be your dessert.” She was wearing a very tight skirt, a low cut short-sleeve blouse and a pair of sexy, stiletto high heels. It didn't take a genius IQ to deduce that Julie Solomon was on the prowl.

While I was pondering Julie's invitation for a potential late-night romp, I noticed there was still one open seat at our table. "It's for a colleague from my group," Julie said, somewhat reserved.

A minute before the seminar started, a petite, drop-dead gorgeous, 5' 3" Asian woman sat down next to me. The moment I cast my eyes on her it felt like the oxygen level in the room had taken a nose dive, making my breathing more labored. No cliché: this girl just took my breath away. I even felt a little light-headed. Small beads of perspiration popped up on my forehead. My palms were sweating, and my heart began to race.

Why is this happening to me? I racked my brain for an answer. It's not like I’d never seen an Asian woman before. Chicago even had its own Chinatown. But back in the 80s, before the wave of Asian immigration, they were not so visible.

Most of the early arrivals worked in low-level jobs. It was not until the following generation that they began the climb, espousing the virtues of higher education as a pathway to upward mobility. There were just a handful at my college, only a few Japanese males at the bank, and none in my social circles. This was my first up close and personal encounter with a real, live, breathing Asian woman.

She was fashionably attired in a light summer dress with a pair of white sandals that had a leather flower perched on the tops. Soon as she sat down, I saw her kick one off exposing the name Gucci stenciled into the top of the sole. She had large brown eyes, flawless white skin, and long jet-black hair tied in a ponytail. Her face had a very natural glow, making it difficult for me to tell if she was wearing any makeup. And then there was that very subtle but enticing scent that reminded me of lavender.

My first thought: *Is she already spoken for?* I nearly got whiplash when my head twisted to zero-in on her ring finger. To my great relief it was bare. The jewelry she did wear included a pair of gold rope style earrings, and a watch with a matching gold rope band, displaying “Cartier” on its face.

The seminar was about to start. There was only enough time to say, "Hello, I'm Sam Lowe, from Chicago."

In a syrup thick accent, she politely responded, "Very nice meet you, Sam. My name Linda Liu.”

And with that my body turned to jelly. I was smitten. A second later, the moderator stepped up to the podium and opened the conference. Not that it really mattered, but I zoned-out the entire seminar introduction. For those two hours all I could think about was the exotic Asian beauty electrifying the air between us.

Years later, when I'd become somewhat indoctrinated into the Asian culture, it was clear to me that this chance meeting was preordained. There were numerous signposts including the following:

Sign A: We met at table 98, which is one of the luckiest number combinations in the Far Eastern culture. Chinese people are, in general, very superstitious. Next time you're out driving and see a license plate with a lot of 8's and 9's in the sequence, peek inside the vehicle and you'll most likely see an Asian person at the wheel. But please be careful, to a degree the stereotype is true: they're not the best drivers. If you don't believe me, and are a real risk taker, drive through any Chinatown in America, but don't say I didn't warn you. (P.S. Okay, that statement is a little unfair. But in the 80s, Asia's economy had not yet blossomed and few of its citizenry were able to afford a vehicle. Thus, most who immigrated here had no prior driving experience whatsoever. Please note, the second-generation drivers are far better than their parents; but I'd still error on the side of caution if I were you.)

Sign B: My last name, Lowe, a common Jewish name, is also a common Chinese surname when spelled Lo. If you spoke to a Sam Lo or Sam Lowe over the phone you might be surprised upon meeting him in person if he was not Asian. In fact, a couple times upon meeting a bank client for the first time, they said to me, “Oh, you're not Chinese?” I thought it slightly odd but never inquired why. I had a slight Chicago accent not an Asian one. I did watch a lot of Charlie Chan movies in my youth. Maybe some of it rubbed off on me?

Sign C: The very unusual turn of events at the bank that sent me to New York.

Sign D: There were almost 1000 attendees at the seminar, but less than a dozen were female. What were the chances that I'd be seated next to two of them, with one being Asian? Romantic that I am, I always believed kismet would someday lead me to my one true love. There was no doubt in my mind that the stars were all in alignment that day, Friday, 9-11-1987.

The speaker finished his discussion, which I think had something to do with new computer software for profit center cost/benefit analysis. I turned to Linda Liu and asked her to join me for a quick drink during the upcoming 30-minute break. Judy chimed in and included herself in what I'd hoped would be a private outing. *Maybe the three of us would be better?* I considered, assessing the situation. *Don't wanna come on too strong and scare Linda off.*

Our two other male colleagues then hopped on the bandwagon inviting themselves to what was now a come one, come all affair. Julie made a face that said, *Beat it kids*, but these keyed-up boys were not to be dissuaded and joined us at The View, a casual bar at the top of the hotel.

The five of us crowded around a circular table suited for four. Linda was very reserved. I wasn't sure if she was shy or if it was a cultural trait. Like a closed book, she wasn't releasing any personal information unless specifically asked; and even then, her answers were short and seemed somewhat guarded. I had to walk a fine line trying to find out more about Linda without making her feel like she was being interrogated by the Gestapo.

My efforts were very short lived. The two sex-starved boys were ferociously competing for the chance to get into Julie's pants. She was doing her best to avoid eye contact with them, and I became the sole object of her attention. There was absolutely no doubt in my mind, if I so desired, Julie would be mine for the evening. She seemed like a nice girl. I didn't want to be insulting by brushing her off, but I also didn't want to give her the wrong idea. I was hoping she wouldn't get more aggressive and send me a stronger signal, like kicking off one of her high heels and rubbing her bare foot against my leg. Or ratchet things up to an even higher level by putting her hand under the table to touch my thigh, then slowly sliding it over to my crotch.

I'd dated enough woman to conclude: The only thing I could say for sure about the female gender is that they're very complicated and unpredictable. It was anyone's guess what would happen next.

Linda was sitting on my right, Julie on my left. Every time I turned toward Linda to try and start a discussion, Julie immediately inserted herself into the conversation, not giving Linda a chance to speak. I could see I was getting nowhere with both present and decided to stop my pursuit, for the moment. I'd wait for a better opportunity, preferably when we were alone, to ask Linda out for dinner.

I realized my situation could get very complicated. Turned out Julie and Linda both worked for Mellon Bank, and I had no clue as to their relationship. I'd have to proceed with caution until I had a better handle on things. I kept glancing at Linda. She caught me staring one time but didn't seem to mind. When she smiled back at me, I felt like I'd explode, both literally and sexually.

I thought it'd be obvious to everyone at the table, and for that matter the entire room, that I was only interested in Linda; but Julie didn't seem to pick up on it.

What a strange feeling, I reckoned. I couldn't explain why, but I was totally intoxicated with this little Asian girl. She was a complete mystery to me. Was she ever married? Did she have children? How old was she? What was her ancestry...Chinese, Japanese, Vietnamese, etc.? Did she have any intolerable quirks? After all, I hadn't heard her laugh yet.

In the past I always made sure to stockpile as much info as possible about a girl before committing to a date...*And I'm already thinking about a relationship! This is sheer insanity!* I knew nothing about Ms. Linda Liu, but a tiny voice deep down inside whispered to me, *This is The One you've been searching for your entire life!* How was this even possible? I'd spent a little under two hours with her and she'd spoken fewer than five sentences. And when she did speak, her accent was so heavy I missed half of what she was saying. I wondered if she'd even pass my two prerequisites.

No. 1 – Was she a college graduate? Linda Liu was working at a bank in a position high enough they were paying for the seminar. She must've been at least an analyst. That required, at minimum, a bachelor’s degree.

No. 2 – Age? She dressed in the style of a 30-something sophisticated woman, but beyond the clothes and jewelry she looked youngish. My guess was 23 or 24.

We finished our drinks, and since I appeared to be the oldest in our group, I picked up the check. Boner move, Julie thanked me for treating her and boldly asked, in front of Linda, "Can I reciprocate by taking you out to dinner tonight?" If I didn’t say something quick, one of two things would likely occur:

(1) I'd end up having dinner alone with Julie, alienating Linda, but most likely getting laid afterwards.

(2) I'd end up having dinner with Julie and her fan club of two drooling adolescents who'd stick to her like tar; not get laid; and really piss off Linda for making her the odd man out.

Unless...I came up with an excuse to get out of spending time with any of them. I was cornered and chose (3): *None of the above*. I figured that sometime before the seminar concluded, I could catch Linda alone and get her phone number.

I produced my best fake yawn—practiced on many a date—and announced to the table, "I'm a little tired from the trip and just wanna go back to my suite, order room service, and turn in early."

Not to be a total party pooper, I did promise to meet up with everyone tomorrow after the day’s wrap-up for another round of drinks in the hotel bar. I was sure I addressed everyone, but for some reason Julie thought I wasn't talking to her.

She flashed a sly smile and said, “Okay Sam, I'll see you later and I look forward to a drink with you...and maybe dinner afterwards?" She then winked at me.

I was again thrown for a loop and didn't know what to say. I'd clearly said *tomorrow*—not tonight. I just half-smiled back at her. Based on how things were going, she probably took my return smile as the signal, *Yes, I am hot for you as well*. This was not going to be an easy ballgame.

We returned to the seminar and a short hour later the speaker made his closing remarks. I could see that Linda was taking her time leaving. I hoped this meant she knew I was interested and wanted to talk. Julie was also taking her sweet time; I assumed for the same reason. The tadpoles were hanging around as well. I thought about informing them we were only three blocks from 42nd Street where $100 could buy a couple hookers. What a dysfunctional table! I didn't want to sit there waiting to see who'd win the stalling contest. I left disappointed. *Another lost opportunity to connect with Linda!*

Instead of heading straight to my room, I took a detour to The View for a night-cap before retiring for the evening. Three vodka tonics later I felt much better. I repaired to my suite, ordered room service and a pay per view movie. I was emotionally drained from the day's activities. It was only 9:00 PM, but I fell asleep just 15 minutes into the movie—*Ishtar*.

I awoke at 10:30 PM to a knock on the door. At first, I thought I was dreaming and ignored it.

KNOCK! KNOCK! KNOCK! Louder this time.

"Who the F's banging on my door at this hour?" I grumbled to myself. Maybe someone stumbled back from the bar and got their room mixed up? I doubted it was room service. Usually they wait until you push the cart outside the door; but with the hotel so full, they may have come early to collect it? Was the maid here for the evening turndown? For sure I'd hung the Do Not Disturb sign on the outside doorknob. I was in my underwear and didn't want to get up and throw on a pair of pants. I ignored the banging expecting the staff person to quickly give up and leave.

I couldn't believe my ears when I heard, "Sam, open up! It's Julie."

Hoffman and Beatty were jabbering on the TV. *Did she hear it?* I told everyone at the table I was tired and going straight to bed. *Did I somehow send her a subliminal message?* My mind was racing to figure out my next move. *How do I get out of this dilemma...or is this an opportunity?* Groggy and a little buzzed from my visit to the bar plus the two glasses of wine I polished off with dinner, my libido had kicked into high gear. I was tempted to fling open the door, pick her up and throw her on the bed. But that thought instantly evaporated as the image of Linda popped back into my head. I'd been thinking of nothing else since I left the conference room.

My situation was like that scene from the movie *Animal House*. I had a devil on one shoulder telling me, "Open the door and screw her brains out!" On the other shoulder stood an angel, who looked a little bit Asian, telling me, "Do the right thing—abstain and wait for the woman you really want!"

The knocking on the door was now a persistent pounding. *This girl is really horny!* Man, I was tempted; but in the end, the angel won out. *Uh-oh, will the sound of the TV encourage her to keep trying until I relent?* I was a little freaked out, so I just laid there still as a church mouse. A minute later the pounding stopped.

I figured, *If Julie asks tomorrow, I'll tell her I had trouble falling asleep. I put on an awful movie, but it didn't help; so I ended up taking a walk around Times Square.* That'd cover tonight, but what about the next couple of nights?

I need to bust a move on Linda soon or she might think I've lost interest...but maybe Julie already told Linda that she has dibs on me—so stay away? I brooded.

In the past few days, I'd gone from a prized stallion to a patsy to the prey of a sexual predator. I wondered what role I'd be playing tomorrow.

The next morning, I went down to the hotel restaurant for an early morning meal. A complimentary continental breakfast was included in my room package. I sat at a table by the window overlooking Broadway and 46th. The waiter walked over, handed me a menu, and poured my coffee. Seconds later, I almost did a spit-take when the lovely Linda Liu entered the room.

I thought I was dreaming when she walked straight to my table and asked, “Hello Sam Lowe. I may sit eat breakfast?”

I awkwardly rose to my feet and beckoned her to the chair across from me. "Uh...yes, please."

She was wearing another stunning summer dress that accentuated all the right curves on her slender body. It was not extremely short, like the skirt Julie wore the previous day; rather there was a slit up one side allowing a breathtaking shot of gorgeous leg, but still left something to the imagination.

The time was 6:15 AM. The restaurant had just opened, and with only a few customers the service was excellent. The waiter returned to our table to take our orders.

Linda, without looking at the menu, asked for a cup of black tea and an omelet. "Spinach. No cheese. No bread. No potato. No bacon."

I ordered my comped continental that included unlimited coffee, a basket with several types of muffins, and a plate of butter with a variety of jams.

We spent the next hour learning about each other. I was having a bit of trouble following her story. Her accent was cumbersome, and she often jumbled up words, making it a challenge to follow. However, I was able to ascertain that she was 26, Chinese, and grew up in Taiwan. She moved to New York by herself two years ago. She was well-read and had already traveled extensively in Europe. When I looked at her face, I saw a little girl with a perfect porcelain complexion, but throughout our conversation I also saw sophistication and confidence. This girl was truly the complete package.

I glanced up at the wall clock: 7:15 AM. The seminar started in 15 minutes. Time was rapidly ticking away so I played my cards: "Linda...will you have dinner with me tonight?"

She blinked her eyes in seeming confusion and replied, "Oh? Why you not ask colleague?”

I stated emphatically, "Julie seems very nice, but she’s *not my type!*"

Linda was toying with me. This was a very intelligent girl. In addition, women are much more attuned to their social environment than men. You must have heard of women’s intuition. You never hear about men's intuition. That's probably because we have none—at least when it comes to the opposite sex. She already knew I'd fallen head over heels for her. I didn't have to tell her that.

Linda Liu agreed to have dinner with me that evening and casually said, "Sam, no need worry. Julie not problem."

I later learned that Linda had already been promoted to an officer position. Julie was still an analyst; therefore, Linda was her boss. Here I was thinking this would play out as a reprise of Alice Schneider-type embarrassment that would include confrontation, awkward moments, nasty glares, and loads of stress. That never happened.

Linda excused herself to use the restroom and cryptically said, "Me see you at table." (Lucky number 98)

Julie never showed up. In fact, I didn't see her even once during the rest of the seminar. An alarm should've gone off in my head alerting me to future enigmas to come, but I was completely off my normal game. The thought that this beautiful young Asian princess could ever be aggressive, imposing or manipulative did not seem possible.

I never got the true story about Julie's mysterious disappearance. I assumed Linda must have reassigned her to another outlying table, or possibly another department; maybe a bank branch in Barrow, Alaska; but who knows for sure?

I was consumed with affection for this exotic creature and totally focused on getting her to fall in love with me as well.

Fast Forward: I don't want to turn this into a steamy romance novel, so I won't go into the lurid details of our courtship and love life. If you are looking for a read that offers plenty of kinky sex you can always buy a copy of *50 Shades of Grey*. But trust me, it would make a very hot read and possibly a blockbuster movie starring Liev Schreiber and Lucy Liu.

Over the next eight months I flew back and forth from Chicago to New York two or three times a month for the sole purpose of weekending with my sweetheart. What choice did I have? My heart truly ached for her; and no matter how many hours I spent in the office or how many dinners I had with friends, there was no other way to quell the yearning. I brought a carry-on to the office with me every other Friday. After work I hopped the Blue Line, which got me to O'Hare in under an hour. Even when I was swamped at the office, forcing me to work over the weekend, I found a way to make the trip. My boss bought me the laptop to get more production out of me. Little did he know that his factious generosity allowed me to follow my heart while still doing my job to and fro on the plane. And the more time I spent with Linda, the harder it was to return to my single life in Chicago.

On March 8, 1988 I flew to New York and proposed to Linda Liu over dinner at Tavern On The Green. She threw her arms around me, and with tears of delight in her eyes, cried yes. However, her acceptance came with two caveats.

Caveat #1 – She'd never live in Chicago. Linda came to visit me a couple times during the 1987 winter. As bad luck would have it, each time she made the trip, the temperature in the Windy City was sub-zero. That was without the wind chill factored in. "Chicago too much cold," she complained. "Me no can go!"

Caveat #2 – I had to get her mother's approval before we could wed. That meant a trip to Taiwan. Linda's dad passed away when she was young. Her family, led by one tough-as nails matriarch, really had to come together to get through some very difficult times. "No have mother's approval, no can marry," she said with finality.

I was so intoxicated with Linda Liu, I would've followed her through the snake-infested jungles of Borneo, if she asked me to. I just hoped I'd pass muster.

First things first; before I could move to New York, I needed to start interviewing for a job in Manhattan's financial sector, aka Wall Street. The plan was to first finalize my employment, then move into her tiny Upper East Side studio for a few months while I tried to sell my Lincoln Park condo. We'd use the funds from the sale to buy a larger place in the city.

Thankfully, things moved posthaste. I landed an officer position in the corporate finance group at The Bank of New York. I have to say that in the end Jack Elliott came through for me. Love conquers all—including him. Jack happily sent my new boss a glowing letter of recommendation. My bumped-up salary was almost twice what I was making in Chicago. However, after factoring in Manhattan's higher cost of living, the increase was not as big a bump as I initially thought.

My first day of work would be August 1, 1988. The office was located at 48 Wall Street which was a snappy 25-minute subway ride from Linda's apartment. With everything in New York now set up, I was anxious to return to Chicago and tie up all the loose ends.

I submitted my official letter of resignation to the HR department. All my friends and colleagues from work threw me a surprise party at King Arthur's Pub. It was the most popular bar in the Loop, famous for its "yards of beer". I couldn't have lasted so long at the bank without that pub therapy to help reduce stress and oftentimes drown my frustrations.

A yard of beer was served in a glass container that was a little over three feet tall. The glass tapered down to a narrow passage that opened into a softball size globe at the bottom. By the time you drank down to the ball you were feeling pretty good or possibly not feeling anything at all. To polish off the last 20 ounces you had to tilt the bottom of the glass up at least 65 degrees to get the fluid to start flowing out from the ball through the tight channel into the large open cylinder of the glass. It was a common and hilarious sight to see an inebriated business professional in an expensive suit and tie take a beer shower.

Even though Jack and Ron didn't show up for my send-off, I'm sure they were both going to miss having me to piss on. No doubt they already had some poor pathetic bastard in their crosshairs. Whoever got the job would also inherit my high-tech laptop computer...and (sucker!) my workaholic weekends.

By the way, I finished Ron's project in just under three months, working 70-80-hour weeks. My efforts on the project ended up saving the bank well over $100 million dollars a year by fine-tuning the processing of several of the bank's commercial products and through my recommendation to shut down the Coin and Currency division. Going forward, that service would be farmed out to a private vendor. Upon completion of the project, I did get a pat on the back—literally. There was no mention of a promotion, bonus or salary increase.

I found a buyer for my condo one month after I left the bank. The next couple of weeks I either sold or Goodwilled everything I owned, except for my clothes. I even said a teary-eyed goodbye to my baby, the 280 Z turbo chick magnet.

Soon after you make the big decision to take the marital plunge, concessions must be made. I'd moved away from my family and friends; gave up my bachelor pad, my club and my ultra-cool sports car. You'd think I'd already made the ultimate sacrifices. Keep reading, this was just the beginning.

SECTION TWO
Introduction to Asia

6. Fly the Smelly Skies

June 7, 1988. I'd already moved to NYC fulfilling Caveat #1. Now it was time to knock out #2: Meet the Liu's on their home turf. My chips were piled high, center table—I was all-in.

While growing up in Chicago, I'd never traveled out of the country. A family vacation was a weekend drive to South Haven, Michigan where my maternal grandma had a modest summer house.

A trip to Taiwan, 20+ hours by plane via Anchorage, Alaska and Hong Kong, was both an exciting an unnerving journey for a Midwesterner with no international experience. This was not a short hop to Mexico or Canada. It'd be an around the world adventure passing through several time zones to a place so foreign that without an escort who spoke the language, this global tenderfoot would've never dared that first step onto the monstrous Boeing 747 heading to parts unknown.

In Asia some call us Caucasians "bai2 gui3", which translates to "white devil". That potential new nickname only ratcheted up my already sky-high fears of flying to Taipei, on a wing and a prayer, to gain the mandatory approval of Linda's mom before we could get hitched.

We arrived by taxi to the international terminal at JFK Airport where we boarded a Tower Air flight to Taipei. At that time in our lives we could only afford the cheapest seats on the thriftiest carrier. Tower Air, aka Terror Air, filed for bankruptcy in 2000 and soon afterwards closed its hanger doors. During the first leg of our trip, it was obvious why they'd eventually fail. It was a true-life lesson, teaching me how important comfort is when making a commitment that confines you for an entire day to an extremely tight and inhospitable environment. It's a decision that should not be taken lightly: Do your research on the seats, food, and safety record before deciding which airline to fly!

To say this was an economical airline would be a gross understatement. In coach class, or more appropriately last class, Tower Air crammed you in. While Linda, a full foot shorter than me, easily fit into her seat, it took some work to squeeze my hulking body into my mini eco-frame covered with cheap, torn and stained fabric. No leg room, no hip room, no built-in TV. Just music from a flimsy headset that required the user to have bat-like hearing since there was very little sound from the right side and dead air on the left. This was my plight for the duration, not including any unexpected delays. The seasoned traveler knows that when it comes to the airlines, "unexpected" means "very likely". If Hell truly exists, it's probably a similar re-creation of this flight. With such bargain basement airfares there was not one empty seat. The exterior door was closed. I was now trapped in a sealed tube with 400 Chinese and just one other white devil heading to the other side of the world.

I was told that the best airline food and service was found on international flights. While the service was good, the food, for my American palate, was inedible. This was mostly related to my unfamiliarity with the various Asian *delicacies* served to this Chicago born, pizza & hotdog eating dude. As soon as we were airborne, even before the wheels were up, I observed passengers reaching into bags, purses, and other small carry-ons, unpacking their own personal food items they'd brought along to consume during the long flight. Soon there were strange smells emanating from every corner of the airplane. The elderly white-haired woman and her husband sitting across the aisle from me opened a plastic box containing some very odd-looking brown shaped objects. I first thought they were oval shaped rubber exercise handballs.

I pointed them out to Linda, who said with glee, “Yummmm, thousand-year old eggs.”

Let’s be clear: not eggs with brown shells but eggs that had some type of jelly-like brown exterior. This was not an appetizing name; especially when it’s well known that eggs spoil rather quickly when not refrigerated.

I whispered to Linda, “I don’t care how organic they are, eggs don’t last more than a week or two—let alone an entire millennium!”

Linda replied, "I know you like. This much popular Taiwan snack.” Later, back in NYC, I dug into my encyclopedia and discovered that they’re made by preserving chicken or duck eggs in a mixture of salt, lime and ash, then wrapping them in rice husks for several weeks. During this time the pH of the eggs rise, transforming them. The chemical process breaks down some of the proteins and fats into smaller, more complex flavors. After curing, the yolks of the eggs turn a dark green offering the *brave and adventurous diner*, "(my addition)" a creamy interior consistency. The whites of the eggs turn amber and gelatinous."

This strange egg preparation dates to the Ming Dynasty, long before modern science clearly understood that bacteria in spoiled food is the main source of food poisoning.

Ask Chinese person." Linda offered, "Say old egg no give stomach ache. Very good eat."

"Well, I'll never know that, for I am a coward, "I retorted." If you've ever had a bad case of salmonella or listeriosis you'll completely understand my reasoning for not putting something that turned from white and bright yellow to brown and dark green in my mouth, especially if it's been sitting unrefrigerated for five weeks on a pantry shelf."

I also witnessed numerous other mysterious victuals popping up in passengers' laps, which Linda identified for me, including such standard Asian fare as chicken feet, scallion pancakes, pickled pigs' ears, jars of soup with a stale sour odor. But by far the worst of them all was a rotten smelling tofu dish. It was so offensive, I felt it necessary to complain to the stewardess.

"I cannot take the intense foul odor," I grimaced, shooting my eyes in the general direction of the sewer-like fetor. "Could you please move us to another part of the plane?"

She was Chinese, like all the other personnel on the plane, and said to me in a very matter-of-fact manner, "What smell, sir?"

And that was the end of that. If only there was a parachute on board; by now I'd have strapped it on and headed for the nearest exit door.

Probably the most tortuous 23 hours of my life later, we were finally landing at Hong Kong International Airport. I had switched with Linda to the window seat (too bad I couldn't have opened it for some fresh air); when the pilot announced that we were beginning our descent. My focus went out the window, looking to find my salvation—the ground, my escape from this flying prison where unsuspecting whitey is subjected to torture by inhumanly designed seats that contort the body, slow starvation due to the unpalatable plane food, and constant subjection to those concentrated vile odors. Yes, in only a few minutes I'd be released from this pressurized tube of horror, but escaping to where? We still had to catch another flight to Taipei.

As the plane lost altitude, I could see the airport in the near distance. *Strange, why are all those tall buildings standing right next to the runway?* They ran parallel to it creating a canyon that looked so narrow I was worried the plane was too wide to fit. Then came a sharp hard turn and we dropped rapidly. I was feeling sick. I didn't know if it was from the rancid smelling food, or just plain fear.

The plane approached the runway, and the tall buildings loomed on both sides of us. I was glued to the window, sure that the tips of the wings were going to cut into the glass and brick facades. The plane's airspeed quickly decelerated to the point where I was actually able to catch glimpses of people in business meetings with colleagues. We were so close, I could differentiate them as being Caucasian or Asian.

After a lengthy period of gut-wrenching anxiety (well, maybe 30 seconds), the wheels touched down on concrete and the plane braked to a stop. I let out a sigh of relief and tried to compose myself for the next flight, leaving for Taipei in 30 minutes.

Good news for all future travelers heading to Hong Kong: the government decided years ago to close Kai Tak Airport and relocate it to a less densely populated area saving many a white-knuckle experience where passengers got the chance to see that special movie short. You know, the one where your life flashes before your eyes. Starting in 1998 the weary international traveler now lands at Hong Kong International Airport on the island of Chek Lap Kock. Unless they have a death wish, I'm sure most airline pilots are also relieved.

I had survived the main leg of the grueling journey. I should've found solace in that the remaining hop to Taipei would take only 50 minutes. Instead, I was bubbling over with anxiety. For soon I'd find myself face-to-face with the person whose blessing I'd need in order to get married: Linda's mom.

7. The Outlaw Meets the In-Laws

The trip had taken its toll on me. I was tired, nauseated and disoriented. Here I thought I was a seasoned flier, but for the first time in my young life I was experiencing major jet lag.

Linda, on the other hand, had traveled back and forth from Asia to the States many times. She had tried to get me to sleep on the plane, so I could reset my internal clock to deal with the 13-hour time change. However, being in such a physically challenged environment, all attempts at slumber were futile. I arrived in Taipei wasted, worn out, unable to comprehend English let alone Mandarin, Cantonese, native Taiwanese or the broken Chinglish that my future in-laws all were about to throw at me. Each one excited for the chance to hone their English language skills and taking full advantage of the opportunity to speak with an American dude. But today I was an American vegetable.

When I exited the air-conditioned terminal, it was like someone smacked me in the face with a hot wet rag. I could feel the life being sucked out of my already weak body. At 6:00 PM it was still 95 degrees with a humidity level of 90+ percent. It took mere seconds before rivulets of sweat were streaming down the sides of my face. It was akin to stepping into a steam sauna fully dressed.

At the curb we were greeted by Linda's oldest sister, her husband and one of her middle sisters. Again, Linda comes from a family with six girls and one boy. In Chinese, you refer to each one with a number, except for the oldest who's called Big Sister.

The Chinese pronunciations I provide throughout the book, such as Da4 jie3, which in English translates to Big Sister, end in numbers that provide the correct intonation to properly enunciate them. For the time being, please disregard them unless you already know how to use the system called "pin yin" for transliterating Chinese ideograms into the Roman alphabet—trust me, very confusing.

After Big Sister, there's Sister Two, the brother, who likes to be called by his Chinese name "Shi2 Hai2", Sister Four, Sister Five, Sister Six (Linda) and the youngest, Sister Seven, who I called Little Sister or Little Ling. Several years later I was given the honor of bestowing English names on all the family members. I resisted the temptation to go with names like Gertrude, Hortense, Flossie, or Wilhelmina. Instead, I picked way cooler ones from a list of inductees into the Rock N Roll Hall of Fame. I was a child of the 70s and just couldn't resist.

In any event, Big Sister, her husband and Sister Four, picked us up in their tiny Taiwan built car, a 1987 Yue Loong Feeling. While the little 1.6-liter Nissan engine ran like a charm, the rest of the car was far inferior to other import options, and just like the airline we flew in on, it was out of business within a few years.

The trunk was smaller than a bread box and could only hold two of the five pieces of luggage we brought. One of those pieces never made it to Taipei. Somewhere in Hong Kong, a Chinese person is wearing my favorite Rolling Stones T-shirt with a picture of Keith Richards and "Let's Get Stoned" printed on the back. I looked at the car, not much bigger than my Z was, trying to figure out how we'd all fit. Solution: three of us squeezed into the back seat and Big Sister's husband piled the other two suitcases on top of me.

It was déjà vu revisited twice again when Sister Four opened a brown paper bag and handed me something to eat.

"Preserved dried plum. Common Asian treat. You try," Linda suggested.

This time, thank heavens, it was odorless. I popped it into my mouth and it slowly dissolved flooding my taste buds with soothing sweet and sour flavors.

At the time I could only say "thank you" and "goodbye" in Mandarin. Naturally I got them mixed up and said bye.

They all had a big laugh on me, which became routine from then on. Each time I tried to speak Chinese, everyone around me would get a big kick out of the goofy American.

The tiny engine of the Feeling came to life and Big Sister's husband drove to my potential mother-in-law's home in Taoyuan, a small town approximately 14 miles from Taipei. I didn't have much chance to look out the window at the passing scenery. I was curious but too tired to lift the cannonball that was my head. Added to that, I was pinned down by both of Linda's

60 lb. suitcases. The motion of the car worked like a sedative and within a few minutes I zonked out.

When we arrived, Linda had to shake me violently to arouse me from my coma-like state. You might think that I'd have slept like a baby that evening, but nothing could be further from the truth. The jet lag had burrowed deep into my soul. I would not get a wink of sleep for the next three days.

My potential mother-in-law's home was three stories and built like a fortress out of steel and concrete. Thanks to earthquakes and typhoons, this was the norm in this part of the world. The house had no air-conditioning; instead, an electric floor fan was set in each room. The first floor had a living/dining room, and a kitchen in the rear. The second floor, where the family all slept, had four tiny bedrooms and one bathroom. The top floor, a converted attic with low angled ceilings, was used for general storage.

Linda's mother, who I was instructed to call "Ma", had no way of knowing that I'd show up both exhausted and nauseated from my trip. She'd spent the entire day preparing a feast for my arrival. Ma had even bought a live chicken, which she killed and butchered in her backyard just a few hours before we landed. She used the fresh chicken meat as an ingredient in several of the traditional Chinese dishes she'd made for the family banquet. There were also two types of fish, numerous green vegetables, none of which I'd ever seen before, and three unrecognizable meat dishes sitting on the table.

SIDEBAR: I'd later learn that, what looked to me like an all-you-can-eat buffet, was in fact an everyday meal for them. And for the life of me, I'll never figure out how they can eat all that chow and stay scarecrow thin?

When I was introduced to Ma, she looked at me in a curious manner, sizing up her daughter's first-round draft pick. I couldn't tell whether she was impressed or intimidated by my height.

Then, walking away, she announced in a sharp tone, "chi1 fan4 le5." Translation: "Time to eat." Ma's proclamation didn't appear to be directed at me, rather the rest of the family.

I whispered to Linda, "Did I do something wrong? Is your mom upset with me?"

"No," she replied, "Just her way. You too much worry."

My stomach was turning summersaults, but I knew I had no choice. If I declined to eat, I might offend Ma. I still needed her approval, and I'd do anything to secure it.

At 7:00 PM it was still close to 90 degrees outside and remained sticky. Inside this concrete hotbox it was even worse. I told Linda, "I seriously need a quick shower."

Big Sister looked at me and announced in butchered English, "You go bedroom three floor. Toilet two floor. You no can sleep Hua Mei." Translation: "Liu house rules—unwed couples sleep apart—nightly bootie calls...Not allowed!"

At least, I was pretty sure that's what she meant. I grabbed my bags and bolted up the stairs directly to the bathroom, barely making it to the toilet before I tossed my cookies.

I recovered somewhat after a soothing, cool shower, but given the house's sauna-like conditions, by the time I got dressed and went down to eat I'd completely sweated through my only shirt, which was starting to smell a little gamey.

I have to say, Ma was a pretty good cook. While I had no idea what I was eating, the dishes offered up to my palate wonderful flavors, and my olfactory system was adjusting to the strange-but-pleasant smells coming from the unidentifiable foods. Things were definitely looking up until I finished supper, and the war in my stomach reengaged. I rocketed up the stairs to the bathroom, kicked open the door, and barely made it in time before I projectile vomited dinner.

There I was, kneeling on the floor with my head halfway in the toilet bowl, when I heard an audible gasp, followed by a loud raspy voice: "Wo3 de5 tian1 na5!" which I was later told is the Chinese equivalent of "Oh my God!"

I turned my head and there stood Ma. No interpreter necessary. The look of pure horror on her face spelled it out for me. I'd just performed the ultimate insult to the woman who'd been cooking all day in preparation for my visit.

A moment later, Linda arrived at the bathroom entrance. Ma stood in place, arms folded, shaking her head and muttering things I was pretty darn sure weren't flattering. Linda knew the real reason I'd ralphed. She conversed with Ma, attempting to explain.

But you know what they say about first impressions. Ma was a tough old bird; I feared I'd just destroyed any chance I had at winning her over. Ma spun on her heels and disappeared. I gargled, then Linda took me by the hand and led me downstairs to the kitchen.

Linda discussed my situation with Big Sister, who decided to brew some special tea to help settle my stomach. She pulled out a handful of dark tea leaves from a steel canister that sat on the kitchen counter.

Ma popped out of nowhere, immediately taking over while loudly spewing out words that clearly meant, *Get out! This is my domain!*

I watched from a safe distance as she placed the leaves into what looked like an oversized thimble which was then inserted into a larger vessel full of hot water. The leaves steeped for a few minutes, and to my amazement, the tea worked like a charm. My tummy soon settled down. But, later that night, alone on the hot and humid top floor of the house, I was unable to fall asleep. My bed was a thin mat not much softer than the hardwood surface underneath. A floor fan only pushed the hot, muggy air around. I was a spoiled American from Chicago, used to sleeping during the summer on my beloved Sealy Posturepedic pillow-top mattress under a lightweight down comforter with the central air running at full blast. But I dared not complain. I was already on razor-thin ice with Ma.

The next day I could aptly be described as a zombie; no sleep and still no appetite. Ma wouldn't look me in the eyes; but with Linda's prodding, she half-heartedly prepared me Congee, a rice dish. Chinese consider this comfort food, but it's also eaten when they're feeling under the weather. Congee is the Asian get-well equivalent to Jewish chicken soup, but with a texture more like our oatmeal. It basically has the flavor of cardboard unless something is added to it. Americans put slices of banana, strawberries, blueberries and brown sugar in their oatmeal. Chinese add chicken stock, scallions, fish, meat; and zha4 cai4, which is a type of pickle from a mustard plant originating in Sichuan, China. Even, *lord have mercy*, slices of the dreaded brown thousand-year-old egg. Both cultures regard their dishes as wholesome, easy on the stomach fare. Afterwards, I felt a trace better, but that night my attempt at sleep once again was for nil.

The following morning, at what must've been 5 or 6 AM, through the open window of my attic-bedroom came an unmistakable sound that stirred me to attention; a sound that by the age of seven had already been indelibly ingrained into the mind of every American child; a sound that immediately fired up all the neurons in our little brains alerting us to the wondrous joy that was rolling down the street in front of our home. If you grew up in the U.S., you know I'm talking about the euphoric musical jingle of the Good Humor truck. *Is it possible that GH ice cream is sold in Taoyuan? And if so, why would the truck be out so damn early? Did I finally fall asleep and now I'm dreaming? In my weakened condition am I starting to hallucinate?* Mine was not to question why, mine was but to eat ice cream or die.

At that moment I felt an incredible surge of energy. A good analogy would be the power rush experienced by a man dying of thirst in the desert when he spots an oasis in the near distance offering water and shade. I hopped up from my simulated bed of nails, threw on my shorts and darted down the stairs, out the front door at breakneck speed, pushing my body past all physical limits toward the Holy Grail, visions of a white coconut ice cream bar dancing in my head. As both a child and an adult, it was my top pick Good Humor treat. Now, I'm not talking about the frozen ice crap they currently peddle from their trucks, but the original, made with real vanilla ice cream and loaded with huge coconut flakes. I don't mean to knock the company's new products, but when it comes to things like that I tend to obsess.

Once outside, I followed the sound down the street to the end of the block and around the corner. I found it somewhat odd there were no signs of children emerging from the houses I passed, filing out one-by-one, running to the truck with money gripped tightly in little hands to get their favorite delight before the vehicle moved on to the next neighborhood. In my state of delirium, my brain was ordering me, *Who cares about the kiddies? I need my fix, and right now nothing else matters!*

The sound grew louder as I jogged down the street, full of hope and anticipation, thinking, *This trip is looking more promising!* My spirits were rising, my stomach felt better, and I was excited about putting something in my mouth that I knew would be cool, delicious, satisfying and psychologically comforting.

I dashed around the corner...and came to a screeching halt, then dropped to my knees in total despair. *What?!* Ixnay Good Humor. It was the morning garbage truck beckoning to the neighborhood's residents to bring out their trash. *What kind of sick twisted mind has garbage trucks playing a children's song offering up the promise of cold creamy delights?* It was only now I noticed various adults carrying bags and boxes of refuse and heading in the same direction.

My spirits totally crushed, I stumbled back to the house. I was too despondent to care about potential repercussions from Ma, and climbed the stairs to the second floor, snuck into Linda's room, and quietly laid down next to her. At 6:15 AM the air was still thick and dense, but the temperature had cooled down to a slightly more reasonable 84 degrees Fahrenheit. Bathed in sweat and unable to sleep, all I could do was lie there wondering, *What other disappointments and embarrassments await me?*

8. Heap Little Medicine Man

Later that morning, with what I assumed was jet lag still holding a vice grip on my haggard body, Linda took me into town for help. We entered a cramped store stocked with myriad small boxes of what appeared to be a vast assortment of dried plants; plus several wooden shelves loaded with glass vials of various sizes, filled with multicolored liquids. The store had a strong but soothing fragrant smell.

Linda introduced me to the herbalist, then explained, "Many centuries, Chinese use herb treat maladies. I think fix you?"

We were standing in front of a long glass counter at the rear of the store; she spoke briefly in Chinese to the diminutive grey-haired old man. To me he looked like a pint-size witch doctor. Of course, I couldn't understand a word, and with skepticism I watched him shake his head, appearing to understand my problem.

He came out from behind the counter and walked around me several times looking me up and down, again nodding his head as if he'd read my detailed medical chart and was aware of all my physical deficiencies. Next, he darted about, surprisingly fast, picking out dried plants from various boxes in the shop; then zipped over to the counter where he pulled down several glass vials from the shelves that lined the store walls. These were placed on the counter where he carefully measured each component before dropping them all into a large round stone mortar. He ground the ingredients into a fine powder with a granite pestle. Once satisfied with the texture of the mixture, he used something that looked like honey to bind the final product then forced the contents into a plastic capsule which he handed over to Linda. The herbalist also prepared a special tea that he brewed in front of us.

I was instructed to swallow the capsule and drink the tea. I did a double take. The capsule looked more like a horse pill. The last time I saw one that large was at the Bronx Zoo, and they were treating a hippopotamus. I had strong reservations whether I could possibly swallow it. If by luck I was able to get it past my tongue and into my throat, I was worried it'd get stuck halfway down. Tomorrow's headline would read: "Funny American commit suicide by self-asphyxiation—Chinese have last laugh!"

With both Linda and the ancient medicine man coaxing me on, I realized I had nothing to lose. After three days without sleep my organs would probably start to shut down anyway. I popped the giant capsule into my mouth, then guzzled the warm tea which somehow pushed it into my esophagus. A cross-eyed swallow later, I could swear I heard a cannonball-like splash when the pill hit my stomach.

On our way back to the house I said to Linda, "No offense, but is there a regular internist I could see?"

Linda shot me a scorching look, then proceeded to give me a lecture on Traditional Chinese Herbal Medicine, concluding with, "Each mixture custom. Cocktail have much good stuff help you." She narrowed her eyes. "Chinese use herb 5,000 years. Why you think fancy American doctor better?"

Later, back in New York, I did a computer search and learned that traditional Chinese medicine has a treatment arsenal of over 300 commonly used herbs, plus other ingredients including, wolf berries, dried rhubarb, peony, astragalus, salvia, and ginger root to name a few—even, literally, snake oil. In Western medicine, they use a growing base of scientific and anatomical knowledge, constantly developing new techniques and approaches to improve diagnosis and treatment. Quite the reverse is true in Traditional Chinese Herbal Medicine where the older the remedy, the more it is used and revered. Though improvements do occasionally come available, they are always built on the foundation of the old recipes. When in doubt, the ancient ways take precedence.

Recently, traditional Chinese herbal medicine has been gaining popularity in the West. Two reasons: (1) It's far less expensive, which makes it available to a much wider demographic, and (2) In almost all cases, it has been found to work.

When we arrived back at Ma's house she was nowhere to be found. Big Sister informed Linda, in English so I would understand, "Ma go neighbor house play Mahjong. She make Congee. Go kitchen eat."

Linda said supportively, "Lucky you. Ma make Sam Congee!" *Oh yeah? If she'd indeed made it especially for me,* I observed, *then why is the entire family eating the same dish for lunch?*

I finished the concoction, then Linda led me upstairs and rubbed an ointment into my shoulders, neck and back. It had the look of Vaseline and smelled like the weight room at my gym. I guess the combination of the jumbo pill, the Congee, special tea and the Chinese ointment, called "Wan4 Jin1 You2", Translation: "10,000 Gold Oil", was what the doctor ordered…I finally fell into a God-blessed sleep. I was out cold a solid 12 hours, waking up the following day feeling incredibly refreshed with all the toxins apparently flushed from my body.

Then and there I vowed; *Never again will I say a skeptical word about Chinese medicine! Oh yes, and before I forget, I'd like to apologize to that wonderful old and wise herbalist about my earlier 'witch doctor' remark. You saved my ass, sir!*

The trauma was over, and I was ready to open my mind and my soul to fully experience life from a very different perspective. This was the first, and certainly not the last of many opinions I would change.

9. Big Breakfast of Little Eats

By mid-morning there was a gnawing hunger in my belly. The family, all fourteen of them (don't worry I'm not going to rattle off each of their numbers) wanted to take me out for a traditional Taiwanese breakfast called "xiao3 chi1". Translation: "little eats". These are small dishes sold at open street food stands or small restaurants.

We walked out of the hot and sticky house into the steamy and stagnant air. Even though I was feeling better my body still hadn't adjusted to the debilitating heat. I assumed the best remedy was to hydrate myself the good ol' Yankee way with ice cold water. Isn't that the normal American protocol? When it's hot, hot, hot, you drink cold, cold, cold to cool the body. Makes perfect sense—right?

The locals stared at the silly American guzzling ice water and shook their heads in amusement. It was now late morning and with the temperature already back up into the 90s the natives were all drinking warm tea. I quickly learned that they were right, and the simpleton from the West was wrong.

Really? Who'd know better? The giant sweaty Caucasian from New York, or the cool and comfortable residents who grew up living day-to-day in the enormous oppressive steam bath? Here's what they already knew: First, temperature influences our thirst indirectly by making us sweat, thereby losing body fluid. Evaporation of this sweat, in turn, produces a cooling affect. So, it has nothing to do with drinking ice-cold water. In fact, when you drink very cold water your system can't immediately process it. The water needs to heat up to your body temperature before it can be absorbed on a cellular level.

In addition, if you drink ice-cold water on a hot day your integumentary system must exert more energy to restore the body temperature back to its normal 98.6 degrees F. There must be some mathematical formula to confirm this theory, and of course we all know how good Asians are at math.

Take Linda, for example. She's wicked smart at anything to do with numbers. Actually, she's wicked smart at almost everything. That's why I'm so well trained. To give you some insight, the Asian husband training program is very similar to its Jewish counterpart. I hope the Jewish and Asian women take this as a compliment. Come to think of it, that may be why there are so many Asian women marrying Caucasian Jewish men. The men assimilate smoothly to the training program, which in most cases is done subliminally. We men don't even know what hit us. See what I mean…wicked smart!

Back to the food; so there I was sitting at the corner neighborhood street stand with all my potential in-laws. It was wide open with only one wall and a roof that sported numerous ceiling fans. They led me up to the counter and instructed me to choose whatever I desired from behind the glass. Several women prepared food on grills and in large kettles. Everything was made fresh right in front of you.

A line of people behind me were waiting to order. I didn't want to be rude, but I also wanted to be safe. I took my time and carefully pointed to various items I could barely identify. I selected something red with egg in it that looked somewhat palatable. There were sandwiches with grayish things inside that turned out to be dried fish. *Yuck!* I also selected the scallion pancakes, which I had before in New York, plus a small assortment of dumplings.

They also offered a cold tofu drink that came plain or sweet. I'm not sure why there's a disconnect between the theory of hot weather warm drinks and the always-cold tofu drink at breakfast. There was also something called "shao1 bing3 you2 tiao2", a long thin deep-fried bread wrapped in a flat baked bread jacket. No barbeque sauce to dip it in, no cheese stuffed inside, no butter or jelly to smear on the top—just bread wrapped with bread? But it was so delicious I had to have one every morning as part of my "xiao3 chi1" little eats breakfast along with a chilled plastic cup of the tofu drink.

With jet lag gone, I was now able to venture out daily with the family to sample the multitude of options at the neighborhood street markets. However, my heart wasn't in it. I came to Taiwan with Linda primarily to prove to her mother I'd be a worthy husband. But Ma continued to cold-shoulder me. When she did acknowledge my presence, it was not with a smile or kind word, rather a grunt or a dismissive glance. Maybe she just didn't want to waste her time trying to communicate with a moronic, ill-mannered white devil who only knew a thimbleful of Chinese words.

I knew if I didn’t find a way to get Ma to accept me, I'd spend each remaining day in Taiwan with the clock running out on my future with the woman I loved.

10. Sizing up Taipei

A week before our return to New York, Big Sister and Linda planned an outing with the family to Taipei; Taiwan's largest metropolis. The trip on the congested single lane highway took over an hour to travel the 15 miles to Sister Four's house in the heart of the city.

At the last minute, Ma decided to join us. I was surprised when she opened the rear door of the tiny Yue Loong Feeling and sat down next to Linda and me. *Is her glacial attitude toward me finally beginning to thaw?* I truly had no clue. During the entire trip she never glanced in my direction, but she did talk nonstop all the way.

At one point, I whispered into Linda's ear, "Does this mean your mom is loosening up?"

"Baby steps, Sam," Linda said under her breath, "baby steps."

Residential and commercial buildings rimmed both sides of the highway. To reduce the traffic in the U.S., the government set up HOV (High Occupancy Vehicle) lanes or, if enough money was available, they'd use eminent domain to tear down houses and expand the highway. In Taiwan they decided to leave the buildings right where they were and build a new viaduct on both sides of the old one, but 40 feet above it. I doubted such a feat would be possible back home. First, the labor unions would strike in protest of the inhospitable working conditions followed by a colossal class-action lawsuit from the thousands of residents whose homes would be cast into darkness by the massive structure.

While we cruised along in heavy traffic at a whopping 15 mph, out the window I saw *hundreds* of men working at a fever's pitch high above me. They were setting forms, pouring concrete and installing steel. No one sat idle.

How is this possible? I wondered. It was almost 100 degrees outside with the humidity so high you'd need a Ginsu knife to cut it. Actually, I think Ginsu is a Japanese knife, but I'd bet the bank that it's made in China along with my phone, stereo, most of my clothes, parts of my Japanese car, and the Boeing jet I flew in on. Sorry, but I digress.

The work ethic of these highway construction workers was remarkable. How could they do such a difficult job in such tough conditions at such a fast pace? On Long Island, close to a home I later owned in Roslyn, NY, they just completed a replacement bridge that runs a half mile, 30 feet above a stream. For *five* years I drove back and forth over that bridge while it was under construction. During that lengthy period, crossing over hundreds of times on an old remaining section, I never saw more than four workers on the project and at least two of them were always sitting on the side with a cup of coffee or a cell phone in their hand. What else would you expect from a government project with a union crew? Just for comparison, the new viaduct I observed that day was 30 miles long and completed in less than two years under intense weather conditions. No disrespect to

American workers, but it's easy to see why, over the past few decades, China's annual economic growth rate has continuously outpaced that of the U.S.

Upon arrival in Taipei we drove to Sister Four's apartment where we planned to stay for a few days. It was a three bedroom flat with a living/dining room combination, a tiny kitchen and a small balcony that housed the washing machine – no dryer. Clothes were removed from the washer, then hung outside on a clothesline to dry. Based on my experiences, walking around Taipei, that seemed to be standard procedure. The entire apartment measured less than 600 square feet. Four people lived there: Sister Four, her husband and their two children, who doubled up leaving one bedroom available. See how considerate my potential in-laws were. Sister Four had even called her daughter an hour before we arrived to make sure she turned on the one window air-conditioner in the flat. Linda told me they almost never used it.

When we entered their studio-size three-bedroom, I cringed as I spotted my probable nightly berth, the two-seater burlap sofa, center living room. With Ma heading back home after dinner, I prayed to *whoeve*r that Sister Four would cut me some slack on the sleeping arrangements.

Taipei (pop. 2 million) is a much bigger city than Taoyuan (pop. 200,000). Therefore, you have a much denser population, plus a lot more concrete buildings which turns it into a human oven roaster during the summer months.

Since the thrifty airline that soon would file for bankruptcy lost my luggage, after we settled in, Linda took me out to a department store to shop for clothes. Four pieces of luggage held Linda's clothes and of course the one they lost held mine. I think I might have been singled out by the airline. Most likely the one other Caucasian's luggage on the flight also disappeared. Whadaya think...payback for complaining to the stewardess about the nasty smells coming from the other passengers?

You don't need a car in Taipei. You can either walk, bike—or hop a taxi. They are everywhere and very inexpensive. We'd decided to walk to the department store, just a few blocks away. Back in 1987 there were very few foreigners living in or visiting Taipei. In addition, since the standard American diet of Cheese Whiz, McDonalds, hot dogs and pizza hadn't yet spread thick roots in Asia, everyone I passed on the streets was very thin—and at least a foot shorter than me. I got a sense of how Gulliver must've felt among the Lilliputians.

We arrived at Ming Yao Department Store and took the escalator upstairs to the men's section. Along the way all the store clerks were bowing to me. At first, I thought that maybe they saw me as a special visitor, like a king from a foreign country. Not to be ungracious, I bowed low in return only to see the look of confusion on their faces. Less than a minute later I realized they were bowing to everyone. Anyway, as a marketing ploy I thought it was a nice touch.

"Qing3 wen4, you3 mei2 you3 ta1 de5 chi3 cun5?" Linda said to one of the sales clerks, gesturing at me. Translation: "Do you carry anything that will fit him?"

The girl surveyed me up and down and replied, “Zhe4 ge1 wai4 guo2 ren2 hen3 gao1 da4,” which loosely translates as: "This foreigner sure is a whopper!"

The two of them disappeared for a few minutes, leaving me standing there alone for everyone to gawk at. They returned with only two pairs of pants and three shirts. “These biggest ones,” Linda said, handing them to me.

In the cramped dressing room, I first put the pants on. The cuffs came above my ankles—I looked like the freakin’ Hulk. Next, the shirts, where the bottoms were above my belly button.

Is Linda doing this on purpose to get a good laugh? I wondered. *Is there a hidden TV crew in the store, and I’m on Chinese Candid Camera?* Then I realized it had to do with sales volume and profits. There was practically nobody like me, the Paul Bunyan size American, buying clothes in Taiwan.

We spent the rest of the day going store to store, fruitlessly searching for the largest clothes available. Though I did find one pair of nerdy plaid pants, and a couple XXXL T-shirts that were still a little tight. Apart from what I had on, these were all the clothes I had to wear for the remaining two weeks of the trip.

By the end of the day we were both exhausted from all the *attempted* shopping. We must’ve gone through half of the clothing stores in Taipei to find my new 3-piece wardrobe. I took after my dad, eating fast, sometimes spilling food and/or drink on my clothing. I'd need to be extra careful not to stain my limited duds and avoid Linda having to constantly remind me, like a little child, "Sammy need be careful. Eat over table."

We returned to the apartment where Sister Four's daughter, Xiang Wen, informed us, "Mom go out. Buy food."

I was anxious to sit back, relax and have a nice simple and quiet home cooked meal. *Hmmm, spaghetti with meatballs, and a nice glass of cabernet sauvignon would be great! Or Veal Marsala with a Chianti Classico Riserva...Yeah, good luck with that!* I should've been excited to explore the culinary delights of a real honest-to-god Chinese meal. However, I was completely brainwashed by the American cuisine marketing machine. I had strong cravings for something high in carbohydrates, fat, salt and sugar. But as long as it wasn't another bowl of Congee, I was ready for almost anything.

Xiang Wen rattled off in Chinese, and Linda translated: "Tonight, all family come. Want meet you."

In all there'd be over 25 people. Everyone was coming out of the woodwork to attend this special event in my honor. So much for a quiet, relaxing evening. I couldn't imagine how this big a crowd could all fit, and how a tiny kitchen with only one burner could pump out enough food.

At 3:30 PM, Ma, Big Sister, Sister Two and Sister Five returned and bee-lined to the kitchen to start readying the meal. Chinese cuisine takes a lot of preparation before you start cooking. Volumes of various vegetables are washed and cut; meats are marinated and/or seasoned then sliced or minced; shrimp is deveined; fish is cleaned and prepped; fresh garlic and ginger are peeled and chopped; and on and on.

The five of them—including Linda, which shocked me because I couldn't recall her cooking anything since I moved in with her—worked in a surprisingly efficient manner preparing the innumerable items that'd be tossed into the jumbo wok.

Sister Four arrived moments later with two more large plastic bags filled with crustaceans. Several of them were moving on their own. Chinese mentality: Start with the freshest ingredients! She put everything down on the kitchen counter, and the sisters went to work, taking the live shrimp, lobsters and crabs from the bags and slaughtering them.

Lucky there isn't a steak dish on the menu! I chortled to myself. All kidding aside, every good cook and professional chef will tell you that the fresher the better. When I was a boy, my mom mostly used frozen or packaged ingredients. She never brought home anything live to cook and we rarely had green vegetables unless you count the frozen peas that were tossed into the beef stew. I'm not saying Mom wasn't a good cook. I loved all the food she prepared including her Jewish chop suey, but tonight I was in for a special treat.

At 6:30 PM sharp, all the in-laws descended on the apartment. Everyone who entered first took off their shoes, standard Chinese tradition, greeted Ma, then me and Linda. I was elated. Why wouldn't I be? I was the guest of honor and with the air-conditioning gunning full blast, the room was approaching comfortable.

With all the in-laws piling into the tiny apartment, the kitchen had to start pumping out the food. I could see by the hungry look on all their faces, these people came to eat!

Ma, who I secretly referred to as "The Little General", ordered all women to the kitchen to assist in the final prep for the family feast.

The guys remained in the living room waiting to be served. Back almost 30 years ago, Taiwanese men were a chauvinistic lot. While Linda, her mother and sisters were slaving in the kitchen, there I was reclining in the cooled down living room with my new buds, downing bottles of Taiwan beer.

In Chinese there's a saying to cover every situation. In this case it could've been "Tian1 xia4 mei2 you3 bai2 chi1 de5 wu3 can1." Translation: "In all the world there is no such thing as a free lunch." I knew it was a mistake when I shot Linda a smug look of sublime satisfaction, as if to say, *I could get used to this life!* Oh yes, a day of reckoning was undoubtedly in my future.

Did I tell you that Linda is not only wicked smart, but like an elephant she never forgets? For a more descriptive analogy, if Ma was The Little General, Linda would be The Little Colonel unless she gets hungry, then she turns into Attila the Hun. Given my current geographical location, maybe a better comparison would be Genghis Khan.

The men all lit up their cigarettes and the room became a smog bank. During that period, most men in Taiwan smoked like factories and my potential brothers-in-law were no exception.

Within minutes from the time I sat down with the boys, I heard a sizzling sound issuing from the kitchen. My curiosity drove me to stand up and walk over toward the tiny packed room to have a peek. The wok, the sole cooking vessel used in the concoction of each and every dish served that evening, was now in high gear. It sat on an oversized burner and was heated slightly before oil was added. Once hot, the oil was dressed up with finely chopped ginger and garlic, giving off a wonderful aroma as it disintegrated into the mix.

Ma barked out the orders, directing each sister, one-by-one, to bring over various ingredients to integrate into the fragrant oil. Sister Four made the mistake of pouring her plate of lobster into the hot steel wok and Ma immediately chastised her, not wanting anyone else doing the actual cooking. She was the master chef and all the girls were her prep crew. Don't get me wrong, Ma was no prima donna. This little tyrant of a woman didn't mind helping with any of the menial tasks that needed doing. After dinner, when it came time for the massive cleanup, she pitched right in with the other girls. While she was only 4-foot-nothing tall, Ma had the presence and voracity of a born leader, hence her military nickname.

The dishes came out in single file and were placed on the table in the dining area. I will not befuddle you with all their

Chinese names. I'll only describe the essence of each dish based on my interpretation using my senses of sight, smell, and taste. The first entree was lobster prepared Cantonese style: lightly coated with a batter of egg, scallion, flour, garlic and ginger.

Many years later I had several Jewish friends over at my house for dinner. One of the more generous couples arrived with ten 2 lb. live lobsters. Sister Four was visiting from Taipei and volunteered to cook that day. She prepared the lobsters two ways—five made in the standard New England style, steamed and served with hot butter, and five made Cantonese style, basted in a special egg batter and cooked in the wok. When dinner was over, we had five lobsters left. I'm sure you've already guessed correctly; they were all the New England style lobsters—case closed. Sorry, but I digress again.

Back to the banquet. The second dish was an intensely green leafy vegetable. Over the years it has become my go-to meat accompaniment—baby snow pea shoots with fresh garlic. Considered expensive in Asian circles, it's eaten only on special occasions. I guess my potential in-laws thought I was worth the splurge.

Up next was fried squares of tofu. A large block of fresh tofu was cut into two-inch squares, covered with some type of bread crumb mix, then dropped into the hot fragrant oil. There was a dipping sauce to accompany the dish made with soy sauce, vinegar and some type of spice. I also tasted a slight plum flavor. When popped into your mouth the contrast between the crispy outside and the soft velvety texture of the hot tofu was truly amazing. This could be presented with a slight twist in Manhattan at one of those trendy fusion restaurants. I can already envision it on the tasting menu at David Chang's Momofuku: "Asian Velvet Tofu & Pork Fat Cubes" $25. For that price you'd only get three small squares.

Next in the lineup was a dish you put together yourself. The ingredients included individual iceberg lettuce leaves laid out on a separate dish, a large bowl of shrimp & water chestnuts diced into tiny pieces, and a second large bowl that contained chopped up "you2 tiao2", the long thin fried bread that I was eating every day for breakfast. I was instructed by Sister Five to take a lettuce leaf, add the shrimp/water chestnuts and fried bread bits, then fold the whole thing over making a small closed pocket. When biting into the mixture, you first get the freshness of the lettuce, then the flavor of the shrimp comes through followed by the crunchy texture of the fried bread and water chestnuts. This one also deserved a gold star. It was looking like I'd soon be adding back the weight I lost during the first few days of the trip.

But hold your horseradish—we were not done yet. Several more dishes were in the works. There was so much food I thought this had to be a once-a-year event. However, I enjoyed several of the same fantastic feasts before Linda and I flew back to New York.

OK, here we go; on came scrambled eggs, chopped scallions and tomatoes all thrown together and cooked in hot oil—very tasty. Following that, two more vegetable dishes, green and bitter; they didn't match up well with my American taste buds which are geared more to the sweet, sour, salty and savory.

We then had a meat dish containing diced chicken. I wasn't sure if this critter was also walking around on its own when it first arrived at the apartment. The poultry was cooked in combination with water chestnuts, green and red peppers and peanuts. It was very, very, very spicy. And, did I say, it was spicy? No one had warned me not to eat the thin purple peppers—Nice! With all those American action movies such as *Rambo*, *The Terminator* and *Die Hard*, maybe my potential Chinese in-laws just wanted to see how tough I really was. Ignorant and trusting, I tossed one into my mouth and bit down on it a couple times then swallowed. I experienced an immediate explosion of heat. It felt like lava was screaming down my throat. My eye-popping facial expression said it all! Everyone was enjoying the show, the whole family burst out laughing.

Imagine my surprise when Ma handed me a cup of hot tea and gestured with her hand to drink. There was no smile or show of sympathy. She provided the assistance in an expressionless, nonchalant manner, then darted into the kitchen before I had the chance to say, "Xie4 xie5" ("Thank you"). Linda later explained that Ma knew not to give me a glass of cold water, which would've increased the sting of the pepper.

Now wouldn't that have been a funny encore if Linda had offered me ice water? It would've been the perfect opportunity to get even for having to slave for me in the kitchen. The hot green brew worked like a miracle elixir. Interesting how you always feel better after a cup.

Ma returned from the kitchen with the last and by far the best dish of all: her *pièce de résistance,* a beautiful whole fish served on a large white porcelain platter.

"This steamed sea bass. Ma chop ginger, cilantro. Add white wine, soy sauce. Make most delicious. You like," Linda whispered to me.

I'd never been big on fish, but this was amazing—so tender, with the flavors from the fresh ginger and sauce all dancing happily together in my mouth.

As I've gotten older, fish has become a staple in my diet. While I've eaten seafood at French, Italian, American and Greek restaurants, I can honestly say that when it comes to cooking fish, no one does it better than the Chinese. Linda would admit that the Japanese also make pretty darn good fish, but it's frequently served raw. I was raised a barbequed meat guy. I don't do raw.

The evening turned out better than I expected. The food was over-the-top fabulous; Linda's family were all warm and hospitable; well, that is, all but Ma, who continued to wear the consummate poker face. I still had no idea where I stood with her.

11. Mahjong-jong-jong-jong

When everyone was finished, the plates were cleared, by the women of course, and the main event of the evening would soon begin. The kitchen table was put back to the center of the dining area.

Linda informed me, "Table have much good desserts. Taiwan fruit and Ma special red bean soup. Sam, you try."

Two folded surfaces, with small plastic drawers on each side, “The Mahjong Tables” were unfolded and placed in the middle of the living room. Eight chairs were carried over and oblong shaped tiles with Chinese characters took center stage. Virtually every inch of the apartment was occupied, and with the opening of the additional tables something had to give. In other words, someone had to leave. Hallelujah, after several relatives graciously took their bows and departed, a few seating options became available. With only one couch, two La-Z-Boy style loungers and several small folding chairs, a majority of the 25+ guests, especially the younger ones, had been standing most of the evening. The vacated spots were filled by remaining family members. Out of respect, and more importantly, to show Ma I was a standup guy, I obligingly maintained my vertical position.

Linda, Ma, Sister Four and her husband, Sister Three and her husband, Big Sister and Sister Two’s husband, (confused yet?) all sat down at the tables and started turning the tiles over in preparation for the opening kickoff. For the rest of the evening, throughout the tiny apartment, issued the loud *CLICK! CLICK! CLICK!* of the tiles.

Mahjong is the national pastime in this part of the world. It is a betting game, but the winnings are only kept when playing with pseudo friends or more serious jongers. When family members or close friends contend, the winnings are spent taking the others out for lunch or dinner. I stood next to Linda to watch and learn.

In Taiwan they play using 13 tiles, which are split up into several runs of three or four. The selection of the correct 14th tile completes the last run providing you with a winning hand. Based on your final tiles, points are tallied, and money is exchanged. If you replaced the tiles with cards, you'd have something similar to Gin Rummy.

I stood there from 8-10 PM absorbing what I could. It was not easy for me to follow—all the information on the tiles was in Chinese. There was such a feeling of ease and familiarity in the way they all played. Each tile had some type of character etched into one side with the opposite side blank. When the game started, all the tiles were placed in the middle of the table with the etched side down. Each player took his or her turn selecting one tile at a time from the center. I was astounded when I realized they knew what the character was as soon as they picked up the tile but before they turned it over. By brushing their finger over the engraved side, they were able to determine what they had. I guess it works the same way for a blind person who reads Braille.

Linda kept insisting, “Sam, you sit. Play with family.”

"They’re betting *real* money. I’m watching them read the tiles without looking. I’d have a better chance at winning the New York Lottery,” I replied, declining her offer.

I stood next to Linda for another half hour or so. Finally, on the verge of death by boredom, I took a seat on the couch and drained a bottle of Taiwan beer while I studied the Chinese language book one of my potential brothers-in-law had been thoughtful enough to buy for me. By now, everyone had left except for eight players who remained fiercely engaged in the game. I figured in an hour they’d pack it in and I could go to our sleeping quarters and pass out. It’d be rude to leave now and hide myself in another room, possibly further irritating Ma.

Linda had prepped me on the flight over: “In Taiwan, family respect for elder is society pillar.”

I never truly understood how passionate the Chinese were about Mahjong until very early the next morning. The eight die-hards played on and on through the night, finally wrapping up around 3:30 AM. If I had the ability to focus for such a long period, continually studying my language book, I might’ve become fluent by the time they all said their final goodbyes. Oh well, we had nothing planned the next day, I mean this day, which was yesterday in New York, or something like that. In any event, I was looking forward to sleeping in, but that was not going to happen. It was too late for Ma to head back to Taoyuan, so she'd be staying the night or the morning or whatever?

The *CLICK! CLICK! CLICK!* of Mahjong tiles for hours on end had left me discombobulated. The dream of sleeping in a separate room, on a regulation mattress, was swindled away. Ma and Linda slept together, and I was relegated to the living room mini four-footer, that would have my legs hanging over one of the armrests. I had a horrible recurring lower back problem and no doubt the couch was going to aggravate it! I injured it in college trying to out-lift a woman body builder at the gym. That's a long story I'll skip except to say that my damn male ego screwed me over again.

Linda knew about my back, but with Ma now sleeping over, there were no options. "Oh Sam, so sorry you stuck on sofa. Bring more pillow. Make better." she offered sympathetically.

"Don't bother, sweetheart, I'll be just fine," I said, resolving I'd have to tough it out. There was no need to make her feel even more guilty. Besides, I'm not supposed to complain. It's an essential part of the Asian husband training program.

Before she kissed me goodnight, Linda reminded me to turn off the air conditioner and open the window. No problem, at this time of the morning it'd be a reasonably cool 83 degrees outside. Sister Four gave me a plastic cover that was two feet too short for my long lanky frame and a lumpy pillow (just like in prison); and everyone else retired to their nice comfy beds.

Finally, I could get some long overdue shut-eye. But I realized I'd forgotten to turn off the air conditioner. I got up, hit the switch and returned to my makeshift bed. Twenty minutes later, unable to sleep, I could feel the room getting warmer. The concrete of the building had sucked up the heat of the day which was now filtering back into the apartment. I got up again to open the window, hoping for a nice cool breeze. The moment I raised the bottom sash, there it was again, *CLICK! CLICK! CLICK!* The games were still on in many of the neighboring apartment buildings. I could see no other option, but to stuff toilet paper in my ears, hoping to stifle the irritating sound. *Nice try loser!* I tossed and turned over the next couple hours finally passing out around 5:30 AM.

The next day, which was the same day, I asked Linda to take me to a pharmacy to buy ear plugs. I was here for two more weeks and needed to gear up for future evenings of Mahjong.

If you're visiting Taipei and decide to take a stroll after dinner, I can guarantee you'll hear the *CLICK! CLICK! CLICK!* practically blaring from open windows throughout the city. Because the game never ends!

12. Hangin' with the Fam'

The next morning, everyone who'd gotten themselves a good night's sleep on their cushy beds, were up by 8:00 AM milling about the tiny apartment. The racket woke me to electric-like pangs spiking out from my aching back. My haggard body was already getting used to operating on vapors. Slowly I crawled off the couch, showered and sat down with Sister Four to have a nice cup of the hot jasmine tea she'd brewed. For the moment, Ma was out of the picture. She was in the kitchen, as to be expected, completely engrossed in cutting and chopping various items for an upcoming meal.

"Zao3 an1" ("Good morning"), I said to Sister Four. My Mandarin was almost nonexistent but ever so slowly improving. It's amusing, whenever you speak a few syllables of someone's native language, they immediately assume you are fluent and converse with you as if you were a local. It went like this with Sister Four. We sat together for 10 minutes sharing the wonderful tea while she rambled on about who knows what? Knowing only a couple dozen words, I hadn't the faintest idea what she was talking about. However, based on what Linda had told me about Sister Four's current interests, it likely entailed her daughter's upcoming marriage, a girlfriend's torrid affair with her sister-in-law's brother, and who was screwing over, or just screwing whom, on her daily soaps.

But Sister Four was kind enough to put us up and host a party in my honor, so I just sat there, smiled, nodded occasionally, and sipped the delicious tea.

A few hours later, Linda's brother, Shi2 Hai2, arrived, and we all headed out for "xiao3 chi1", our little eats breakfast.

Ma decided we needed a change and informed everyone we'd be dining on Dim Sum instead. There were no dissenters in the ranks, and even if there were, Ma was the boss and her word was law. Dim Sum it would be.

Ma's husband had "disappeared" many years ago when Linda was eleven. In fact, he was blown to kingdom come in an explosion at a fireworks factory just outside Taipei. Like most Taiwanese men, a chain smoker, Dad forgot to stub out his cigarette at the end of his lunch break and walked back onto the factory floor with the butt still smoldering between his lips. Some people want to go out with a bang...but c'mon. And I probably don't have to tell you: No firecrackers for the Liu clan to celebrate Chinese New Year. They all just snap their fingers. Husband gone, Ma had to put every ounce of her being into providing for her large family. Therefore, she never had the chance to get a higher education, especially back in the day when the male chauvinistic machine was in full throttle. But Ma was strong willed and smart all the same. She raised seven well-adjusted children through some difficult times. Now they took care of her. She was surrounded by family who all showered her with love and respect. Except when staring in my direction, Ma always seemed happy. But if you crossed that line, better run for the hills.

In the East, Dim Sum is all about variety and taking your time. It's the ultimate in tasting menus giving the customer complete control to personalize the dining experience. Most Asians take a couple hours to eat, slowly sipping their hot green, black or jasmine tea with only a few dishes on the table at any given time. If you see a group of Caucasians in the restaurant, they'll usually have 8 to 10 dishes on the table all at once. By the time they get to many of them they're already cold. We, on the other hand, all had a sumptuous meal together that seemed to never end.

Shi2 Hai2, wanted to test his English on me. With an ear-to-ear grin on his face, he practically shouted, "Sam, good shit. Right damn Yankee boy?"

"Right on, bro" I said, on the verge of cracking up, "really good shit."

My Chinese was still in the infant stages, but I was slowly picking up words here and there. My repertoire had grown to about thirty and I was adding a few more each day.

Shi2 Hai2 translated a familiar, derogatory phrase I'd often heard Linda use when chatting with her girlfriends and family: *ben4 dan4*. "Mean stupid egg."

I shot Linda a question mark expression. But even my native-born Chinese sweetie didn't know why they put the *egg* in after *stupid.*

I discovered that in Chinese society "ben4 dan4" (stupid egg) is so commonly used that no one really seems to notice or care if they hear it paired with their name during a conversation. A final observation: I did hear it more often being used by women than men, but no surprise there.

Strange how whenever anyone learns a new language, it seems they always get the curse words down first. And in Shi2 Hai2 I had a good tutor. Of the 30 words I knew, 75% were offensive. Linda and her Asian girlfriends would now have to be careful what they said around me, especially when talking about their husbands.

The rest of the day Linda and I went window shopping in a few of the large indoor malls. I still couldn't get enough of the department stores with clerks all bowing to me, giving me a taste of what it was like to be royalty.

By late afternoon we were both famished. Linda called Sister Four to inform her that we'd soon return to have dinner with the family. Even though taxis were cheap, we were living on a budget and walked the mile or so back to the apartment.

When we arrived, Sister Four opened the door with a big grin aimed at me. She quipped, "Gan3 kuai4 lai2, ni3 kan4 wo3 dai4 le5 shen2 me5 hao3 dong1 xi5 gei3 ni3" ("Come quickly and see what I brought for you.")

I stepped into the apartment and my eyes torpedoed in on two large flat cardboard boxes sitting on the dining room table. On the top of each I noted red labels with blue and white dots, and white lettering. There was something so familiar about them, but the long walk back in the oppressive heat had somewhat dulled my senses. As I moved closer to the table, the white letters came into focus and my heart started racing when I read: "Domino's Pizza".

How'd they know I was longing for a slice of Americana? While I'd been enjoying most of the new and different Asian cuisine, at the same time I was dying for something heavy, filling, greasy and loaded with cholesterol. I was practically foaming at the mouth, anticipating the thick crust topped with cheese, pepperoni, sausage, bacon and maybe even one vegetable, like onions—but *no mushrooms,* thank you! I never got that Good Humor coconut ice cream bar, and a few wedges of pizza would totally make up for it.

But not so fast—after our mile-plus stroll through the Taipei steam machine, I desperately needed a shower. I wanted to be clean and comfortable before sitting down to this thoughtful gift from the Liu's. My shower probably set a world record; I was dressed within seconds—remember I'm a man—and now ready for my fantasy meal.

Linda asked me to wait for her and hopped in the shower right after my exit. Will somebody please explain how a woman's smaller body takes 10 times longer to wash? Because *the longest 45 minutes of my life* later she came out of the bathroom dressed for dinner.

The insufferable wait was over, and we all sat down to eat. This time there'd be no strange bitter vegetables, no creepy crawlers, no spicy killer peppers, and nothing un-American, just two great big pizza pies topped off with a cold bottle of Taiwan beer. I was even envisioning the cold leftover slices that I could have the following morning for breakfast.

In my head there was a drum roll playing as Sister Four reached over and popped open the pizza boxes lids.

What?!!? Are you shitting me? Please, someone slap me awake from this nightmare! How can this be happening to me again? Is this some cruel hazing ritual Chinese families pull on unsuspecting foreigners? I stared at the two pies on the table, and while I had a make-believe smile on my face, on the inside was a sick feeling of surrender deep down in the pit of my gravely disappointed stomach. The toppings on my Dominos Pizzas were chunks of mackerel and squid. I think I might've even seen a fish head.

Ma was sitting to one side watching me like a hawk. I dare not insult the Liu's, but it was unfathomable to expose my poor taste buds to the horror-show that sat before me.

Solution? Pound down several bottles of Taiwan beer, and hope the buzz takes my mind off the desecration of my beloved American staple.

I whispered to Linda, "We should make a toast to your family for this wonderful surprise." Shi2 Hai2's tutoring provided me with a few key words for the occasion. "Gan1 bei1"

("Empty your glass" or "drink up"), I said to the room, holding up my bottle.

“Good call,” Linda said.

“Good damn Yankee boy,” Shi2 Hai2 exclaimed.

And with that, everyone raised their bottle or glass of beer and proceeded to empty their vessel.

Several toasts later, I felt confident I'd reached an adequate level of inebriation, but after forcing down several bites of the nasty fishy-cheesy flavored crust, my stomach began to protest. Nausea took over turning my face a pale grey.

“Linda, I don’t feel so good,” I eked out. Before she had the chance to respond, I darted for the bathroom. *This is becoming a bad habit*, I thought en route.

Linda explained to the stunned family, “Ta1 de1 wei4 bu4 hao3” ("He has a weak stomach.")

Upon my return, Ma shot me an if-looks-could-kill look. It could just as well have been written on her forehead: *Food not up to your standards...ungracious white devil!”*

Another day, another screw up. My chances at winning her over now seemed none, and more none.

13. Similar Circumstances

[DELETED]

(See Chapter 3½)

14. The Hot Seat

If Tokyo is famous for its Ginza and sushi, New York for its Statue of Liberty and ethnic diversity, Paris for its Eiffel Tower and night lights, Rome for its Spanish Steps and city fountains, and Moscow for its Saint Basils Cathedral and Red Square; then I'd have to say that Taipei should be famous for its world class Chinese food and Palace Museum.

Ah yes, the National Palace Museum is a truly amazing place, housing one of the largest collections of Chinese art anywhere.

Please bear with me on the history lesson: In 1949, Mao Zedong led the Communists to victory against the Nationalists after more than 20 years of civil war, then proclaimed the founding of the People's Republic of China. That same year, Chiang Kai-Shek and his followers fled China for Taiwan to escape the vice grip of the new communist regime. They brought with them a trove of the country's greatest treasures. Almost two decades later, during the Cultural Revolution (1966-1976), Mao Zedong instituted policies that led to the destruction of much of the nation's historical relics and artifacts. Cultural and religious sites were ransacked and most art, including musical instruments and ancient calligraphy, was lost forever. If not for Chiang Kai-Shek's actions, Mao's communist dictatorship probably would have erased from existence most tangible evidence of China's rich and profound heritage. Years later, as Mainland China became a global economic powerhouse, the government's attitude toward its own cultural treasures evolved. They now push to protect and preserve all of China's precious antiquities.

The Palace Museum is quite large, housing an enormous number of rare cultural artifacts. The full collection, some 700,000 pieces, spans many dynasties. At any given time, the museum displays less than 1% of its valuable stash with exhibits constantly rotated in and out of storage every three months. At that rate, it would take decades to cycle through the entire collection. The other 99% is stored in temperature and humidity controlled massive vaults that lie in lower stratums beneath the museum. Lesson over...Do I hear a sigh of relief?

Since it was my first trip to Taiwan, Linda decided that some education was in order. The museum would be the first stop on our laundry list of activities. She was proud of her Chinese heritage and excited to take me to see, what's undoubtedly, the greatest collection of ancient Chinese art in the world. Just like the early Romans and Greeks, during its heyday ancient China was the most advanced civilization on earth. This early supremacy was well represented through the various exhibits on display.

On this weekday morning traffic was light, so we decided to take a taxi to the museum. While the automobile count was low, our vehicle was still surrounded by a multitude of various two-wheel conveyances including motorcycles, mopeds, scooters and bicycle hybrids that'd been cleverly outfitted with a tiny motor attached to the metal cog of the rear wheel. It was spooky how close they were cruising right alongside us.

Linda didn't seem the least bit concerned, while I was constantly worried that any slight jostle of the steering wheel by our driver would start a domino effect of destruction with bikes toppling over each other in the tightly packed formation. But whenever the cab moved back and forth between lanes, the dozens of contiguous two-wheel vehicles mimicked us as if they were somehow psychically linked together, like a flock of blackbirds in flight, weaving back and forth, constant, smooth and continuous. This was how people here got around. They were completely in tune with this compressed traffic pattern.

Twenty minutes later we arrived at the museum. I was pleasantly surprised to see it was not crowded. No interminable line to buy tickets. Linda couldn't wait to show me the museum's feature attraction—possibly the most famous treasure in all of Asia. Hardly larger than a human fist, the Jadeite Cabbage is a perfect carving made from an imperfect, cracked stone. Does this sound familiar? (Michelangelo's masterpiece, David, perfectly carved from a piece of flawed marble). This diminutive sculpture, measuring only 7.4" long by 3.6" wide by 2" deep, is a masterpiece partly because it stands apart from a long tradition of idealized perfection in jade carving. A jade masterwork is typically flawless, cut from a stone without cracks or variations in color. The piece of jadeite, from which the cabbage was carved, was not only fraught with cracks but also came with cloudy, opaque patches visible in the white part of the cabbage's stalk. Rather than letting the stone's flaws be a deterrent, the artist used the cracks in the jade as leaf edges then carefully incorporated the natural color variations of the stone into the cabbage design.

"Jadeite much hard stone," Linda filled me in. "Sculptor use more harder sand from ruby and garnet. Carve most beautiful."

On closer inspection, I noticed two tiny grasshoppers perched atop the cabbage, with their reaching antennae and long spindly legs. The cabbage stood for purity of family, while the grasshoppers were the symbol of many children. This makes perfect sense since it was given as part of a dowry back in the late 1800s.

Years later, a renowned New York art collector told me, "The Cabbage could possibly be the most valuable piece of art in the world."

We passed so many incredible exhibits, stopping periodically to check out only the ones that caught our eye, otherwise it'd take you weeks to get through the place. Interestingly enough, though at the time I didn't know that one day I was going to be a writer, the part of the museum I enjoyed the most was the Chinese calligraphy.

Wen Zheng Ming was one of China's most celebrated calligraphers. He lived during the Ming Dynasty and passed away in 1559. Linda adored his paintings and calligraphy. Wen spent his entire life practicing morning to night, mastering his brush strokes to create perfect characters. When I say perfect, I don't mean a mirror image of some standard design. Each artist's writings were unique to their own hand, much like fingerprints are never identical. I was blown away by the simplicity and beauty of the handwriting and astonished how the artist could control the brush stroke to such a degree that recurring characters looked as if they were printed off a press.

Even though I was unable to read Chinese, and didn't understand the message, I became enveloped in the sheer splendor of the characters' flowing lines, each one possessing the particular spirit of the artist. I had a similar feeling standing in front of a huge Jackson Pollack at the Art Institute of Chicago. As I gazed upon this large canvas filled with a mix of paint drips, pours and brush lines, I found myself lost in the moment, unable to step away.

With enough practice, it's truly amazing the heights a human being can reach. Malcolm Gladwell's book, *Outliers*, discusses the "10,000 Hour Rule": The key to achieving world class expertise in any skill, is to a large extent, a matter of practicing the correct way for a total of around 10,000 hours. With calligraphy, if you practiced only 10,000 hours, you'd still be considered a rank amateur. Most of the great calligraphy masters started practicing their brush strokes in their childhood and continued 10+ hours a day into adulthood clocking over 200,000 hours. In sum, to master calligraphy, you'd need to follow the 100,000+ Hour Rule.

About an hour and a half before closing, I was completely drained, while Linda was still going strong. Plus, my back was killing me from riding the couch last night. If I didn't say something, we'd be here until they locked the doors. "Honey, I had such a great time, but I think we should head back. I'm sure your family is waiting dinner on us." I figured food would provide the necessary nudge and I was right.

"Okay Sam," she said with a smidgen of disappointment, "but first need use bathroom."

We located the closest restroom and she scooted in. I stood there waiting for over 20 minutes. One of Linda's little peccadilloes was that she lost track of time while sitting on the john—especially if equipped with reading material—and she was carrying quite a fistful of museum brochures.

I had to get off my feet. I spotted a couple comfortable looking old wooden chairs. There was no rope cordoning them off, and I plunked myself down on one. Instantly, I heard a shrill woman's voice screaming, "Bu4 xing2 bu4 xing2 kuai4 dian3 zhan4 qi3 lai2" (Translation: "Not allowed! Not allowed! Get up, right now!) It was only then I noticed that one end of a rope, protecting the priceless Ming Dynasty pear wood chairs, had been knocked off its metal stanchion. The lady scurried off, and I figured for sure she was going to report me.

I rushed to the restroom entrance and called out, "Linda?" but there was no response. I leaned my head in to try again; but before I could get her name out, I heard a loud police whistle and nearly jumped out of my socks.

Next thing I knew, two guards grabbed me by each arm and using Kung Fu, I presume, had me face-first on the floor, applying handcuffs. They both barked at me in rapid-fire Chinese.

I yelled in pain, "It was a mistake! I didn't mean to..."

Well, when it's time for action, I have to hand it to Linda. She was out of the RR like a bat out of you-know-where, screaming at the guards and pointing at me. The only two words I could make out were "Sam" and "fiancé".

A minute later, the guards, all apologetic-like, removed the handcuffs and helped me to my feet. After assuring Linda I was okay, we headed for the exit.

On the way I asked, "What did you tell them about the chair?"

"What chair?" Linda looked at me funny. "They see you poke head into woman toilet. Think you pervert."

Oh my God, I thought, *just what I need. If Ma somehow catches wind of this, my goose is nuked!*

15. Please, Just Shoot Me

I was drowning in a gigantic metal mop bucket. Above the rim I caught glimpses of people looking down at me. I yelled for help, but no one seemed to care about my predicament. A moment later the handle at the top started cranking. Next thing I knew, the tail of my shirt was caught in the rollers of the wringer, drawing me closer and closer. I screamed, *Please! Someone help me!"* The people above just stood there, shrugging shoulders or shaking their heads. My body was inches away from being pancaked when…

"Sam, Sam, Sam. Need wake up!"

I cracked open an eyelid to see it was still dark out. Linda stood over me.

Why is she waking me so damn early? I could barely lift my head, exhausted from another long listless night. Linda was chattering away about something, but in my near-comatose state, I couldn't comprehend a syllable.

"Sam, Sam, Sam. Why you no rise, shine."

"Wazzz up," I slurred my words.

"Honey, today have big surprise," Linda said, bubbling over with excitement. "Quick! Put on clothes. No can be late. We 7:00 AM arrive. Must eat big breakfast. No time eat lunch."

I could hear pans clattering in the kitchen. Ma was already on the job and the sound of something sizzling in hot oil was having an enticing effect on my empty stomach. Her one-night sojourn had already stretched into an entire week. I suspected she stayed to keep an eye on me—*the evil eye.*

I dragged myself upright and headed to the bathroom, my body was slightly contorted from another night on the torture rack that was my bed. A quick rinse, tea, three scrambled eggs with scallions wrapped in fried dough, and I was ready for my gonzo surprise adventure.

“Linda, where are you taking me today?” I demanded to know.

“You wait see. Much fun!,” was all she allowed, her face glowing with anticipation.

We left the house and hopped a taxi. Fifteen minutes later we pulled up in front of a store featuring large windows plastered from top to bottom with pictures of couples dressed in a variety of costumes. An enormous black plastic camera was mounted over the main entrance.

“Where are we? What's the big secret?” I was stupefied.

"This big exciting! Since little girl want do this." And then, with certified pride: "Today, take wedding pictures!”

I was now totally confused. Wedding??? Pictures??? I didn't even have the stamp of approval from the Liu clan’s supreme ruler yet. We’d made no plans to get married. I was over-the-hills in love with Linda and definitely hoping to spend the rest of my life with her, but wedding pictures…now? How was that possible without an actual ceremony? Was she planning on throwing a surprise wedding with all her family attending, without giving me prior notice? Was the *Chinese Candid Camera* going to film the video to be played, along with my earlier shopping spree, on comedy shows throughout Asia? Even more worrisome: *Is the big event going to take place at Sister Four's tiny place?*

Linda saw the look of confusion on my face and explained, "No worry. Only take pictures make keepsake album."

I let lose an internal sigh of relief. At least no other family members were to be involved and there'd be no wedding taking place in Sister Four's dollhouse masquerading as an apartment.

Linda play-slugged my arm. "Silly boy, no need worry. Everything already set up. Just wait see. You be big-happy we do this." And then pointedly, "*We have much special thing! Look at whole life!*" (Famous last words...as you'll see later.)

My first impulse was to take her advice and relax, but my natural defensive instinct kicked in and the feeling of calm evaporated like water in Death Valley. Through the numerous reassurances and urgent tone in her voice I knew in my bones that today was not going to be easy.

We were served tea then directed to a table near the front of the store where dozens of books featuring wedding photo samples were neatly stacked. Our first task was to peruse the albums and pass on all our comments to the assistant who'd relay them to the photographer and set designer. This information would guide them in customizing the final product to Linda's tastes. I did not matter since I was a man and had no taste.

I sat there for an hour nodding my head in agreement, the few times she turned to me and asked, "How you think?" In reality, I didn't have a clue what I was agreeing to or what the result would be. Near as I could tell, I was brought there so Linda would have someone standing next to her in the photos (aka a stooge). Only a few years out of college with several student loans hanging over my head, I had little money to spare. But if I had the financial means, I would've gladly hired someone as a stand-in. I was beginning to think, *Being subjected to a 24-hour continuous loop of Hee Haw reruns would be preferable over today's outing.*

Someone famous once said if you always tell the truth nothing bad will come of it. I wondered, *When George Washington admitted to cutting down that cherry tree, did his dad really let him slide?*

I quickly disposed of the notion, forced a smile, and said to Linda, "What a great idea having our pictures taken together."

My little white lie worked. Linda was ecstatic. "Oh Sam, you see, this be trip high point!"

My following thought: *The phrase "grin and bear it" must've been coined by a man in love.*

The next step in the fake wedding picture process was to pick the clothes we'd wear for the photo shoot. The store had an extensive wardrobe. With the assistant's guidance, I'd be suiting up in whatever Linda had picked out for me. However, not being the size of your average Chinese man, the options were extremely limited. Linda, on the other hand, with her size 2 body fitting the archetype perfectly, had countless choices available.

The staff did their best to accommodate my awkward body type, XXX-large. They were able to scrounge up a tuxedo that was snug on the top, but the pants were over 6 inches too short. They didn't have a traditional Chinese wedding garment in my size, so they took the largest they could find and did a quick tailoring job, opening up the back and shoulder seams then pinning the whole caboodle to my undershirt.

When the pictures were processed, Linda is in a different outfit for every picture. I'm in the same tight-fitting tuxedo or the one traditional Chinese man-dress. In some of the pictures Linda is seen standing on a box or sitting on a high chair with her feet dangling. Anything and everything was done to avoid shooting me from the knees down.

Next, the photographer took us outside to snap more photos in front of some of Taipei's most important landmarks, like the Chiang Kai-Shek Memorial and the Taipei Confucius Temple. It was 100 degrees in the shade and there we were, my beautiful fiancée in a light chiffon short sleeve dress; and me in a black tuxedo complete with frilly shirt, bow tie, cummerbund, and those atrocious black high-water pants. People walking by were all quite interested in me and my strangely tailored getup. I was embarrassment personified.

What made matters worse was the incredible humidity that day. Within 10 minutes the sweat was pouring out of me. I wanted to rip off the tuxedo, run naked to the nearest fountain, and dive in. Somehow, I was able to tough it out for almost two hours. Every time I thought we were done the photographer called out, “zai4 zhao4 yi1 zhang1 jiu4 hao3 le5.” Translation: "Just one more shot."

I was about ready to tear the camera from his hands and smash it on the ground when he finally told Linda, and she translated for me, “Outside finish. Now go back store. Continue take pictures.”

Continue? I wanted to scream. *What more can there possibly be?* By the time we reentered the shop my fancy frilly tuxedo shirt had flattened out and was badly stained by the black bow tie which, after soaking up all the sweat, had bled its color onto the area around the collar. If it’s true the human body is composed of about 60% water, there could only have been 40% of me left.

I glanced at my wristwatch: *Have we really been at this for only 4 ½ hours?* It felt like 4 ½ *days*. A brief tea break, and we started up again at 2:00. The rest of the afternoon he shot us inside with different backgrounds and props for each picture. There was one that had us inside a church standing next to a 5-foot Styrofoam wedding cake. Others included the Eiffel Tower, a field of sunflowers, on the deck of a cruise ship with a glacier behind us, and on and on and on. I lost count after 20. In every shot there was my perfect looking fiancée in her fresh new outfit; and standing next to her was Lurch from the Addams Family. We finished well after 6:00 PM.

I was completely shot (pun intended) and begged Linda for an evening of doing ZIP-ity-do-dah, save for a long cool shower.

Fast Forward: Two albums were assembled and shipped to our New York apartment. Four weeks after our return, they arrived via DHL. We looked at them ONCE, then stuck them in some closet, never to be viewed again.

That night in Taipei, under the stream of soothing water, I found religion. Before I knew it, a prayer had escaped my lips: "Lord, if there is to be a worst day of my life, please, please, please, let this be it!"

Man-oh-man...the things we do for love!

16. A Fish Story

With only a couple days left before heading back to New York, Linda told me that the Liu clan was discussing options for the final family outing. Tomorrow, we'd head to one of their cherished idyllic destinations.

"Cool. Where do you think they'll take us?" I asked.

Linda shrugged. "Me not know. Ma decide. Now go shopping. You home alone, okay?" she asked, part loving concern, part statement.

"Of course," I assured her. "I'm a big boy. You girls go have fun."

Little did she know I was relishing some solitary to catch up on my sleep in an actual bedroom on a real mattress. The girls would be gone several hours, shopping for the copious ingredients required to prepare tonight's standard multi-course feast. When we were back in New York, I expected it'd be a tough transition to our normal single course meal.

An hour after they left, I was woken by a loud knock at the door. I opened it to Linda's brother, and said, "What's up, Shi2 Hai2, my man?"

"Feeling good, Mr. Yankee boy," he grinned.

He was doing his best to communicate, but the next batch of words he threw at me were a convoluted jumble of Chinese and English; but I caught the drift. "Mr. Yankee man, tomorrow, wo3 men5 qu4 chi1 yi1 ge5 te4 bie2 de5 yu2, get big fish!"

"Really? You're taking me fishing? Awesome," I said.

“Awesome me too,” he replied.

He had stopped in to speak to Ma about something; when I told him she and the girls went grocery shopping, he knew where to find her and dashed out.

Dinner that night was the usual 10+ course bonanza. I was starving and ended up overeating, resulting in a bad case of gas. I couldn’t hold it in and ripped off a loud fart. Everyone laughed—except Ma.

I knew that for many Eastern cultures, burping was considered a high compliment to the host. So, wouldn't flatulence be pretty much the same thing? Apparently not: I translated the look on Ma’s face to read: “Disgusting American Pig! How could my little girl do this to me?”

In anticipation of an early start tomorrow, the compulsory Mahjong game was cut short at midnight. I passed out the moment my head hit the so-called pillow (I think it was really a half-inch thick seat cushion). Around 5:30 AM, I was woken by a hard slap alongside my head. I looked up in shock to see Ma standing over me. She said in a loud, harsh tone, “Lan3 chong2, qi3 lai2 chi1 fan4 le5!” Translation: "Get up lazy bum. Time to eat!" Or something like that. Despite the rude awakening, I was wildly excited about today's fishing expedition.

After breakfast with the family, who had all arrived prior to my rise and not shine, we all piled into the three tiny cars that would ferry the 16 of us. I didn't see any rods and reels, but I assumed, for lack of space, we'd rent them at the bait shop.

I asked Linda, “What's the name of this place we're going?”

"Shi2 Men2 Shui3 Ku4," she replied, then translated: "Stone Gate Dam and Reservoir. Close Fusing village.”

A brief pause for some detailed information: Stone Gate Dam crosses the Dahan River in Taoyuan, County, Taiwan. The dam’s main purposes are water supply, flood control and hydroelectricity generation, and it holds the Shimen Reservoir, Taiwan’s third largest artificial lake. Completed in 1964, the dam and reservoir now supply water to more than three million people in northern Taiwan.

It was about an hour and a half ride. With 16 of us sardined into the three small vehicles, two of which appeared to be designed to carry four pygmies, it was the epitome of a tight squeeze. Our group that day included Ma, Big Sister, her husband and their two boys; Sister Two, her husband and their three children; Sister Four, her husband and their two children and let’s not forget me and my potential bride to be. We had to stack several kids on our laps to all fit.

Earlier, Linda had informed me that we'd be riding with Sister Two in their brand-new Nissan Pintara, which looked like a shoe box on four wheels. With my limited Chinese vocabulary, I complimented Sister Two on her purchase: "Ni3 de5 che1 zi5 hao3 bang4!" ("Your car is great!")

Lickety-split, I was corrected by Sister Two’s husband: "Shi4 wo3 de5!" (Translation: "It’s mine!")

He felt a burning need to clarify whose name was on the title. This again reminded me that, at the time, Taiwan was still a male-dominated society. Sister Two was never allowed to drive the car. She didn't even have a license. If her husband was not available, she either hiked or biked to her destination.

There's a silver lining to everything. Since her husband drove everywhere, he got no exercise and developed an unsightly potbelly. Sister Two's hike-bike regimen kept her thin, strong and attractive.

SIDEBAR: She later learned to drive when she stayed with us in New York. Unfortunately, the body of my beloved Chevy Camaro IROC Coupe suffered dearly from the experience.

That day I was lucky to be in Sister Two's *HUSBAND'S* car, because she brought along for the ride some interesting Asian "fast food" snacks including: fried wasabi green peas, spicy beef jerky, dried pieces of fermented tofu, and mango coconut jelly strips. They were all packaged in cellophane bags. I savored the nice crunch of the peas, and boy did they clear your sinuses. There must've been something in the recipe that made them addictive. The more I ate the bigger my craving. She only packed one bag which I scarfed down in record time. I'm guessing their American snack counterparts would be fried spicy pork rinds, Slim Jims, Doritos, Cheetos and Gummy Bears.

The highway cut through the urban landscape ascending into the central mountains of Taiwan toward the town of Fusing, which was a frequent retreat of Chang Kai-Shek, Taiwan's first president. The mountains were carpeted in bamboo and palm trees with winding roads threading between numerous quaint villages.

Sister Two, through my personal interpreter Linda Liu, informed me, “Fusing sweet white peach most famous.”

Upon our arrival, we took a short tour through one of the orchards, built on terraces that ran up the side of the mountain. The Liu's purchased three full baskets to bring back to Taipei. Compared to the dark reddish-yellow peaches I bought back in the States, these were substantially larger. They had a gorgeous light yellow and orange hue on the outside and were sweeter, less acidic and juicier. You had to take extra care; we were there at the height of the picking season; with each bite the juice shot out both sides of your mouth, down your chin and onto your clothes.

From there, we walked into the town where I expected we’d stop to pick up our fishing gear. But instead of entering a bait shop, the family, like moths to a flame, headed for a restaurant.

"I thought we were going fishing," I protested, still full from all the snacks and peaches. "Your brother said I'd catch a big fish."

"Why you no have patience?" Linda giggled. "No worry. Today, get big fish!"

Does this family ever think about anything except food? I marveled. *As soon as one meal is over, they're busy planning the next.*

My first impression: *What a dive!* But by now I should've known better. In Taiwan the restaurants were all about the food, not atmosphere, especially in the rural areas outside Taipei.

The room was packed…always a good sign. Sister Four's husband waived the waiter over to discuss the limited table options. He chose a large one near the back of the restaurant where there was an opening in the wall allowing for the occasional cool breeze. We were up in the mountains, so the temperature during the day was just 85 degrees F. Two weeks in the Taipei blast furnace made the weather in Fusing seem quite comfortable. All sixteen of us bellied up around the large round table, and warm tea was immediately served.

Ten minutes had passed when Sister Four's and Sister Two's husbands both rose from the table. Hub #2 said to me, "Mr. Sam, gen1 wo3 men5 lai2." ("Come with us.")

I shot Linda a hesitant look, but she waved me on, along with an encouraging smile.

I followed the husbands to the back of the restaurant. I thought we might be going to the restroom. In America, women always go in pairs. *Perhaps in China, men go in threes?*

Instead, we met up with one of the waiters. He guided us through a narrow passageway at the rear of the kitchen. I could hear the splashing of water coming from outside. By then I was completely perplexed. *What? Are we going swimming now?*

We exited into bright sunlight and soon were standing in front of a huge fresh water pond. I estimated it covered almost an acre of land. You couldn't see it from the street because it was hidden behind the store facades which had all been built with connecting walls.

Three men wearing hip waders stood in knee deep water. I actually jumped when I noticed they were all holding large wooden clubs. The husbands beckoned to one of the men and the three of them held a brief discussion. At the same time, they were all pointing at various places in the water. I stepped to the pond's edge and got down on my knees to have a closer look.

"Holy mackerel," I gasped, noticing the pond was stocked with hundreds—maybe thousands—of gargantuan fish. There were so many, and they were so HUGE with sharp barracuda-like teeth protruding from their mouths.

When I was a child, my dad often took me fishing. We'd sit on a long pier that jutted out into Lake Michigan hoping to catch Coho Salmon. Some of the big ones we reeled in tipped the scale at 15 lbs. The fish in this pond made those salmon look like guppies. By my estimate they had to be well over 25 lbs.

A few more minutes of back and forth conversation, then one of the husbands made a decision and took control. He pointed at a particularly large fish that was swimming away from them and toward me.

Hub Four was yelling something in Chinese at the worker standing in the water while Two was running along the side of the pond following the fish that was steering in my direction. They were both jumping up and down with excitement. The man with the club was short and fat, but he moved surprising fast through the water. He was heading straight for me with the club raised high above his head. This caught me off guard. My mind was in a state of confusion, and for a couple seconds my brain was unable to communicate with my body. I froze, unable to get to my feet and back away.

And then, just like in the movies, everything was happening in slow motion...the short fat man came to a stop directly in front of me…here's the part where my life passes before me…his large wooden club was now sweeping downward…I followed the arc of the club with my eyes…it missed my head by a mere two inches…then came the sickening *CRUNCH!* as it slammed into the skull of the giant fish.

Back to real-time: The water erupted in a huge splash that hit me in the face along with what I presumed to be fish brains. I fell back onto my butt, stunned, but feeling lucky to be alive.

We were done here. It was time to return to the family. I took a detour to the restroom and cleaned off all the fish splatter from my face and clothes. By the time I reached the table, my loose-lipped potential brothers-in-law had already told the funny story about the big brave American who froze like a frightened little girl at the water's edge only to get splashed with fish gunk. At least that's what I presumed with everyone talking and laughing. I now had about 80 Chinese words in my repertoire, but they all seemed to be speaking at super human speed. Everything just sort of melted together into an up and down pitched humming sound. However, I did pick up on two words I knew very well: “ben4 dan4”…stupid egg. Que sera, sera, I was again the butt of the joke.

Linda tried to blunt the embarrassment that was evident on my face. "Sam, think much good sign. Brother-in-law say you catch biggest one!"

"You Chinese sure have a kooky way of goin' fishin'," I said, and joined in the laughter.

Ten minutes later, after polishing off my second bottle of Taiwan Beer, the dishes started to arrive. We began with fried fish covered in chili and oyster sauce, followed by two green leafy vegetables. The first one was simply cooked in hot oil with fresh garlic and the second one was topped off with a crab meat mixture.

Second, a large piece of steamed fish served with a black bean and ginger sauce. Awesome!

Third, a good size chunk of braised fish smothered in a sweet and sour sauce.

Fourth, spicy ground pork—*What...no fish?*—wrapped in cabbage.

Fifth, a baked chunk of fish prepared with cilantro, soy sauce, sesame oil, green onions and ginger.

Sixth, the last dish of the meal, small bite-size pieces of fish swimming in a deep rich broth along with spring onions, Chinese parsley, some other green leafy vegetable, minced pork and what appeared to be ikan bilis, or as they are called where I come from: anchovies.

I'd never tasted fish so tender and fresh. Like I said, I was always a burger and fries' guy. My idea of a fish dinner was the Filet-O-Fish sandwich at McDonalds. Need I say all the dishes were cooked perfectly and tasted wonderful? And no surprise they were all prepared from the same behemoth that only 30 minutes ago was whacked by the little fat man in the pond behind the restaurant. I still had the stains on my shirt to prove it. With my very limited wardrobe, I just prayed they'd come out in the wash.

Our three-hour feast and fishing trip was over. We were ready to head home. With the huge quantity of delicious food, we'd all consumed, maybe it was my imagination, but it sure seemed a bit more difficult squeezing back into the three pint-size vehicles. I was extremely full, but not in a bloated uncomfortable way, like I'd be after polishing off an extra-large pizza. This was closer to a feeling of deep satisfaction that put a smile on your face, then ever so slowly (i.e., the standard one-hour later) faded back to a mild hunger.

All the way home, sure enough, the talk centered around, "What's for dinner?"

17. The So-Awesome Din Tai Fung

My initial idea, for what I call "scribble therapy", was to set down for posterity all my experiences on the indoctrination of an ignorant white male into Asian culture. If you think I've been moving in a direction more closely aligned with the culinary adventures of the late great chef Anthony Bourdain on his television show *Parts Unknown*, in many ways your thoughts would be correct. But what was I to do? Chinese society has a passionate love affair with food. It's an integral part of their heritage and daily life. To top it all off, my potential in-laws just happen to live in one of the world's greatest food meccas. So, let's see what's cookin'...

On my last night in Taipei the family wanted to take me out to the original Din Tai Fung. At the time, many people living in Taiwan would rate it Taipei's best restaurant. They don't take reservations and the queue for both lunch and dinner can be seemingly endless.

"Last week, I want go there, eat lunch," Linda said wistfully. "But long-long outside wait. Too much hot."

Everyone gathered at Sister Four's apartment for pre-dinner drinks, which included a type of clear alcoholic beverage called Gaoliang. It looked like vodka, but I later learned it was stronger, with an alcohol content near 60% (U.S. equivalent: 120 proof). Ma pulled out a fresh bottle of the stuff, took a big swig, and spat something at me in Chinese. From my minimal grasp of the language, I thought she was talking about a pig in Taipei.

I asked Linda, sitting next to me, “What the heck is Ma talking about? Did she just call *me* a pig?”

“No dear,” Linda covered her mouth to stifle a laugh, “she ask, you one day want *live* here.”

My callow ears still could not differentiate between the five speaking tones. Apparently, the words *pig* and *live* sound the same except for the intonation, or the tone. I wondered how many people I’d insulted over the past couple of weeks, butchering the words by speaking in the wrong tones. I’d received some pretty strange looks from several of the locals I tried to converse with.

Ma passed me a shot glass full of the clear alcohol. Linda quickly threw out a warning: “Sam, that drink too much strong. Think Taiwan beer better. You no want ruin tonight special dinner.”

The seldom-used, rational voice in my head said: *Listen to your better and smarter half.* I waved off the shot and grabbed a brewsky.

I held up my bottle in a *Cheers!* gesture to Ma, but she was clearly displeased by my rejection.

Ma blurted out a few words in a grating tone, and the room erupted in laughter. Likely Translation: "Can you believe the big galoot chickened out on a little ol' lady?" She then chugged half the bottle like it was tap water.

When the giggling and guffaws died down, the clan rose to their feet. Time to head over to the restaurant and queue up for what I hoped would be my most memorable Taiwan food experience. Too far to walk, so we had to call for a fleet of taxis. As we approached Din Tai Fung, I could already see the long line of people. It started at the entrance, wrapped around the corner, and continued down the block, ending...who knew where? It was similar to what I'd seen at the Manhattan movie premier of *Back to the Future*.

The heat of the day was still making its presence felt, especially if you were standing on the concrete with no shade. I cringed at the thought of waiting there interminably for a table. Plus, I could guarantee it wouldn't be long before my poor lower back raised a protest.

We sprang out of the taxis and followed Sister Five. It made me very uncomfortable when we marched past all the people waiting patiently for their turn to get seated. At any moment I expected to hear insults hurled at us right before they turned into an unruly mob. In New York, we'd be lucky to get away without an ugly fight resulting in bruises and broken bones.

When we arrived at the front of the line, there stood four nieces and nephews. They'd been given the onerous task of waiting almost two hours in the grueling hot sun to grab a table for the family. At least they'd be rewarded with a fantastic meal for their suffering.

I found this type of sacrifice common practice in Chinese culture. Children's respect toward their parents was ingrained at an early age. In Chinese, terms such as "ke4 qi5" and "xiao4 shun4" which respectively mean politeness and filial piety or obedience to one's parents, both have deep roots in Taiwan family life. I'm quite sure that's part of the reason Chinese kids from Taiwan do so well in school. They truly want their parent's praise and, therefore, work harder to earn it. This very structured homogenous society is all about respect for your elders.

All 12 adults cut into the front of the line with the kids. No one behind us said a word. The people of Taiwan are well educated and civil. However, there are exceptions to every rule. Just like anyone else, on occasion, they do show their temper.

SIDEBAR: If you've ever seen a YouTube video featuring heated brawls, often resorting to fisticuffs, between the two parties in Taiwan's Parliament, you'll know what I mean. Sometimes I get so frustrated with our namby-pamby elected officials here in the U.S., I wish the Republicans and Democrats would take a cue and duke it out on the floor of Congress. Who knows, maybe a lot more would get done that way?

Thanks to my gracious nieces and nephews, we were escorted right in to a large round table. By the way, if you truly want to enjoy great dinner conversation, a circular table is a must. Most of the homes I've visited in the U.S., including my own, have a rectangular dining table where you only have the option of talking to the person directly across from you, or craning your neck from side to side to converse with the person to your right or left.

No doubt about it, my next dining table would be round; but that night I could've been sitting at a triangular table and it wouldn't have improved my ability to engage in conversation. Everyone was jabbering Chinese in Uzi machine-gun pulses, and with my embryonic language skills, the shape of the table offered no benefit.

I'd heard so much about this place and was birthday-boy excited to finally have the chance to experience it. On the way to our table, I surveyed my surroundings, doing my best to soak in the ambiance. The restaurant was impeccably clean. The young female waitresses buzzed around tables like bees, ever vigilant to the needs of their customers. The male chefs, dressed stem to stern in white, including their hats and face masks, prepared the delicious food inside a huge open kitchen. The staff was like a blur: fast and efficient. Whenever a customer's cup was over half empty, a waitress would magically appear to top it off before they had a chance to ask. The place truly ran like a well-oiled machine. But in order to handle the steady stream of patrons, I suppose it had to.

The instant we sat down, a very young and probably new waitress arrived with menus and asked what tea we preferred.

Ma piped up, "Xiang1 pian4 cha2" (jasmine tea) and an eye-blink later it was delivered to our table.

I opened the menu and was astonished to see I'd been given one written in both Chinese and English. The waitress also snatched my chopsticks and put a metal fork in its place. But I felt I needed the practice. I said politely, handing it back, “Bu4 hao3 y4 si4, wo3 bu4 xu1 yao4 cha1 zi5”. ("Excuse me, I don’t need a fork.") She shot Linda a look of confusion and sputtered, “Ta1 yao4 yong4 shou3 chi1 ma5?”

"What did she say?" I asked Linda out of the corner of my mouth, maintaining eye contact and a smile with our waitress.

Linda had to bite her tongue to keep from laughing out loud. "She ask, you want use hands eat."

The kids couldn't help themselves and were snickering. The adults were doing their utmost to stifle guffaws.

Linda clarified my request to the waitress. The girl, clearly embarrassed for me, nodded her head up and down like a bobble doll, and said to Linda, "O4, dui4 bu5 qi3 wo3 dong3 le5." ("Oh, so sorry, I understand.")

She quickly placed the chopsticks back beside my plate like they were lit sticks of dynamite, then hurried away.

Weary of being scrutinized—I guess the kids were still learning not to stare—I buried my face in the menu. *Wow! So many options*. Since we were a sizeable group the dining experience would be far better. It’d allow us to order and sample a much larger variety of dishes.

The family members didn’t bother to look at the menu. They were all so familiar with the food and each one had their own special dish. Just about everything on the menu sounded amazing to me, so I followed Linda's whispered suggestion that I stay out of the way and let the seasoned pros take charge. There was back and forth banter that lasted a few minutes before final decisions were made. Shi2 Hai2 gave the waitress our order and we waited for the feast to arrive.

You can relax. I'm not going to describe each of the tantalizing items on the menu. Instead, I'm singling out a few of my most relished choices, and the restaurant's specialty, their famous "xiao3 long2 bao1" (little soup dumplings). They come in a multitude of varieties. We'd ordered just two types, pork and crab. Both were divine.

Okay, this is a bit far-fetched, but let's say I was on Death Row. The warden offers me *anything* I want for my last meal…*Hmmm, what should I ask for?* Actually, there'd be no hesitation. Hands down: "The pork and crab little soup dumplings from Din Tai Fung." (Plus, shipping them over from Taiwan would buy me some more time.)

And today, 30 years later, now in my late-fifties, having traveled to many parts of the world, experiencing an incredible variety of amazing dishes, my answer would still be the same. Din Tai Fung's little soup dumplings simply can't be beat! The skin is exceptionally thin. Inside you have a varied mixture of meat, seafood and vegetable that sits in a luscious rich broth—simply awesome!!

How to Eat a Little Soup Dumpling – Sam Lowe's Six-Step Method

Step #1 – Carefully pick it up with a small pair of metal tongs, provided with your order. You have to be both agile and gentle to avoid tearing the dumpling's delicate translucent skin; this would result in the loss of the rich flavorful broth contained therein.

Step #2 – Gently place the dumpling in a large porcelain spoon.

Step #3 – Avoid burning the inside of your mouth along with your throat, esophagus and possibly your entire intestinal track by taking a small bite from the top to release the steam inside. This dramatically reduces the temperature of the burning hot interior.

SIDEBAR: Over the years I've seen many inexperienced diners plop the entire dumpling into their mouth. It's similar to swallowing a burning hot charcoal right out of a barbecue grill…"ben4 dan4", stupid egg.

No warnings are posted. Its buyer beware…eat at your own risk!

Step 3 ½ – Once you have the dumpling safely nestled in the spoon, and steam is rising out of the bite-size escape hatch, you ladle on a small amount of a soy/vinegar sauce, then top it with a few thin-sliced strips of fresh ginger.

Step #5 – You need to wait a minute to allow the dumpling to cool down a bit more (perhaps do a drum roll with your fingers to pass the time and heighten the anticipation).

Step #6 – At this point, you can either pop the whole thing in your mouth (my preferred method) or eat it in small bites.

Either way, once the combination of ingredients hits your taste buds, there's an explosion of flavor like nothing else you've ever tasted, or ever will. The soup and crab or pork marries perfectly with the tang from the sauce, and the sharp spicy smack from the fresh ginger. Ahhh! Perfection on a spoon! Once you've eaten a properly prepared and dressed up soup dumpling, I guarantee you'll be hooked for life.

Linda noticed me inhaling them and cautioned, "No eat too much. Still many dish coming." I knew I should listen to her since she's always right. I later learned that even when Linda's wrong she's right—my little secret to marriage longevity.

I heeded her advice and drew to a halt at my sixth dumpling. I think there's general agreement on the notion that variety enhances the dining experience. Thank heavens I listened to Linda. Each and every dish that hit our table was mouth-watering good...the steamed vegetable dumplings, the shrimp & pork shao1 mai5 (stuffed steamed dumplings), the chili oil wontons, the steamed fresh chicken and noodle soup, a braised beef noodle dish, the exquisite fried rice, a crispy but juicy fried pork chop, the sweet & sour spare ribs, the 8 treasure sticky rice…so sorry, I got carried away and broke my promise to refrain from a viand recitation. But I was wallowing in food heaven and couldn't restrain myself.

And now...the grand finale: a platter with a selection of sweet taro, red bean and sesame buns. When the waitress set it down in the center of the table, Linda said, “Sam, please try. I know you like eat.”

On occasion the Chinese do eat dessert, but they are not known for having a voracious sweet tooth like many Westerners. This was one of the few confections I’d enjoyed since leaving New York. Like an All-American, I popped four buns in my mouth as if they were M&M's. When I reached for a fifth, Ma deflected my hand and pointed at the children, who were patiently waiting their turn. The way I'd attacked the plate, they were probably afraid they’d lose a finger. Ma mumbled something under her breath. Linda, my trusty translator, had left for the restroom; so I'd have to guess it was "Three strikes...yer out!"

18. Night Market Moves

I was so full, I thought I'd have to be forklifted to a taxi. But the family insisted on showing me the Shilin night market.

Part flea market, part food court, part carnival, part social nexus; vendors set up over 200 temporary booths along Ji He Road to peddle their goods. Night markets were open from 5:00 PM till 2:00 AM. All Taiwanese towns and cities had them, but we were strolling the most famous and largest in Taipei.

At 8:00 PM the narrow street where we entered was already packed with people. We wended our way down the aisles stopping periodically to examine a store's inventory. Vendors hawked a rainbow of brightly colored clothes, exotic jewelry, odd-looking luggage, books by the thousands, every electronic device ever invented, outré art and sculptures peddled by the artisans themselves; and if you were short one, I'd bet you could even find a kitchen sink. But the main attraction was the hordes of food carts selling local specialties. Even though everyone was completely sated from dinner, we couldn't resist occasionally stopping to watch vendors preparing popular street fare such as: candied tomatoes and strawberries, spicy pig blood on a stick, oyster omelets, deep fried prawns wrapped in dragon whisker noodles, oyster vermicelli and virtually the entire anatomy of every animal found on earth. For example, in addition to the standard fowl parts (legs, thighs, wings and breasts), vendors hawk fried duck tongue, chicken feet, butt, and the red somatic cap on the head of cartoon's favorite son, Foghorn Leghorn. It's called the comb and has a tough rubbery texture. At Taiwan's night markets, if it's chewable, it's saleable. Wake-up Proctor & Gamble! You're missing a lucrative venue for Pepto Bismol.

Then there were the gazillion fortunetellers, baiting people passing by with "Suan4 ming4 san1 shi2 kuai4 qian2." Translation: "Your future for only 30 Taiwan dollars!" (equivalent to $1 U.S.) I noticed that quite a few of their booths were occupied. But probably not the ones *fourth* from the corner, next to *44* Ji He Road, or in front of a *four*-story building (See Chapter 3½). Even in today's China, superstition dies hard.

Back then, Taiwan had a practically nonexistent crime rate; at no time was I ever worried about pickpockets or thugs assaulting me. Actually, it was quite the opposite. With my eclipsing size, I often noticed the natives shirking away from me. My height had the same effect as being radioactive. It turned out my only worry was the high possibility of getting plowed into by a bicycle or motor scooter, which were as thick as fleas on a mangy dog. It was common practice for riders to zip through the tightly packed night market aisles.

Shilin was busy as usual that night. I had to slowly squeeze my way down the center, stopping and starting with the ebb and flow of people. At one point I heard the sound of engines behind me followed by blaring horns. I almost shit my pants when two motor scooters passed by me on either side; so close their handlebars grazed my hips. I had to bite my tongue to prevent myself from screaming, "Assholes!" That would've made me the bad guy—not them. I kept waiting for the crowd to rip both riders off their vehicles, but clear as day, no other soul minded—or even seemed to notice—the intrusion…just a normal night at the market.

Then there were the illegal street markets, staffed by unregistered vendors. They filled the adjacent side streets selling knock-offs: "Rolex watches…only 300 Taiwan dollars!" ($10 U.S.) Warranty? Yeah right. They might work all the way till you got home.

What I found amazing was how quickly the illegal vendors could pack up all their wares and vanish into thin air when they got a signal from their spotters that the cops were coming. Mere seconds after the police left…*POOF!* Back in business.

"Every night play same joy-luck game," Linda said good-humoredly. "Over, over again."

Two hours of walking the market and Sister Four asked if anyone wanted to stop somewhere for dessert.

I was hoping: *Maybe we could all get a Bubble Tea?*

If you've never had one before, a description is in order: Bubble Tea is a Taiwanese beverage containing a tea base mixed with fruit or fruit syrup and/or milk and small chewy white, clear, or black tapioca balls, called "pearls", that sit on the bottom of the cup. You can also order it with taro or lychee. Bubble Tea is to Taiwan what iced-coffee drinks or Coca-Cola is to the West. The plastic cup is filled with the mixture then put in a machine that applies a thin plastic wrap on top sealing the contents inside. You take a plastic straw that is angle cut on one end and poke it through the plastic. The straw is extra thick to provide access to the tapioca balls. One thing I can tell you about Bubble Tea, it's very addicting. If you've ever had one, you'll be ready to commit mayhem for another.

Majority ruled, and we were going to the famous ice cream store, Xin Fa Ting, for their specialty: mango flavored shaved ice. There are many variations to this dessert. Instead of mango you could have pineapple or lychee or multiple fruit toppings. You could also add almond jello and/or red bean.

In my honor, Sister Four decided to treat everyone. She purchased several bowls, handed me one and said, "Chao1 hao3 chi1 de5", which Linda loosely translated as "This to die for."

I looked down at the shaved flakes of ice, covered with condensed milk and chunks of sweet ripe mango. At first, I had my doubts, until the combination of rich, sweet and cool all exploded together in my mouth. I love Bubble Tea, but I was delighted that Sister Four introduced me to this fantastic treat. It was the perfect end to the evening—until reality broadsided me like a cement truck: Tomorrow we boarded the plane for NYC. How was I going to marry the love of my life? Twelve hours left, but it felt like the NBA's 24-second clock was running out on me, and I wasn't even close to having a shot at winning Ma's blessing.

19. TICK...TICK...TICK...

Our flight on Terror Air was scheduled to leave at 4:30 PM the next day. We got back to the apartment; I was the third in the door and the Mahjong table was already pulled out with the tiles plopped on top. Our planned departure would have no effect on the family's routine evening Mahjong game. It proceeded as usual, ending a little after 1:30 AM.

Not a problem, I thought. *This time I have my ear plugs at the ready.* With the game in full swing, I seized the opportunity to pack up our luggage. The typical Asian man would rather undergo torture than do the packing. Maybe it's a Jewish thing? I assume it must be written somewhere in the Old Testament: *Thou wife shall shop, and thou husband shall pack*; or it could just be a tradition in my family. Whatever the source, I can tell you that I packed, my father packed, my grandfather packed and so on and so on all the way back to Adam when he and Eve decamped Eden.

Afterwards, I returned to the living room. Ma was standing there holding a glass of clear liquid in each hand. In a raspy, booming voice, she said to me, "Gen1 wo3 he1 jiu3."

Linda translated: "She want goodbye drink with you."

"This is interesting," I replied. *Is Ma extending me an olive branch? Or is this a challenge to a drinking contest?* From the sour look on her face, I was betting on the latter.

She shoved the glass into my hand and bellowed, "Gan1 bei1" ("Drink up!")

I remembered the last time Ma offered me Gaoliang and I chickened out. *Not today!* I held up the glass in a salute. *Game on!*

Round One – In one quick gulp, Ma polished off the entire contents of her glass. I recalled doing watermelon shots in college. But I quickly discovered that *this* booze was nothing whatsoever like the sweet, low-alcohol party beverage. No siree! This was caustic, 120-proof battery acid. Men much tougher than me had woken up in an unfamiliar motel room, with a strange bedfellow, for drinking less. With the alcohol level so high I caught an intense buzz after just one shot.

Round Two – Ma filled her glass and pounded down another like she was drinking tea. She refilled my glass and again shouted, "Gan1 bei1."

Linda issued a warning, "Careful, Sam. That much-strong stuff."

"You kidding me?" my macho kicked in, "I'm three times your mom's size." And with that, I threw back my second glass of Taiwanese rot gut. I was starting to get used to the burning sensation in my throat and stomach.

Ma refilled, polished off another glassful of the ethanol, then shot me a devious grin. She couldn't have been more than 85 lbs., but damn! She had the alcoholic tolerance of a 300 lb. NFL lineman.

Round Three – I was just about to hold out my glass for a third shot when a dense fog enveloped my head. Most likely, all the neurons in my brain were now sloshing around in a gasoline-ish fluid, rapidly shutting down one by one. The room began to spin, faster and faster, like an out-of-control carousel. I felt the floor slip-slide away beneath me, and my world turned black and silent.

Game over! Ma, the reigning champion, retains her belt.

Post-game recap (later reported by Linda): A moment after I hit the floor unconscious, Ma's jovial laugh reverberated throughout the building. She took another hearty swig from the bottle, stepped around the lump on the floor, which was me, and headed for the kitchen to make a late-night victory snack. The men each grabbed an appendage and uploaded me onto the couch. Tonight, I'd have no need for ear plugs.

I was awakened at 10:00 AM to the sound of many voices gabbing in Chinese. I opened my bloodshot eyes to find the entire family congregated in the room; some sitting, some standing. I slowly hauled myself up to a sitting position. The front of my head was throbbing, and the back felt like it was being attacked by a blowtorch.

Linda squeezed through the crowd to check up on me. "You no feel okey dokey, sweetie-pie?" she asked, tenderly massaging my shoulders.

"I know, I know, I should've listened to you last night." I shook my head pitifully. "When it comes to drinking...hell, when it comes to anything, your mom's like the Rock of Gibraltar."

"Well, no fret." Linda gestured to the room. "Family all here. They come say goodbye before we go airport."

Wow! The entire Liu clan had stopped by to give Linda and me a proper Chinese send-off. The plan was we'd all sit down together, but due to the laws of physics (tiny apartment vs. numerous people), most everyone ended up standing, to eat fried homemade dumplings Ma had prepared from scratch an hour earlier.

Linda informed me that it was considered good luck to eat dumplings prior to a long journey. I'm not superstitious by nature, but who was I to argue with a few thousand years of Chinese tradition? Needless to say, Ma's handmade dumplings were delicious!

Afterwards, we loaded our luggage into the car and were ready to head for the airport. I said goodbye to all of Linda's family. I was saddened to think that this could be the last time I'd ever see them.

"Mr. Sam!" came the harsh, raspy voice from behind me.

I spun around and there was Ma, staring up at me with that special scowl reserved just for moi. She grabbed my shirt sleeve and pulled me down until we were face to face. Then...*KA-POW!* Ma slapped my face hard, forcing my head to the side, then yelled in my ear, "Damn good Yankee boy!"

I was stunned for a second, then I straightened up and turned to Linda in bewilderment.

A big smile spread across her face. "Oh my God. Sam…Ma give her blessing!"

And the crowd went wild! Laughing, cheering, jumping up and down, backslapping, shaking my hand, bowing to me, and on and on. For a moment I thought they were going to hoist me up on their shoulders and carry me around the block for a victory lap.

Well...the plane ride as expected was awful once again, but this time it'd be bearable. Bless her heart, Linda had gotten us exit row seats. I'd now be able to grab a few hours of sleep without my knees stationed practically under my chin.

Bad weather had delayed us for almost an hour on the first leg to Hong Kong. We were concerned about making it in time to catch the connecting flight to JFK; but alas here we were.

A split-second after the "fasten seatbelts" light clicked off, I bent down and pulled out my carry-on bag from under the seat. I was licking my lips as I removed a plastic box containing tea eggs, several leftover fried dumplings from breakfast, and two bags of wasabi coated dried green peas...but of course no smelly tofu!

There was a Caucasian passenger in a business suit sitting in the seat across the aisle from me. His facial expression made it clear that he was deeply offended by the various pungent odors now wafting through the cabin from about a hundred just-opened containers. When he covered his nose with his tie-matching breast pocket handkerchief, I chuckled to myself, *Rookie!*

While Linda did not see the need to convert to Judaism, I evidently had started my conversion to Chinese.

SECTION THREE
The Great Chinese Invasion

20. Calm Before the Storm

One week after our return home, Linda Liu was pronounced my wife at a private ceremony in the home of an ultra-reformed rabbi who cut through all the religious red tape. The event was attended by four people: the rabbi, his wife who served as the witness; and as you'd expect, the bride and groom.

My parents were still in utter disbelief that I left Chicago to, as they put it, "Shack up with an alien from the other side of the world." Mom and Dad had called almost daily hoping to dissuade me. They truly believed my relationship with "that China woman" would not last; and I'd soon wake up from my dream (and their nightmare). But I was head over heels for Ms. Liu and nothing they could say would change my mind.

We didn't want to spend our life savings on a super colossal expensive wedding, so we decided to make things simple and elope. The honeymoon would have to wait. We'd just returned from an overseas trip and were now focused on building a life together in New York.

A month later we pooled our money and bought our first apartment on Manhattan's upper west side. From Monday to Friday our day was fairly routine. I woke up before Linda, at 5:30 AM, had my two coffee super-chargers, then hopped on the downtown #3 subway to the Financial District arriving at my office by 6:45. Most days I worked until 7:30 or 8:00 PM, engrossed in a business valuation project, stuck at an inter-departmental meeting, or working overtime to prepare for a morning one-on-one with a client. I didn't want Linda to wait dinner for me and often ate mine at my desk.

Linda worked in Mellon Bank's internal profitability division. Her day was lightweight by comparison. She rose around 7:30 AM. Her boss, Jerry Adler, commuted in from Scarsdale and always showed up after 9:00. She could drift in any time prior to his arrival. At 5:00 PM sharp, her workday was over, and Linda was out the door like a speeding bullet, headed for the subway.

On occasion we'd meet up for a late-night bite at a restaurant close to our apartment such as Empire Szechuan or Dan Tempura House. I missed my little eats breakfast and the home cooked Chinese feasts Ma and my (now official) sisters-in-law made. However, living in a city with the largest Chinese population in the country, we did have access to some decent Asian cuisine.

On a Saturday or Sunday morning we'd take the B train to Chinatown or the 7 train to Flushing, Queens for a Dim Sum breakfast. You could get many of the same items I was introduced to in Taiwan, but they weren't quite up to snuff. In addition, there wasn't nearly as much variety. Flushing did have a few restaurants that served my Death Row soup dumplings, but they couldn't compete with Din Tai Fung.

Speaking of access to Asian fare, it's a well-known fact that wherever there's a large concentration of Jewish people, Chinese restaurants propagate. For example, in the heart of LA's Jewish neighborhood (Fairfax) there's a restaurant serving a Jewish-Chinese hybrid cuisine, called Genghis Cohen. The unique fusion menu offers some interesting options, including Krispy Kanton Knish, Shalom Pork and New York Style Eggrolls. I don't have the statistics handy to prove it, but it's possible that the Jews were the ones behind the popularization of Chinese food across this great country. However, be fair warned, there's a huge difference between a Chinese restaurant where the clientele is largely Asian and one where they're mostly Caucasian. All Chinese restaurant food is not created equal. Having sampled Taipei's gastronomic heaven, I learned the difference between *Caucasian* Chinese food (sweet and sour pork, sesame chicken, egg foo young, battered fried shrimp, General Tsao's Chicken, etc.) tainted by the white man's cravings for sugar and fat; and *real* Chinese food (made-to-order dumplings, steamed fish, stir fried green vegetables, seafood soup, etc.) which is all about fresh ingredients, variety and cooking technique. Had I turned into a sort of Chinese cuisine snob?

While I ended up enjoying the days of hanging out with my wife's family at Ma's and Sister Four's place, I was happy to once again have an apartment to ourselves. For the first time in weeks I didn't have to share the bathroom. I could read my newspaper in quiet solitude. I walked around in my underwear without worrying about startling my in-laws. I could grab a quick snack in the kitchen, prepared exactly how I liked it, without my sisters-in-law appearing out of nowhere to see if I wanted something else, constantly eyeing me to commandeer a second helping. I came and went as I pleased without disturbing anyone. Anti-Mahjong ear plugs were no longer standard equipment for a decent night's slumber. But most of all, I could "legally" sleep in the same bed (on a for-real mattress) with Linda.

The next couple months were life as usual. Linda called Ma once a week to see how everyone was doing. Out of respect, I got on the phone and said a few words. I was still studying Chinese at least an hour a day—both by the book and with my live-in tutor. Ma got a big kick out of hearing me butcher the language, but occasionally a blunder offended her. Like the time I mixed up the words young and old, and Jekyll turned into Hyde: "Ni3 bu2 zhao4 zhao4 jing4 zi5. Kan4 kan5 zi4 ji3 you3 duo1 lao3, ben4 dan4!"

Linda got a kick out of translating it for me: "Hold up mirror! You look ten years older than me, stupid egg!"

But overall, now satisfied that daughter #6 had married well, or at least well enough, Ma's acerbic attitude toward me mellowed appreciably. When Linda was on the phone talking to one of her sisters, I often heard Ma laughing in the background. Either she truly led a blissful life, or she was hitting the sauce a little too much. I remembered how Ma never missed her daily glass of *Gaoliang* (Chinese fire water).

One Friday evening in early October 1988, my secretary buzzed me on the intercom and said, “Mr. Lowe, your wife is on line 2.”

“Hi honey, what’s up?” I said sweetly, happy for the interruption.

"What time finish?" Linda inquired with restrained excitement. "You want meet eat dinner? Have very great news!"

My curiosity piqued. “What news is that?”

“I talk later, darling,” she responded coolly.

Here we go again, I thought to myself. *I know exactly what’s going on.* Linda does this all the time. She was either baiting me, or softening me up for having something her way, or getting something from me she wanted, or tricking me into thinking it was my idea in the first place. *And the sad part is, it works every time.* No matter how hard I pressed, Linda wouldn’t reveal the “very great news” until she was damn good and ready. She must know I’d happily give her just about anything she wanted without the manipulation, but I think she enjoyed the game. *Women!*

We agreed to meet for dinner at Café Fiorello, an Italian restaurant near Lincoln Center. On the subway heading uptown all I could think about was the cryptic secret. By the time I reached my stop I had it all figured out: A month earlier we’d spent a whole day shopping for a new living room sofa. At Maurice Villency, my wife fell in love with a light beige fabric sectional with red, yellow and green piping. But the price was a little too steep for our pocketbook, and we sadly crossed it off the list. I remembered seeing an advertisement for a Maurice Villency floor sample sale in the *New York Times Magazine* the previous week. It featured the exact sofa we wanted, and being a floor model, we could likely get a deep discount. Linda had hopped out of bed early that morning to share a couple rounds of coffee before I left for work. I completely forgot to mention the magazine ad. No matter, I knew Linda was a *New York Times* junkie and rarely missed anything. My money was on her knowing about the sale, and she'd already gone down to the store to put a deposit on the sofa. This, for a change, was going to be a good revelation, and by the time I got off the #1 train at 66th and Broadway, I was confident I'd nailed the correct conclusion.

I was famished, looking forward to a satisfying meal and seeing Linda light up when she told me about the sweet deal she scored on the sofa. I'd act all wide-eyed surprised when I received the good news.

We met at the front of Café Fiorello. It was a gorgeous evening, so we decided it'd be more enjoyable to dine under the stars. Even though I'd made a reservation, outside tables were in hot demand and we'd have to wait for one to open up. We spent the next 15 minutes talking about her day, the new 19th and 20th Century Chinese painting exhibition at the Metropolitan Museum, and *The Music Teacher*, a foreign film that just opened at the Lincoln Plaza Cinema. Three times I tried to steer her toward a discussion that hinted living room furniture, but she played it cool, always changing the subject.

Finally, the hostess informed us that our table was ready. I'd missed lunch and was anxious to order. A waiter seated us. Minutes later, the bread, water and menus were all delivered, but still not a word had crossed Linda's lips about the mysterious topic she wouldn't discuss over the phone.

I couldn't take the suspense anymore and just asked her outright, "Okay, so what's this big surprise?"

Linda acted a little nervous, fidgeting with the bracelet on her arm, still not divulging, "Uh…well…you see…"

The waiter reappeared and asked if we wanted to hear the specials. My wife breathed a sigh of relief at the interruption.

I waived him away and said, "We need a few minutes."

I was starving by now, but I wanted to get past the surprise so we could relax and enjoy our meal together. I took the lead again, ending the tension and spilling the beans, "Linda, I already know you bought the sofa, and it's fine with me. I loved it the moment I saw it, and even if the discounted price is still a bit high, it'll be perfect in our apartment."

She had a confused look on her face. "How you think that? Today I no buy sofa." Linda looked at me like I was a creature from Mars. "Yes, I know have sample sale. But store clerk say already sold."

"Then what is it?" I demanded. "Oh my God…" my eyes lit up, "You're not preg…"

She shook her head vehemently, cutting me off. “No, Sam. We agree wait more later.”

“Then what is it?” I threw my hands up in defeat.

“Visitor coming…” Linda said tentatively.

“Let me guess…is it someone from Taiwan?”

LINDA: “Yes.”

ME: “Big Sister?”

LINDA: “You much cold…”

ME: “Sister Five?”

LINDA: “More warm…”

ME: “Sister Four?”

LINDA: “More warmer…”

ME: “I got it! It’s Little Sister.”

LINDA: “Yes!”

ME: “And she’ll be staying for what, a couple weeks?”

LINDA: “You colder…”

ME: “One week?”

LINDA: “More colder…”

ME: “I surrender. Just tell me!”

LINDA: “She move in.”

Turned out Little Sister, aka Little Ling, had decided to go to college here in New York City; and the semester started in two weeks.

You know how it is when you get one of those premonitions…The sprinkle of rain before the tsunami…The sneeze before the avalanche…Well, the invasion had begun. The first wave would soon be landing on the island of Manhattan. I gave her the ol' fake smile; I hadn't used it in quite some time, so it might've been a little rusty; and said, "Gee Linda…I can hardly wait!"

21. D-DAY

On the evening of October 17, 1988, we drove to JFK International Airport to pick up my sister-in-law, Little Ling. She'd be staying in our second bedroom, which meant I'd be losing my home office. My wife was concerned she might get lost in the airport, so we parked the car and met her inside the terminal.

Little Ling had only one large suitcase with her, but it must have weighed 100 lbs. This was before the airlines started charging passengers for checked bags over 50 pounds. If the limit had been in place, I can guarantee Little Ling would have worn the other 50 lbs., in multiple layers, on the plane. Like the rest of the Liu clan she was incredibly frugal.

The family's unrelenting efforts not to waste anything came from their meager upbringing. Absent a father, this large family of eight had to sustain themselves on whatever the government provided, subsidized only by "Da4 jie3" Big Sister's job at The Mattel Corporation where she worked as a laborer making Barbie Dolls. Before they moved to their more spacious multi-story home in Taoyuan, they'd lived for 12 years in government housing, occupying a tiny one-level three-room shack. The makeshift kitchen was outside, and it didn't even have a refrigerator. Food was purchased and consumed each day. In this burning hot environment, with giant flying roaches and no cold storage, leftovers were not an option.

There was no plumbing, heat or air-conditioning. Water had to be drawn from a community well and carried back to the shack. Their space was built contiguous to several other identical three-room abodes forming what would be considered a very basic row house. There was a vast rice paddy behind the building.

Linda told me stories about how they could always hear their neighbors through the thin cardboard partitions. Sometimes the children poked small holes in the walls to spy on them (i.e., primitive Chinese Reality TV).

And their bathroom-less shanty required a walk outside of 300 yards to a communal outhouse. The children all dreaded having to use that facility, especially after dusk. A night trek to the bathroom in pitch blackness might well include an encounter with a snake. And the Taiwanese varmints were generally poisonous.

Interestingly enough, when her sisters all got together and recounted that period of their lives, they all described it as some of their happiest times. It made perfect sense to me. For one thing, they'd never experienced any other type of life. The basic necessities don't seem so basic if you've never had anything better. They had food, a roof over their head, and the adversity strengthened their love and support for one another.

My family also didn't have much money. When I was a child, we lived in a small two-bedroom walkup apartment in Chicago. I had to share a room with my sister until I was eight.

At least our apartment had two bathrooms, a kitchen with a refrigerator, heat, two window A/C units, and not a snake in sight. When it came down to who grew up poorer, I was completely out gunned. By the way, I'm also very frugal, at least I thought I was until I met my in-laws. They were the dictionary definition of *spendthrift.*

Back to Little Ling. When she moved in with us, she was a very naive 25-year-old. Our friends thought she looked (and acted) closer to 16. That had as much to do with her physical appearance as her childish nature. The clothes she wore followed teenage fashion trends; she jumped up and down and clapped her hands when excited; and made a pouty face when upset. We also had to worry about strangers because our gullible Little Ling believed everything she was told.

No idea how it started, but she was addicted to horror movies. Night after night, Little Ling watched them in our living room with the TV blaring. She'd scream almost loud enough to shatter the windows at all the climactic moments. Time and again I'd rocket out of bed thinking an intruder had broken into our home.

Her English was nominal. Even when she came close to speaking the words correctly, her viscous Chinese accent made it near impossible for me to understand. One night, Linda and I were discussing the music appreciation class Little Ling was taking at school, when out of the blue she shouted, "Mr. Sam, me like sex!"

My face reddened, and I said, "Uh, that's nice, Little Ling, but are you interested in learning to play an instrument?"

"Me sink sex be fun!" she insisted again.

Dumbfounded, I looked over at my wife.

"Sax, Sam," Linda clarified, "she want play saxophone."

Trying to communicate in Chinese with the natives in Taiwan gave me a taste of what her days must have been like attending classes at Baruch College. I have to give my little sister a lot of credit. It must have been very difficult for her, but she was not a quitter. Still, Linda and I were both concerned about her ability to adjust to a new life in NYC. She always seemed to be walking around in a fog, shuffling her feet, likely to drift aimlessly into traffic at any moment. We never really knew how bright or dim her bulb burned. In the beginning she struggled at school, but with the determination of an ancient Spartan soldier she persevered, eventually making the Dean's List.

I adjusted as best I could to our new occupant. For one thing, I'd once again need to tolerate a long wait to use the bathroom. Two bathrooms plus two women equals *NO* bathroom for Sam. Lucky for me, I had a healthy set of kidneys.

I was also forced to become a part-time plumber, constantly removing clumps of hair from clogged drains. I was just starting to deal with my own slowly receding hairline. These women both had beautiful healthy heads of shiny long jet-black hair. Every month I was pulling yards of it out of the sink, tub and shower drains. Enough hair to weave rugs that'd carpet all our floors. It just wasn't fair. Maybe God is a female entity and it's *Her* way of getting even with men for childbirth and Sunday Night Football?

My next gripe: the two bedrooms were adjacent to each other with an adjoining wall. For the next year of cohabitation, I had the sex life of a Tibetan monk. This was by far the hardest part for both of us. We were married just two months prior to my sister-in-law's arrival, so we were still in the honeymoon phase. At least I had a heavy workload at the bank to keep me preoccupied, plus the periodic cold shower…on the rare occasion I got use of a bathroom.

I really shouldn't complain. Little Ling was an endearing, wonderful person, and Linda was so happy to have her baby sister around. However, I was seriously concerned she'd be with us for the duration of her college education. And what if she graduated and couldn't find work, or landed a low paying job and was unable to afford her own apartment? Maybe she'd never meet anyone, become an old maid, and end up living with us until she qualified for a retirement home?

22. I Can't Breathe

Six months that felt like six years after Little Ling arrived at our doorstep, my wife hung up from a conversation with Ma, then turned to me with a big smile. "Sam, you guess what? Big Sister, two sons, and Sister Two daughter all coming!"

"And…" I warily asked my wife, "where are they all gonna stay?"

Linda raised an are-you-kidding-me? eyebrow.

Swell. Now I just had to find a place to put the Mahjong table then locate the ear plugs I buried away following our return from Taiwan.

After their arrival, the sleeping arrangements were as follows: Big Sister and Linda's niece slept with Little Ling in my converted study, and the two boys bunked on the new Maurice Villency sofa that my wife rushed out to buy (at full price) to make sure there'd be a comfortable place for our nephews to sleep.

SIDEBAR: After just a few weeks, our $12,000 designer sofa looked like something you'd pick up for $50 bucks at the Salvation Army.

Linda slept like a baby in our master bedroom. And still a newlywed with my sex drive in high gear, I *pretended* to sleep beside her.

For the duration of my in-law induced detention, it felt like we were back living in Sister Four's cracker box apartment in Taiwan. My wife's family was so miserly we almost never went out to eat, except for the periodic weekend trip to Flushing for Dim Sum or little eats. The purpose of that trip was *second*: to enjoy a relaxing Asian style breakfast, and *first*: to purchase and haul back to our apartment bags and bags of Chinese provisions. Our small four burner stove never had such a workout. During their stay with us, I do not remember ever seeing a time something wasn't cooking on it. My gas bill rivaled that of a Pittsburg steel foundry.

Now there were *three women and Sis-2's teenage daughter* using the two bathrooms. And my second job, the plumbing and hair disposal service, was becoming full-time. These women were shedding more hair than the Westminster Kennel Club. Besides clogged sinks and bathtub drains, it was all over the floors, the furniture, and sometimes on the walls and in the food. I couldn't help but wonder if this was some seasonal molting period that coincided with the fall foliage; or was this a normal year-round phenomenon? How could they lose so much hair and not be completely bald? I kept sneaking glances at the top of their heads expecting to see wide swaths of exposed skin, but all I ever saw was thick, shiny jet-black full heads of hair.

Next, I had to be extremely careful how I conducted myself in my own apartment. With my sisters-in-law and young niece now living with us, I had to make sure I was always reasonably clothed. No more refrigerator visits for a midnight snack in my whitey-tighties. And with two young impressionable boys, I also had to watch my language. When you're trying to tolerate intolerable conditions, sometimes those four-letter words just slip out.

I felt like a bug under a microscope, especially when I went anywhere near the kitchen. I could never just grab a quick bite without someone popping up to investigate what I was eating. Soon as I closed the refrigerator door, Big Sister would materialize out of nowhere.

She'd always ask me the same questions. "Oh, Mr. Sam, hungry? Mr. Sam, I make you something eat!" Then, for some strange reason, she needed to see what I had in my hand, so she could tell me what I already knew I was eating.

For example, if I grabbed a peach, she'd say, "Oh look, Mr. Sam, eat peach," purposely speaking loud enough to make sure everyone in the apartment knew exactly what I was about to consume. Who knows—maybe this was her way of informing the family of the remaining food inventory? Or maybe she didn't want me snacking on anything she didn't personally prepare—as if she was shirking what she considered her duty?

I never did figure out that idiosyncrasy. Whenever I asked about it, they'd just laugh themselves silly.

So, there I was, living in my own home and feeling funny about taking the food—which I paid for—out of my own refrigerator. Whenever I ventured in or around the kitchen, I had this eerie feeling I was being spied upon. I guess I now had a little taste of what Big Sister must've felt living under Ma's roof back in Taoyuan.

We had just one television in the apartment, which was stationed in the living room. Prior to the arrival of my adopted Asian family, I'd love to come home after a long day at the office, kick back on the couch, and watch the evening news. *Say goodbye to TV, Sam.* My two nephews (ages 7 and 9) who were essentially glued to my new designer sofa, were always watching cartoons. While they were wonderful tykes, well trained to be polite to their elders, I still felt suffocated.

The net result was, I ended up putting in a lot more time at the office. I left extra early before anyone was up and came home quite late. If you look for it, there's always a silver lining in almost every predicament. I was spending so much time at the office; my boss had no choice but to promote me. He also raised my salary twice.

But no matter what time I came home, Big Sister always had food waiting for me. She'd gotten a handle on which Chinese dishes I liked; and the ones I preferred they stayed in China. I think cooking for everyone was her biggest joy in life—especially now that she didn't have Ma (aka The Little General) standing sentry, just waiting to chastise her for any minor slipup. She was now "Captain Cook" and there was no one to second guess her decisions.

One evening, I was sitting by myself eating a late dinner. I asked Big Sister, hovering nearby, why she made the decision to come to New York with her two boys. Her English was worse than Little Ling's. However, with both of us speaking to each other in a hybrid form of language that straddled the line between Mandarin and English, we were able to communicate. From what I was able to comprehend, the education system in Taiwan was rigorous and competitive. Children had to focus intensely on their school work. If they did well, they'd gain their parent's love and respect, which was paramount to them. Students in primary school, grades 1 through 8, were in class from 8:00 AM to 5:00 PM. Most parents were out working, and the children stayed after school, often as late at 8 PM, to finish their homework.

The curriculum for junior high through high school was even more demanding. Students came home late every night and often worked until the wee hours studying and preparing for the next day. The grownups had it easy. There were no parent-teacher conferences to attend, no PTA meetings and no field trips to chaperone. Their kids' self-discipline was a done deal. The children all wore the same school uniform, saving parents the hassle of constant shopping to keep up with current teenage clothing fads. Never was there any emotional trauma associated with the ongoing fashion competition between girls. No tantrums over not having Dolce & Gabbana sunglasses, the alligator Prada bag, or the Michael Kors shoes.

In addition to the heavy workload, competition to get into the top tier high schools and colleges was fierce. The gap between the best and worst schools was Grand Canyon wide. Therefore, either you went to a mediocre school or a stellar one.

With each child's thirst for parental praise and respect, the battle to the top was ulcer-level stressful. If your offspring were to succeed, they couldn't have the carefree childhood that many American children take for granted. In the end, there'd either be sheer exuberance or bitter disappointment. Big Sister did not want to subject her children to that life. She bolted Taiwan, leaving behind family and friends to sacrifice everything for her two boys.

And with that final note of praise on Linda's selfless Big Sister, I turned my head to see my two nephews passed out on the couch, the younger with drool hanging from his mouth and the other with a Hershey bar in his hand, partially melted, now staining the delicate light fabric.

My thoughts? *Will those stains ever come out, and if not, will there be any resale value? Will I ever get my private TV haven back?* A wave of emotion swept through me, and I felt my eyes start to water. If you wait a minute, you're likely to see a grown man cry.

23. Hair-Raising Experience

Most days and weekends my wife and Big Sister went house hunting. They were fishing for something in or close to Flushing, Queens where my in-laws would have access to the products and services offered in this burgeoning Chinese community. I kept quiet about it, but I longed for the day when I could reclaim my solitude on an island of chaos. Of late my only escape was my office at 48 Wall Street. The tumult I was fleeing from showcased in my apartment 24/7.

Monday, March 12, 1990, I woke up as usual around 5:30 AM. Not wanting to wake Linda, I slowly rose from the bed, grabbed my suit, tie, etc., then headed to the bathroom, quietly closing the door behind me. I planned on sneaking out before anyone woke up. Today I was treating myself to a good ol' American breakfast: coffee, sausage and egg croissant topped off with a strawberry jam infused Danish, which I'd consume at the privacy of my desk.

When I exited the bathroom, Linda rolled over and said, "Hey, early bird. You sneak out eat greasy American breakfast?"

"Yep, you know me all too well. Sorry I woke you." I bent down and gave her a loving smooch.

Linda knew my office had become my port in a storm and felt bad I was spending so much time there. I hoped that realization would push her harder on the family's search for the perfect property. Just like she'd manipulated me, Linda sweet-talked her puppy dog boss into giving her a three-month sabbatical to help integrate the new arrivals into their foreign environment.

I fought off a look of disappointment when she said, "Honey...today need house-hunt break. Take family Flushing. Buy groceries. Eat breakfast."

They'd been looking for two months with no success. With the recent tidal wave of Chinese immigrants landing in New York, the competition for property in and around Flushing was cutthroat. Finding a good deal on anything that hit the market was like looking for a Baskin Robbins in Hades.

I gave her my now-perfected phony smile. "Sounds great, sweetheart. Enjoy the day off with your sister." But in the back of my mind was the little voice that always spoke my truth: *Get your ass back to house hunting and find something quick before I go ape-shit.* Usually when you start hearing little voices in your head the insanity has already taken root.

Later that afternoon, I was in my office working the final income projections on a business valuation to establish an Employee Stock Ownership Plan for a private company that made computer aided design equipment. The higher-ups were using my department's expertise as a tool to pull the company in as a new customer. With annual sales of over $1 billion dollars, the bank president was personally involved. I had high hopes that if I landed this client, it'd fast-track my career. But was I again being naïve, or could the stress at home and lack of sleep have dimmed my senses? I'd be presenting the final numbers to the company's CEO in the morning.

I called my wife to let her know I was working late again. I didn't want Linda or the family waiting up for me. On an assignment of this magnitude, I'd follow my normal protocol and order in fast food to eat at my desk.

My nephew answered the phone. He and his younger brother were both learning English incredibly fast. I found it fascinating that their young brains could pick up a new language just by watching cartoons on TV. After a person gets past his or her teenage years, something in the brain stalls out and language learning becomes much more difficult. I could sit in front of a TV watching Chinese programming 24 hours a day for 10 years and not pick up much more than "hello" and "goodbye". My young nephews watched so many hours of cartoons their little brains had become saturated with Looney Tunes vernacular. They were mastering the language through *educational* programming like the *Road Runner*, *Scooby Doo* and *Bugs Bunny*.

There was a long silence after my nephew picked up. Apparently, he hadn't mastered American phone etiquette yet, so I prompted: "Hello?"

"What's up, Doc?" he said with glee.

I asked, "Hi, Xiao3 Pong1?" (Translation: "Little Pong"—the older nephew) "Is Aunt Linda home?"

"Sufferin' succotash, Uncle Sam. Aunt and Mom no here."

I heard the younger one in the background imitating his brother word for word. “I see. Did they go to Flushing today?”

“Yabba dabba doo,” he replied.

“Okay,” I said. “Thanks, Little Pong.”

“Th-th-th-that’s all folks!” Then I heard a click and the line went dead.

I found it strange but somewhat comforting they went to Queens without the kids. I hoped that meant they’d decided to look at more houses after all. Linda was radar sensitive and picked up on everything. *Did she hear that little voice in my head? Maybe today is my lucky day and they’ll find something?*

That evening I left the office very late, arriving home around 11:00 PM. I was planning on quietly sneaking in, taking a hot shower and hopping into bed without any human interaction. As I was approaching the door, it shot open and my two nephews, niece, and Little Sister were all standing in front of me, wearing big grins. So much for my late-night clandestine ops. The whole family had waited up for me. I suspected they might’ve been a little upset that I’d slipped by them in the morning: A missed opportunity to feed a family member!

My wife came out of the bedroom with Big Sister.

“How’d your day go?” I asked hopefully.

“Well,” she responded. “I meet friend Taiwanese restaurant. Eat famous stinky tofu.”

I think Linda felt a little guilty and added that last twist, so I wouldn't be envious. I was wishing she'd surprise me with good news on the house front.

Instead, she concluded with, "Finish day get hair wash."

Big Sister chimed in with a gleam in her eye, "Hungry, Mr. Sam?"

No surprise there.

"Bu2 yao4, xie4 xie5," ("No thank you,") I said, then explained, "Since my group all stayed late tonight, I ordered in pizza for everyone. I couldn't eat another bite."

I was exhausted from the extra-long day finalizing my presentation for tomorrow's early morning meeting. I just wanted to get out of my suit and into bed.

Linda asked me to come back out after I changed. "I bring special treat! Buy most fave childhood sweet from Flushing street vendor," she said excitedly, "Dou4 hua1."

I later found out it translates to "Bean Flower" and has no real meaning in English.

Anyway, I knew better than to argue; I changed into sweats, then sat down with my in-laws at our dining room table. Small porcelain bowls were parceled out to each of us. There were three plastic containers stationed in the middle of the table. The largest one held pure white steamed tofu. The second in size was some odd type of softened peanuts. The smallest container had a thick honey-ginger sauce.

My wife knew I was shot and got up to serve me. I immediately became worried she was going to hit me with some more bad news. The last time she served me was in Taiwan at Sister Four's apartment under Ma's iron fist.

Fortunately, that was not the case tonight. This time Linda was doing it out of pure guilt. She had a nice relaxing outing with her sister. They'd both been pampered all day long in the traditional Chinese way while I dealt with a killer 12-hour marathon at the office.

Back to the dessert. First, my loving wife scooped up the steamed tofu and put it in my bowl. Next, she ladled the honey-ginger sauce over the tofu, then topped it off with two spoonfuls of the soft peanuts.

Once everyone had been served, Linda instructed me to dig my spoon deep into the mixture, making sure to pick up all the ingredients at once. I did as told and popped the entire contents into my mouth. A fat smile erupted on my face. The combination of the smooth tofu, sweetness of the honey, bite of the ginger and tapioca-like texture of the soft peanuts was no doubt one of the greatest desserts to ever treat my taste buds in all my 28 years on Earth…*Wow!! Crème Brule, chocolate soufflé, cheesecake and tiramisu, you've all been outclassed!*

This Chinese wonder of wonders would not only make my Top Ten list of all-time greatest desserts, it became my number one. In addition to the pure and utter enjoyment, this scrumptious indulgence was very low fat and deliciously healthy…

Deliciously healthy, isn't that an oxymoron? If there was or is a God, this definitely would be His or Her heavenly dessert.

I wolfed down my second bowl, sat back, and had a crazy thought: *If my in-laws aren't able to find a house, maybe they can just live with us?* A moment later, my euphoric state of mind went even more haywire: *My wife can now spend money freely, put more dents in the car, invite more in-laws to New York—even her mother—and I do not care. She'll only need to ply me with my new fix, a bowl of "Dou4 Hua1" and all will be instantly forgiven.* I wondered if this stuff was laced with some type of hallucinogen.

After dessert I went to bed and slept like a bear in winter. In a dream I saw myself diving into a swimming pool filled with steamed tofu, sweet honey, ginger and soft peanuts.

I woke up the next morning refreshed and ready to take on the world. Today that planet would be FIDA Corp. (Fully Integrated Design Automation), the new client my bank was targeting. I'd spearheaded the entire operation with virtually zero input from the department head, Charles Satch III. My presentation lasted over two hours.

FIDA's CEO must've been quite impressed with my work. Soon as I wrapped up, he turned to the bank president and said, "Damn good job! Have your people send my people the paperwork to execute."

It seems things never work out as planned. Charles Satch *the third* stepped in and took full credit for *my hard work, all my planning and all my smarts*. If you've seen one asshole corporate executive, you've seen them all. Same bullshit, different department! Did I have this upward mobility thing all backwards? Maybe the Type A Leader (The Inspirer) should be labeled "The Pushover"; the Type B Leader (The Prick)—this one still rings true; and the Type C Leader (The Stealthanator) "Future CEO". *Food for thought?*

Having been stripped of my chance to bask in the glory of my gargantuan contribution to today's victory, I decided to leave work early. I called Linda to vent about the afternoon's events. "Hi sweetheart, I'll be home within the hour. The presentation was a home run." I then told her about Chucky III's intervention and concluded, "I've got a bad feeling my boss may screw me out of a bonus."

"Sam, no be glum. You one day get hard work reward. Future more better," offered Ms. Perpetual Optimism. "I have big idea: Tomorrow we go Flushing. Take family. Make fun day."

The thought of traveling to Queens with all my live-in Chinese roomies did not seem like any sort of a celebration. But after the office smackdown, maybe I needed a distraction?

The next morning, reminiscent of my road trip with the family in Taiwan, the six of us (Big Sister, her boys, Little Ling, Linda and I) crammed into my two-door Camaro and motored over the Triborough Bridge to Flushing. My teenage niece had taken off an hour earlier to who knows where? She was decidedly introverted and kept mostly to herself. As I try to recollect, other than the conventional polite niceties, I don't think I ever had a real in-depth conversation with her. She maneuvered through life as if somebody's shadow.

We lunched at Joe's Shanghai restaurant, famous for its pork and crab soup dumplings. The place had a huge following and just opened this second store. After an hour wait, we were seated at a huge round table.

A quick family discussion in Mandarin, with Linda providing translation, then Big Sister placed the order. Everything was amazingly good—especially the shredded pork with pickled cabbage noodle soup, prawns in shell with chili sauce, and shredded turnip shortcake. Big Sister also ordered a braised sea cucumber. For a Midwestern fast food simpleton this was a new one on me.

I turned to Linda. "Really? Chinese grow cucumbers in the ocean?" I was supposed to be resting my over-taxed brain from last week's epic work session, but I now had numerous questions buzzing around my skull. "Are these like the land version but saltier? How deep down do you plant them? Do you need scuba gear to harvest them?"

Linda giggled. "Silly boy. These cucumbers crawl."

Turns out I was not a fan of this strange marine bottom dweller. It had a mushy texture and was bland. However, I enjoyed all the other dishes, losing all self-control, eating way too much until my body needed a short intermission. Linda said,

“Da4 jie3 (Big Sister) take Little Ling and boys videogame arcade. Then go market, buy groceries. No take car. Come back later. Sam, we go now." She began pulling me by the hand.

"Go where?"

"Salon, lucky you. Get wash and cut,” she said with a twinkle in her eye.

"I don’t know,” I resisted as she kept tugging, “I have my own barber just down the street from the bank.”

"You see. Much big treat!” She let go of my hand and marched off. What else could I do but follow?

I was unclear why Linda thought this would be anything other than a bore fest for me. What’s so special about a hair wash? From my previous barbershop experience, they crank you down in a reclining chair so your head rests in a sink for a quick wash and rinse, 1-2-3. Then *BOING!* you’re cranked back up to cut and style. Of all the words that could be used to describe it, “treat” does not come to mind. It was just another of the many tasks that periodically had to be done, like going to the dentist to get your teeth cleaned. Or to the ophthalmologist to have your eyes examined for your driver’s license renewal. Or to the proctologist for—you know…

But I should’ve known better after my recent almost surreal tofu dessert experience: When a Chinese person uses the word “treat” it refers to something out of the ordinary. We walked several blocks, past rows of contiguous store fronts. I felt like I was in one of my nephews’ old cartoon shows where the character is moving, but the same background keeps going by. We eventually stopped in front of a shabby wooden doorway.

Linda announced, "We here."

I looked left and right but didn't see any hair salon. There was a Chinese pharmacy at ground level to the right of the doorway, a bank, restaurant and eye center on the left. We walked through the entrance and ascended a steep set of worn wooden stairs. At the top landing were two doors. The first was an accountant's office with the signage written in English (Liberty Accounting & Tax Preparation—Notary Public Services) with Chinese characters above, which I assumed had the identical meaning. I'd noticed the names of most stores in the neighborhood were printed in both languages. However, if only one was used, it'd be Chinese characters.

Linda and I entered the salon. My wife must have been a regular customer; when the staff saw her, they immediately jumped up, greeted her by name and did that rapid bowing thing. They seemed deliriously happy we'd graced them with our presence. I later learned that their glee in seeing Linda resulted primarily from her being an above average tipper.

Today I'd get the full treatment. A teenage girl took me by the hand and led me to a standard barber chair. In an American salon they first bring you to the back to wash your hair, but the training clicked in and I didn't ask questions.

Another young Chinese girl came over and asked me in Mandarin, "Ni3 yao4 cha2 ma5?" ("Would you like tea?")

I was not only able to understand her but capable of answering back: "Hao3, xie4 xie5." ("OK, thank you.")

My wife sat in the chair next to me to observe. I decided to grab a magazine off a nearby rack to occupy my time while they cut my hair, but I should've known, it was written in Chinese. A minute digging through their inventory and I found one in English. I was hoping for *Sports Illustrated*, *Time* or *Rolling Stone*, but my magazine reading today would be a two-year-old edition of *Ebony*.

The girl returned with my cup of black oolong tea. Yet another girl arrived and asked me to remove my dress shirt, leaving my tank top in place. She then put a plastic sheet over my undershirt to protect it from the water and shampoo. So far, this was standard hair salon procedure. But from there on the experience switched gears. She applied a cream to my forearms, then massaged with each hand working its way up to my shoulder, ending at my neck. The girl's technique was a firm constant kneading motion, similar to a deep tissue massage at one of those exclusive overpriced spas. This lasted for 15 minutes.

After the partial body massage, she brought over two plastic squeeze bottles, one with shampoo, one water. She dribbled some of each on my head, then massaged the fluids into my hair. This was not your typical American hair wash. I was getting a deep scalp massage that lasted 20 minutes. My body was so relaxed I was on the verge of somnia.

I was brought back to consciousness by a tap on the shoulder whereupon the girl pointed to the rinse station at the back of the salon. Obviously, you couldn't get your hair rinsed while sitting upright in a chair, but at the same time, I didn't think it was possible to get your hair washed there either.

In a blissful state, I shuffled over to a standard-issue reclining chair. My hair was rinsed, again shampooed, rinsed again then conditioned and rinsed one last time before I was sent back to where I started. A different, older girl appeared before me, scissors in hand, to do the haircut.

I said, "Ni3 hao3" ("hello"). I'd forgotten that if you say two words to a Chinese person, they think you're fluent.

She unleashed a torrent of Mandarin; I mean it came pouring out of her like water from a burst dam. I couldn't understand a single word. I tried speaking to her in English, but it was as if she'd just stepped off the boat; she didn't understand one word.

I was now in a panic. I worked in a professional environment where wearing a hat was not an option. A bad styling job could mean weeks of embarrassing comments from my colleagues: "Hey Sam, what'd they use to style your hair…an egg beater?" Or, "Oh well, you know what they say…Hair today—gone tomorrow." Or, "Looks like they let the cat out of the bag and it landed in your hair." And good ol' Larry, the office clown, would probably pat his lips to make an

Indian war hoop: “Woo-woo-woo-woo…Nice hatchet job, Sam!”

I didn’t want to take any chances, so I asked my wife to interpret. Even so, I walked out of the store with my beautiful head of curly Jewish hair blown out straight and piled on top of my head like a big fluffy cream puff.

Linda and I walked back to the grocery store where Big Sister, Little Ling and the boys were waiting next to a mountain of bagged produce. I loaded the trunk to full capacity, plus the backseat passengers all had bags on their laps; and off we drove.

I could feel my new puffy hairdo rubbing against the ceiling. I looked over at my wife and Big Sister; for the first time I noticed that their hairdos had the same pompadour look. I guess this was the trendy style offered by most of the Chinese hair salons. Next time, maybe I’d just call it quits after the wash and massage.

“Back to the city now, or do you want to catch a matinee?" I asked Linda.

“Neither,” she said, pointing in the direction of the Long Island Expressway. "Want go see house.”

“Really?” I said, fighting back an ear-to-ear grin. “I thought you were taking a break from house hunting.”

“In *Times* read, 'Queens New Construction'. Good location. Flushing not far. Go now take peek.”

“And?” I said, boiling inside like a pressure cooker with anticipation.

"And, house maybe work. But cost too many dollar," Linda replied, steely-eyed.

"Well, let's go have us a look-see," I said, pressing a little harder on the gas pedal. I was overwhelmed with the prospect of saying sayonara to my perpetual house guests. But I cautioned myself; it was too early to claim a victory. I knew that Linda and her family were looking for a Mercedes but only wanted to pay the price of a Chevy.

We arrived at the Bayside property 10 minutes later: A two family house with an almost identical three-bedroom layout on floors one and two, plus a finished basement with a full-size washer and dryer and a separate side entrance. The house also had a two-car garage which sat directly underneath the first floor. The interior finishes were reasonable, and the layout worked well. Most important, the local public school was one of the best in Queens, and the proximity to Flushing would make it easy for my in-laws to acclimate to their new life in New York.

At some point while I was zoning in the salon chair, Linda had called ahead, and Andrew Posner, the builder, was waiting for us out front. We completed our walk-thru and told Mr. Posner we'd discuss it further and get back to him.

Before leaving, Linda casually mentioned to him, "This weekend, have many see. Already make two offer."

In reality, my wife had zip to look at, and everything they'd seen over the past three months was either priced too high or not worth making an offer. She was wearing her best poker face that day.

We'd barely pulled out of the driveway before deciding this was "the one" and we'd be putting in a bid. The house was listed at $595,000. Big Sister insisted we submit $399,999, a good Chinese number, but a pretty dismal-price.

Based on my later perusal of the area's sale listings, this brand-new home had been sitting on the market for over six months. After three reductions it was priced to sell. I assumed the builder overextended himself and was very motivated. Superstition kept Big Sister out of the $400,000s range, but a number below that was ridiculous. I could not bear the thought of losing it. Before we submitted the offer, I negotiated head-on with Big Sister who finally agreed to pay $508,000.

One week later, after some intense haggling back and forth, the contract was signed, and we'd close on the property within 60 days. I said "we" because it turned out to be a family purchase, and I was now part of the family. How lucky for me. Linda and I made the initial down payment, and Big Sister would contribute to the monthly mortgage. This house would become their family compound. In two months—and yes, I'd be counting each day—I'd have my apartment back. Now I just had to find a way to keep my wits about me till close of escrow.

With no credit history my in-laws couldn't get a bank loan, so the mortgage was put in my name. In addition, I'd recently taken out a loan on our Manhattan apartment, so the bank now required a much larger down payment, which took our cash reserves to nil. Believe me, the loan officer never received a completed application so quickly. I hounded him every week, practically begging him to do whatever he could to expedite the approval process. Forty-five days later the house was officially ours and my wife's family moved out.

I had not cried since falling off a bike and breaking my arm when I was ten. However, that first day, after stepping into my quiet and empty apartment, the ecstasy of solitude overwhelmed me. There were tears of joy running down my face. It was like five massive boulders had been lifted from my shoulders. I'd again enjoy the NYC American restaurant scene and get back my home office. The second bathroom freed up just for me. I could sit on my threadbare chocolate coated designer sofa and watch the evening news. Sometimes the simplest pleasures are the best.

Linda looked at me and asked, "Sam okay? Why you cry?"

"It's nothing, I'm just going to miss all of them," I said straight-faced. I fought it, but I couldn't contain it completely; the crook of a smile slowly emerged.

"No can fool me," Linda said. But then she surprised the hell out of me: "I miss too. But now only us. How you say, 'groovy'." She winked. "Hope neighbor no complain, when find out I'm screamer."

I'd never heard Linda talk like that before. But, like the preacher's daughter, the longer a girl is suppressed, the more she rebels and the wilder she becomes.

Linda grabbed my hand, and almost gave me whiplash, yanking me toward the bedroom.

A month later Linda called me at work to find out when I'd be home, and added, "Tonight want make romantic dinner."

Linda rarely cooked, so I knew something was up. When I entered the apartment, I didn't see her, but I did notice the table set for two with candles and our guest dishes and silverware. A moment later she sauntered out of the bedroom in a sexy black negligee.

"What's this all about?" I said, a little suspicious.

"Have very great news," she beamed.

I'd heard that line before and knew exactly what it meant. "You're kidding me, right? We're going to be housing another of your relatives?" I said in exasperation.

"Yes Sam, another relative," she said evenly.

"Let me guess," I said bitterly, "Sister Four with her entire contingent?"

"No, my love. Someone else coming."

I couldn't take it any longer. "No more guessing games, please. Just tell me who."

Linda patted her tummy and said, "Sammy Junior."

24. The Incredible Dumpling Machine

"We're going to be a dad? I mean, I'm gonna be a dad, and you're gonna be a mom?" I said, shocked but elated at the incredible news. Linda's face was glowing with love and sheer exuberance at the prospect of the new arrival. She'd prepared a special dinner, but I was so excited about the baby I could hardly eat a bite.

Afterwards, Linda spent well over three hours on the phone calling each of her in-laws in Taiwan. I couldn't decipher most of the lighting speed Chinese, but I frequently made out the word "ying1 er2" ("baby").

Back then we didn't have Vonage. We paid an obscenely high rate of $.53 per minute, but I was on such a high I didn't care about the cost. Okay, maybe I cared a little bit; especially when the bill arrived, a whopping $695.58. At least there were no 4's to fret over in the outstanding balance. Soon to be a father, I was perched on cloud nine.

When Linda concluded the calls, her expression changed perceptively, reflecting a more somber tone.

Oh boy, here it comes, I said to myself. Did I tell you that Linda was a master of timing?

"Sam..." (PAUSE—take my hand to brace me for the news) "I discuss with family. Make much important decision..." (PAUSE—flash a loving smile to soften me up) "Need help with baby so...(PAUSE—look deep into my eyes, daring me to object) "Ma coming."

Time stood still. Linda looked at me solicitously, waiting for my reaction.

Rule #1: Don't ever argue with your wife on the day she tells you she's with child.

Rule #2: When discussing family issues, especially in-laws, always think before you speak.

Looking back, I'd further modify that rule to: Always think long and hard before you open your flapper, especially if your wife is the one who carries the big stick. This was a lesson I inevitably learned the hard way. I don't really understand why, but for some reason I couldn't stop myself. The words originated somewhere deep in the left hemisphere of my brain, passed through my vocal tract, fell onto my lips and out my big mouth: "I hope you're not planning on having her stay *here*. I think it's fantastic Ma's coming to help, but we just got this place to ourselves again. There's plenty room for her at the Bayside house. Ma will be much more comfortable living there with Big Sister and the kids."

Linda's eyes hardened at my recommendation of having Ma shipped out to Queens. She shook her head emphatically. "No, no, no. Why you no understand? Ma need move here. One year…maybe two. Help raise baby." The icy challenge turned glacial.

What happened next should have been an Oscar-winning performance. Upon realizing my faux pas, I put on my bogus smile and reversed gears: "Oh, of course...I see, whatever makes you happy dear, I love the idea."

Linda saw right through my act, but let it go. Maybe she felt I'd suffer enough over the next two years under The Little General's own form of Sharia Law.

I never truly accepted the notion of a place called heaven, but I was starting to believe in hell, curses, voodoo magic and witchcraft. Somewhere, somehow, at some time during my relatively short life, I must have pissed off the wrong deity.

Oh…one last surprise (how much more can a hard-working stiff take?), three weeks prior to Ma's arrival, Linda would be sending the family's personal taxi service (who else?) back to the airport to pick up Big Sister's husband. He'd also decided to pack up and move to Queens, leaving behind a mediocre low paying job in the yarn division of the Far East Textile company. My brother-in-law was moving here with no job prospects, but at least he was college educated and spoke passable English. Thanks to me, there was a nice roomy house in Queens waiting for him.

The upstairs had been rented out to a single Caucasian man to help pay the mortgage. Big Sister said no to several Chinese families who wanted the apartment. She was concerned they'd soon overrun the place, inviting more and more relatives to move in with them—sound familiar? Big Sister would only rent to a non-Asian single or couple—no children or pets. In a way, she'd become a reverse racist.

The Liu family had the first floor and the basement to accommodate their needs. Following a phone conversation with Big Sister, Linda turned to me and said, "Need buy more furniture. How can live? House too much empty."

With my savings account nearly sucked dry from the hefty down payment on the new family compound, I begged the bank to float me a short-term loan. Our finances were getting tighter and tighter. There's an exception to every rule: In this case, Linda's timing couldn't have been worse. Ma called a couple weeks before her arrival. She insisted the pressure at work was not good for Linda or the baby and convinced my wife to just up and quit, which took a sizeable chunk out of our monthly income. Her burden was not really alleviated, it was just shifted—*onto me!*

Now the sole bread winner, I had to make monthly payments on two mortgages, a car payment, an upcoming short-term loan for my in-laws' new furniture and the remaining 18 installments on the Maurice Villency sofa, which by now was not even Goodwill-able. Ma was 8000 miles away, but the effects of her rule were already altering my life. One of my eyeballs started to shimmy periodically. Word traveled like a wild fire through the Liu family grapevine. Ma phoned in her decision: She was concerned I might have some type of virus that could infect mother and child. I was forbidden to set foot in my own apartment until I got checked out. Later that day, the ophthalmologist diagnosed me with "high stress disorder". Well, at least Linda and Junior were safe.

On occasion, Little Ling would stay with us in the city. It was easier for her to get to classes at Baruch, and it comforted my wife to have her around. However, after almost a year of living in close quarters with my Chinese relatives, for me it was a hellish nightmare watching our dream of privacy trampled on by the potential horde of in-laws trickling back. Silver Lining? None for me, but having our sexual escapades once again on hold, at least our neighbors would have more restful nights.

With my wife now incubating our first child, I felt my sole purpose in life was to keep her clam happy. This was likely related to some type of guilt induced behavior subliminally programmed into the unsuspecting male by their superior female counterpart. Until I married a Chinese girl, I thought Jewish women were the masters of this domain. I later learned from someone really smart, whose name and qualifications I can't recall, so I can't be held responsible for anything I might say, this skill is innate to all women from birth. It's widely known, but seldom admitted, that men are the weaker sex. If one day women found a way to produce their own sperm, male Homo sapiens would find themselves placed on the endangered species list. Maybe that's why the male dominated Catholic Church condemns stem cell research and cloning? It's a survival tactic.

The in-laws were currently using one of three mattresses I purchased (on credit) from Macys for living room furniture. To make the place habitable, Linda took Big Sister and her husband on a shopping spree. Thanks to the mountain of debt, the bank denied my request for the short-term loan. With no other options, Linda opened and maxed out a new credit card to furnish the entire house including a large screen TV. The next week we brought in a cable company from Flushing to install a special box that allowed them to get Chinese TV stations with English subtitles. I was hoping they'd take the hint and learn English ASAP so there'd be fewer misunderstandings.

Initially they didn't have a car, but a bus stop was conveniently located just a couple blocks away. The bus came frequently and took only 15 minutes to get to Flushing where they could buy groceries, on occasion eat at a restaurant that served authentic Taiwanese style food and get their mandatory Chinese hair wash.

Six plus months after Big Sister's husband arrived, I helped them get a loan to purchase a laundromat and a mini-van for pickup and deliveries. Since I acted as guarantor, my butt was again on the line. I hoped and prayed the business survived.

Mirroring the Jewish stereotype, and being a financial whiz, I took pride in my ability to broker super deals. But Big Sister put me to shame. I'd never before seen such a crackerjack negotiator. And I'd worked alongside some of the best in the banking business. I went with her and Linda to a Chrysler dealership to assist in purchasing the mini-van. She worked with a linebacker sized salesman to pick out the type, color and options. Afterwards we all sat down and waited while he tabulated the total. In a loud, boisterous voice he said, "With all the extras I can let you take it off my hands for $28,450."

Big Sister looked him straight in the eyes and said with absolutely no hesitation, "Too many dollar. Give half. $14,000 top price. OK to go, Joe?"

Hearing the insane number, the salesman did a double take, then blurted out, "Say what?"

My sister-in-law was taking the art of the deal to a whole new level. I had to squelch a laugh when I heard the offer matter-of-factly roll off her lips. The salesman had a confused look on his face. I tried to imagine what was going through his mind. Probably something like, *This broad is totally BONKERS!*

I was a little bit embarrassed by the whole scene. I said to Linda and Big Sister, "Well, it looks to me like the negotiations are in good hands," then fled the dealership for some fresh air.

A half hour later, the Asian tag team walked out the showroom door carrying a signed receipt for the truck. It'd be ready for pickup in three days. The final sales price, including tax, license & registration, plates, undercoating and a final paint seal coat was $19,800—the exact price Big Sister had intended to pay when she walked in the door.

Through the window I could see the salesman slumped over his desk with a rather exasperated look on his face. These two slight Chinese women had worked the big bad salesman over the coals until they broke his spirit and reduced his commission to pocket change. I felt like going in to console him; to let him know that he was not alone. He should've considered himself lucky that day. He only had to haggle with the two of them. It could have been much worse. Ma hadn't yet arrived. If the poor salesman had to deal with her too, he probably would've quit the business.

SIDEBAR: A year later, Sister Five moved to New York and took up residence in the Bayside house. Soon after, she decided to buy a new car. Big Sister told her about the great deal she got from the Caucasian salesman at the Chrysler dealership. That day, good fortune shined on the salesman. Sister five had a preference for Japanese cars and ended up purchasing a Toyota Rav4 instead.

The great Chinese invasion continued. Two weeks later I was back at JFK to pick up Ma. The family would not let her fly alone. Oh sure, tough-as-nails Ma could've easily flown solo. It was a respect thing, and like a Mafia don, she'd be traveling with an entourage: Sister Two and her husband who'd be spending their six-week vacation at the family compound in Queens.

I initially thought the purchase of the Bayside property would be a true blessing for Linda and me. However, when it came to my wife's family, there were no boundaries. In their minds, their house was my house and vice versa. In addition, with the upper floor now occupied by a tenant, housing options needed to be found for the continued flow, like running water, of in-laws. Since I couldn't afford the down payment for an additional dwelling, my apartment became the family's Plan B.

With all the in-and-out activity at the Bayside abode, neighbors soon started grumbling. I suspect they also took offense to the strange odors that emanated from the kitchen which was in round-the-clock operation. It was probably like living next door to a restaurant "Open 24 Hours." My in-laws were subjected to several visits by agents from the NYC Department of Buildings and Safety and The Department of Health. One or more neighbors had filed a complaint alleging that the two-family house had been illegally converted into a multi-residential dwelling. The agents made their inspections, confirmed it was one very large family—all related—living there and left without issuing any violations.

After the initial surge of spot checks by the city, for some unknown reason, the official visits abruptly stopped. It's possible that over time the neighbors' olfactory systems adjusted to the pungent aromas. They really had no choice but to adapt. A year after my in-laws moved in, another Chinese family bought the house across the street. Thanks to the proximity of Flushing, this ultra-white conservative middle-class neighborhood would soon be hit by a mass migration of Asian families.

We picked up Ma, Sister Two and her husband at the airport and drove them all to Bayside for a family reunion. Two and hub were crazy excited to see their daughter and thrilled to spend time with Big Sister and the boys, who'd arrived almost a year earlier. Ma was also anxious to see her oldest child, but even more excited to see my wife who, after three months into the pregnancy, was starting to show.

Over the years, Ma had become the go-to person whenever anyone in the family was expecting. She provided support as both a private chef and nutritionist; and after the birth, a nanny to her new grandchild. Thank God (or whoever's in charge) I'd insisted on ordering takeout for the family reunion that day. With each bite of the inferior, American-tasting Chinese food, Ma unabashedly made a face of disapproval.

Hallelujah! My blunder inadvertently caused Ma to reconsider her initial housing game plan. For the time being, *chef* took preference over *early-stage nursemaid***.** With Big Sister and her husband spending most of their time at the laundromat, she now saw an immediate need to make sure there'd always be an ample supply of Ma-cooked food for the clan.

But my climb to the top of Mt. Euphoria made a sharp U-turn, then plummeted into the valley of despair. Ma informed Linda she planned on staying with us over the weekends to make sure she was eating properly, thus providing the proper sustenance for the little one in her belly. For Big Sister, that weekly two-day reprieve from her overlord was like an all-expense paid tropical island vacation.

Sometimes Friday night, but more often Saturday morning, I was delegated the task of driving out to Bayside to pick up Ma. On the way back to the city we often stopped in Flushing for breakfast then shopped at the Chinese grocery to purchase the provisions Ma needed to prepare the weekend meals and the additional ones she made to hold Linda over during the week when she wasn't there.

I think its common knowledge that the Chinese diet is much healthier than its American counterpart. Hypothetically, if Ma's wok could pump out enough food to feed the entire U.S. population, the obesity epidemic would disappear, and the cost of health care would plummet.

With Ma here on the weekends, I once again said goodbye to fine NYC dining; eating all our meals at home. These included the ones Ma made for us onsite, and the excess crammed into the refrigerator prior to her chauffeured departure back to Queens. On occasion I'd work late just to avoid another premade Chinese meal, such as her "jiu3 cai4 he2 zi5"; like a hot pocket, but the cheese and pepperoni are substituted with Chinese chives, bean curd, chopped eggs, glass noodles and mini-dried shrimp with their heads still on—*Gross!* There were also several other of Ma's vegetarian meals I either didn't like or had gotten tired of. On those days I savored a cheeseburger, kielbasa, or a footlong hotdog smothered in ketchup and mustard that I purchased from a street vendor, while Linda dined on her beloved homemade mommy fixins.

Another Friday arrived, and once again I'd transform from businessman to cabbie. I left work early, picked up my car, and drove to the front of our building where Linda was waiting. I jumped out to open the door and ease her into the front seat. She'd already put on 20 lbs., and I was a little nervous about her stability. I clicked in her seat belt.

Linda put her hand on my cheek and said, "Oh Sam, you too much good to me."

I followed with, "That's not possible for Sammie Junior's mom."

She returned a weak smile which caused me to wonder if she intuitively knew something I didn't regarding the gender of our child.

We fought the nasty weekend traffic for over an hour and a half, finally arriving in Bayside at 7:30 PM to pick up Ma—the Lowe family's Chef de Cuisine. She was waiting out front pacing back and forth, clearly annoyed by the delay.

"Ni3 hao3," (Hi) Ma," I shouted, giving her my best toothy smile.

She hit me with one of her patented menacing stares and rattled off, "Hei1!, ben4 dan4, ni3 lai2 guo4 hen3 duo1 ci4. Zen3 me5 hai2 hui4 mi2 lu4?"

"Linda, tell me what she said and don't sugarcoat it."

"Okay, you ask for it: 'Hey, stupid egg. Come so many times. How you get lost?' "

Ma was not an easy read. Yes, I'd received her blessing, but I was unsure if she actually liked me or looked upon me solely as a provider for her daughter and a stud to make grandchildren.

Currently, Ma's main function was to provide sustenance for the weekend and restock the fridge for weekdays. During her pregnancy, Linda routinely ate only Ma's home cooked food—which worked out fine for her. After all, it was what she grew up on. I, on the other hand, soon grew tired of Ma's 3x a day meals—to the point where even airline food would've been a welcome change.

"Linda, I need a break from Chinese," I pleaded. "Can we go grab some American, Italian, India, Polish, German, Russian...*anything* that isn't served with chopsticks?"

"But Sam," she cooed, "Have much good Ma cooked food. Why you want go outside eat? Besides, not know what in food, even so-called *Chinese* restaurant. You no want baby have best?"

"You're always right, honey," I responded in a slightly irritable tone. People start getting edgy when they're hungry. However, Linda could always trump me by playing the pregnancy card. *C'est la vie!*

There was never the slightest chance we'd run out of food. The second my mother-in-law stepped into our apartment the human dumpling machine went into mass production. Ma's skill at pumping them out was without equal.

First, she prepared all the ingredients that'd comprise the interior's contents. Next came the dough, which she made completely from scratch, then rolled out and cut into circles using the proper sized drinking glass. Ma placed a scoop of the ingredients (a mix of minced pork or shrimp and a vegetable) in the center of the circle then picked up the ends pinching them together in one swift machine-like motion and *voila*—one down—hundreds more to go.

The process time ran a good three plus hours, producing at least 500 at a crack. Some were set aside for weekend consumption, but the majority were placed in large plastic bags that took up every inch of our freezer. Whenever hungry, Linda pulled out a bag of 25 and dropped them into a pan of hot vegetable oil where they'd cook roughly 5 minutes until one side turned a crispy brown. To finish them off she poured a large glass of water into the pan then covered it tightly with a lid. When the evaporation was complete the dumplings were ready for consumption. I personally liked the added flavor from my own version of Worcestershire, sesame oil and soy sauce. Ma's dumplings were lip smakin' good, but after eating the same thing every day for weeks on end, no matter how amazing, an aversion leading to revulsion develops.

Three months after Ma arrived, I'd eaten enough dumplings to last two lifetimes. Linda was getting bigger, and with Ma absent during the week, she didn't want to lift a finger. Save-the-day dumplings were so easy to prepare, they became her express option. I was dying to sneak myself something else to eat, but my culinary skill set ended at pushing down the lever on the toaster.

Contingency Plan: Find a way to slow down production, or at least use up the almost infinite supply.

"Dear, Ma's dumplings are so good," I said, hatching a scheme. "Would you mind if I gave a few to my colleagues at the office?"

"Of course, Sam. Take plenty. Ma make more."

That thought kept me up half the night.

The next morning, I grabbed nine large bags (225 dumplings) from the freezer, which barely put a dent in our inventory. In the end, only one of my colleagues took a bag. (He owed me a favor.) I chucked the rest in the dumpster behind the bank.

I was in a quandary. The more dumplings I disposed of the more Ma would produce. If I stopped eating them altogether, I might insult her cooking, which I'd already done in Taiwan, and I didn't want a repeat of that history lesson.

Ma immediately discovered the slight reduction in her dumpling arsenal. She asked Linda, "Shei2 chi1 wo3 de5 shui3 jiao3?" (Who is eating all my dumplings?)

"Sam's tong2 shi4 hen3 xi3 huan1!" ("Sam's colleagues love them!") Linda replied.

Ma's face lit up like a sunburst. The notion that Americans enjoyed her cooking made her day and she increased production to supply the entire bank. When I got home from work, not only were the nine bags from the freezer replenished, but the entire refrigerator was filled. My disposal scheme had backfired big time! What was I thinking? There's just no outsmarting Ma.

On Saturday, February 9, 1991, while shopping for a new sofa to replace our other new sofa, which defied cleaning even by professionals, Linda went into labor. Initially we were both fooled by the Braxton Hicks (false labor), but nine hours later I was hailing a taxi to take us to Mount Sinai hospital. At 10 PM she gave birth to a healthy baby girl. We'd tossed around names for months. Unquestionably, Samuel if a boy. If a girl, we had an A-Z list, but I kept insisting it should be Linda. We were about to finalize our decision when Murphy's Law kicked in; I received a phone call from my boss and had to take it. I excused myself and left the room. It took almost an hour before I was able to straighten out *his* mess. I returned to Linda's room, apologizing profusely, but she immediately cut me off.

"You no here. So, I make executive decision," Linda said firmly, and handed me the completed birth certificate application.

I fell in love with my wife all over again when I read the name she'd chosen, that'd never occurred to me: *Samantha.*

We lived directly across the park from the hospital. On doctor's orders, Linda would be staying the night. I decided to head home to try and get some sleep. In my euphoric and energized state of mind I made the bonehead decision to walk back to our apartment, completely forgetting about the dangers of crossing Central Park in the pitch black of night. This was during the Dinkin's Administration. I don't mean to cast aspersions on Mayor Dinkins, but at that time, certain parts of

NYC were much more dangerous than today. Strolling through the park at midnight was not the action of a sane person, but irrational choices are often the norm for a first-time dad. I was about halfway across when a burly guy, approximately six inches shorter than me, seemed to appear out of nowhere. He blocked my path and held a gun 12 inches from my face.

I put my hands up and did my best to play it cool. "What do you want?"

The mugger's eyes immediately went to my gold Movado. "Everything. But let's start with that watch."

It had been presented to me by the Liu clan. Gold was the traditional Chinese wedding gift symbolizing wealth and prosperity. As directed by Ma, the entire family pooled their resources to make the purchase. And that started me thinking about everything I'd gone through and put up with over the past year. I could feel it all boiling inside of me, ready to explode.

By this time, I'd removed the watch from my left wrist and was holding it wrapped around the fingers of my right hand. Talk about irrational...I looked the mugger in the eye and said, "You want the watch? I'll give you the watch."

I blocked the gun away with my left hand and used the Movado like brass knuckles to smash the mugger in the nose. Blood squirted out like a geyser, and the gun dropped to the ground when he grasped his face with both hands, howling in pain. I put my foot on the gun and feinted another punch; the clown turned and took off running. With immense pride, I pulled the watch back over my left wrist and snapped the band.

Just to be safe, I picked up the gun with my handkerchief, to avoid fingerprints, and tossed it into a pond on the way home. When I entered my apartment, by now, reality had settled in: *I could've been shot and killed!* I was both an emotional and physical wreck; couldn't even make it to the bedroom and crashed on the couch.

I woke up the next morning realizing I'd overslept. Linda would probably be wondering where I was. I shot out of my building and ran down a cab.

Upon entering the hospital waiting area, I was met by a host of strange stares. The triage nurse hurried over and said, "Do you need a wheelchair?"

A security guard asked what happened, and could I identify the assailant.

Confused by all the attention, I dashed into a nearby restroom and looked in the mirror; my face and shirt were splattered with specs of dried blood. I washed up, went to the desk, and had Linda's doctor paged. After I explained what had happened, he agreed it was probably best that I didn't upset Linda and keep it to myself, at least for now. We were about the same size, and he lent me the dress shirt he was wearing under his white coat.

I entered Linda's room. She smiled, then shot a glance at the wall clock. "Somebody up late celebrating?"

"Perhaps a little," I allowed.

"How your night, hon?"

I affected an English accent and said, "My dear, it was absolutely smashing."

The day before I brought my wife and little Samantha home from the hospital, I drove to Bayside to pick up my mother-in-law. Ma was moving in with us *permanently*—that is, until she was satisfied we could get along without her. I imagined that might be when our daughter turned 21. Ma had no hesitation leaving the family to live with us. Her golden rule was that babies always come first. God help me if Linda wanted to follow in her mom's footsteps and have seven children.

On the plus side, Ma was the perfect infant caregiver. My daughter was a colicky little one who had to be constantly comforted otherwise the crying was nonstop. In my inexperienced arms she'd squirm and shriek until my head was ready to go *KABLOOEY!* But with Ma always at the ready, I could hand her over and as if by magic, she'd instantly calm down and nod off.

I wanted to take off from work the day after my daughter came home, but I was in the midst of completing a business valuation related to an acquisition by one of the bank's largest commercial clients. There were several important meetings I had to attend. I rose extra early, coffeed up and headed downtown to prepare. Even knowing that my wife was in good hands, I felt guilty for leaving her.

My meetings went surprisingly well, and third-Charles told me point-blank he didn't want to see me around the office until the following week. It was already Friday, so I wasn't sure if he was kidding me. My boss's actions continued supporting the notion that he was either a *Prick,* a *Stealthanator,* or some nasty combination.

Stacy, his secretary, left me a message that I was to report to the executive conference room Monday at 3:00 PM to meet with him and one of the bank's corporate clients to make a pitch for new business. At least Chucky III wasn't asking me to work the weekend.

Prior to finding out about the Monday meeting I was going to ask for a one week leave of absence. Women get maternity leave—it's not fair there's no such thing as paternity leave. Shouldn't the father deserve some time off too? Since that was now off the table, I'd try to enjoy the weekend and hope no dire emergencies flared up before Monday. Little did I know that an hour later, I'd be ready to turn around and head straight back to the office.

On the way home, I picked up a dozen roses for Linda. Given how hard she'd worked delivering the baby, I knew in my heart she deserved an expensive piece of jewelry, but as I stated earlier, I come from a long line of misers. The lovely Linda also was tightfisted with a buck—except when it came to designer clothes, shoes, purses and of course Tiffany jewelry. Although when she did buy any high-ticket item, it was either on sale—or she created her own personal sale by bargaining the price down. Afterwards, few things in life gave Linda more pleasure than telling me how much money she saved us on the purchase. Since my gal had exceptional taste in everything and I had none, tonight the roses would have to do.

I arrived at my building, the Vaux Condominium, around 5:00 PM and took the elevator up to the sixth floor. The moment I stepped into the hallway my olfactory senses picked up on a foreign essence. Initially, I didn't give it much thought. At all times, the Vaux had a symphony of strange smells emanating from most apartments. The complex housed a plethora of very old rent-controlled tenants, which may have been the reason so many of the hallways smelled like mothballs. We also had several East Indian families, meaning a strong scent of curry and sometimes the nasty smell of asafetida, an Indian spice also known as devil's dung. We'd been residents of the condominium for almost two years and were just starting to get used to its pungent aromas, but nothing could've prepared me for this vicious attack on my nostrils.

Our apartment was located at the end of the hallway, the farthest from the elevator. With each step closer to my door the smell grew exponentially stronger. It was an odor that was hard to pin down. It had a tear-inducing fragrant part, but not like a strong perfume. A better comparison would be the musky odor of a skunk. I detected another part that had a sour stale smell with a hint of something organic that died some time ago and was now in the final stages of decay. Limburger cheese, by comparison, was ambrosia. And I soon found out that I'd have to live with this funky stench every day for the next month. When I opened the door, the smell met me like a shock wave and nearly knocked me back out into the hallway on my ass.

Ma was in the kitchen stirring a pot exuding a brownish-yellowish-greyish smoke.

"Linda…what's that stench?" I asked, wiping my stinging eyes.

"Sheng1 hua4 tang1," (literal translation: "birth transformation soup") she replied nonchalantly. "Chinese use three hundred years more. Ma boil herbs and plant root make special soup. Flush out toxins. Heal body. Bring back blood and Qi."

I discovered it had permeated everything in the apartment including all my business suits. I wondered what people at my office would be saying about me behind closed doors. I figured my colleagues would discreetly hide things for me to find in and around my desk—you know, odor eaters, underarm deodorants, bottles of cologne and packages of those scented Christmas trees people hang from the rear-view mirror in their car.

That night I turned my bed around, so the top was against the window. My wife, in case of an emergency, was sleeping with Ma, so whatever crazy, insane methods I deployed did not raise her objection. The stone sill was slightly higher than the mattress, but with three pillows in place my nose was at the perfect height. I then removed the screen. Just my luck, it was the dead of winter. Every night for the next three weeks, I slept with my head in a ski mask and hanging partially out the window.

25. Who Are You?

Prior to moving to New York, none of my in-laws had English names. Why would they? They were all Chinese down to their bone marrow. However, given the difficulty of correctly pronouncing their Mandarin names, an English one would be helpful with their assimilation to life in America.

My wife completely agreed with this logic. She had taken one just a week after arriving in New York. Liu Hua Mei told me, "I deserve name Linda as in Linda Carter—Wonder Woman."

How interesting is that? Confident? Narcissistic? I never heard of an Asian named Clark Kent. That moniker should've been my first indication of what I was in for, but blind love clouded my reasoning.

When it came to the naming of the rest of my wife's family, the honor was bestowed upon me. There was Ma, five sisters and one brother. Since I didn't know any of them that well, I thought it best to use a theme. Headphones and a Sony Walkman was often my escape when the Mandarin was machine-gunning back and forth in my apartment. So, I decided to use famous female rock stars of the 80s for my name pool. I selected singers who offered up characteristics that reminded me of each in-law. The ceremony took place at a dinner in our apartment two weeks after the birth of Samantha.

Here are the matchups:

Ma (The Little General and/or Mrs. Genghis Khan)—both well suited to her pugnacious temperament. I didn't have a death wish so I kept this one to myself. Besides, Ma would always be "Ma" to everyone concerned. However, if I did pick a name, I would've gone with Joan Jett, who had a similar brash presence. Additionally, the name of her band, The Black Hearts, tied in with my inability to break all the way through to Ma's soft side, if one existed.

Big Sister – the oldest: Sarah (Sarah McLachlan) carbon copy with high arched eyebrows.

Sister Two – second oldest: Melissa (Melissa Etheridge) same raspy voice.

Sister Four – fourth oldest: Joan (Joan Baez) dead ringer but with an Asian flair.

Sister Five – fifth oldest: Tina (Tina Turner) vivacious to a tee.

Sister Six – sixth oldest: the enchanting Linda Liu (already anointed Linda after Linda Carter, alias Wonder Woman—super at having her way).

Sister Seven – the youngest: Patricia (Patricia Mae Andrzejewski, aka Pat Benatar, aka Little Ling) the identical short haircut which Ling copied right after seeing Benatar perform in concert in Taipei.

The Brother – third oldest: Stevie (Stevie Nicks). I was already pulling female names from my 80's memory bank, and it was simpler to follow suit. Nicks was the only female vocalist I liked with a gender-neutral name. Linda's brother was your archetypal Taiwanese male chauvinist, so I didn't tell him he was named after a girl.

One day, my brother-in-law caught me off-guard, wanting to know the who and why. In fact, none of them knew their namesakes; no explanation was necessary; except for Little Ling who was flattered to share a name with her rock idol.

"Stevie, as in..." I had to make up something fast, "uh...Stevie...Wonder."

"And why?" he pressed.

"Well... because..." my brain quickly rolodexed through song titles, "because you are the sunshine of my life."

Corny? Yes. Did he buy it? I'll never know.

26. Eye of Newt, Toe of Frog

Having lived with or visited my in-laws for many years, I can tell you firsthand that Chinese people truly have a love affair with their soup. It's a staple in their life and seems to accompany almost every meal. They even have it for breakfast.

Millions of Americans often enjoy cold soup for breakfast. They call it cereal. It's usually very sweet and comes loaded with all sorts of wonderful chemicals, colorful dyes and often more sugar than grain. Americans also eat hot cereal (oatmeal, Cream of Wheat, and grits), but because of its viscous nature, I wouldn't classify it as a soup.

Chinese breakfast soup is hot and has noodles, vegetables and meats kerplunked into the base. You'd think it was much healthier than its American counterpart, but that depends on what was added and how long it was sitting unheated on the stove.

After the family moved into our apartment there was always a large pot of soup simmering in the kitchen. When I looked down into the metal vessel, the mixture inside often had an opaque grayish cloudy appearance with various unrecognizable items bobbing up and down, breaking the surface. Hence, I dubbed it "Swamp Soup".

It became apparent to me that Ma and my sisters-in-law never threw anything out. Paying no attention to expiration dates or bacterial growth, all leftovers were fair game to become ingredients for the witches' brew that hid unknown quantities of aging food items unconsumed from meals long forgotten. This concoction sat on the stovetop all day, every day, ready for whoever dared ingest its occult contents. It was a sort of Chinese pot luck chunky liquid surprise.

I remember from my childhood, Mom always reminding us to put the leftovers from dinner back into the refrigerator after they had thoroughly cooled off. This home cooked Chinese pottage was the definitive exception to that rule. Maybe that's why it always had a somewhat foul stale odor.

"Oh my God! You see that?" Linda screamed in panic.

"See what?" I rushed over to find her frozen in place.

"Something gray! Long tail! Run across kitchen floor! Go behind fridge!" she eked out in a terror-stricken voice.

I inched back the refrigerator and spied a small mouse hunkering in the corner.

"Lao3 shu3! Lao3 shu3!" ("Mouse! Mouse!"), Big Sister yelled, shouldering me aside, wielding a broom. In one quick thrust, she struck with the wood pole end, KO'ing the poor little guy. "Dai3 dao4 le5," ("Got ya,") she proudly exclaimed.

This was the first one I'd seen in the apartment. With all the bags and boxes of food piled up in the pantry closet, and the numerous cooking scraps that had fallen behind the stove and cabinets, we apparently now had a serious mouse problem. Man of the house, I considered it my duty to pick up the deceased creature by the tail and deposit it in the garbage.

That evening, after finishing our dinner of Swamp Soup, fortunately complemented by other dishes, I performed my nightly duty—disposing of the garbage into the hallway refuse chute. While slowly pouring out the can's contents, I morbidly kept an eye peeled for the dead mouse. To my horror, it wasn't there.

I gasped in disbelief, *You gotta be shitting me!* Did one of my in-laws really fish it out of the trash and toss it into you-know-where!? I dashed to the bathroom, shoved my finger down my throat, and puked up dinner.

The next day, I overheard a conversation between Big Sister and Little Ling. Turned out Little Ling saw the dead mouse splayed out on top of the garbage, was grossed out, and flushed it down the toilet.

Our mouse problem continued until my in-laws moved out. But as long as Big Sister's frugality didn't lead to stir-fried rodent on the menu, I could live with it.

27. Scram for the Exits

Everyone has something they abhor eating. George Bush Sr. couldn't stand broccoli. Bill Clinton despised pecan pie. The Obamas requested the White House chef never prepare anything with beets. Woody Allen hates oysters, insisting his food must be dead prior to consumption. And based on information leaked during the 2016 Republican presidential primaries, Donald Trump might have a phobia about Mexican food; or maybe that's just Mexicans in general.

I on the other hand, will eat almost anything. I'm so very lucky to live in New York City where there's a plethora of food options. I always try to keep an open mind when it comes to sampling new cuisine. However, there is one dish I was introduced to, up close and personal, during my first visit to Taipei that I'd never have the intestinal fortitude to taste. You've heard me mention it before...chou4 dou4 fu5, which I will describe in a couple minutes. But first a backstory...

During our initial visit to Taiwan, Linda took me out to the Hua Xi night market. Just like other Chinese street fairs, the Hua Xi offered a multitude of local snacks and numerous small seafood restaurants serving delicious Taiwanese dishes. But the big difference between the Hua Xi and other night markets are the scads of vendors who sell food products made from the bountiful snake population.

According to native beliefs, snake is a healthy source of vital nutrients, and thus very nourishing for the human body.

Snake meat is served in soup, cooked dishes, and is also used in medicines.

At Hua Xi, visitors are introduced to live snakes. Some vendors put them in a cage with a chicken or a large rat, providing gruesome theater for the tourists. Linda and I stood with a group of patrons in front of one vendor watching him pull back the lid of an enormous glass aquarium, housing a huge snake with brownish blotches covering its skin.

One of the spectators said something to him in Chinese and he replied, "Mang3 she2."

"What did he say?" I asked Linda.

"Python," she replied.

"Are those local to Taiwan?" I asked, taking a half step back.

"No, but have plenty other deadly snakes," she said matter-of-factly. The vendor grabbed a live squawking chicken and with a wide grin, that showcased an incomplete set of yellowish-brown teeth, he thrust it into the cage and pushed the lid back in place. The chicken immediately sensed danger, fleeing to a far corner. The snake's head turned toward its prey then it stopped and remained motionless. The chicken, frantically running back and forth at the opposite end of the aquarium, kept knocking into the glass trying to escape. Then the frenzied, clucking bird made a fatal mistake and veered toward the snake. The python shot like an unleashed spring, grabbing the chicken's wing with its mouth, coiled its powerful body around its prey, and the squawking turned to silence.

I nudged Linda. "How about we skip the third act where he swallows the bird whole?"

"Who the chicken now?" Linda chuckled. "Okay. No want spoil your appetite."

I raised up to my full height. “Well, I’m just glad we’re at the top of the food chain.”

“Hungry yet?” Linda, who could eat anything, anytime, asked.

My stomach was a bit queasy from the live-dead show. “Not really, I think I’ll wait for dinner. You up for vegetarian tonight?” I asked hopefully.

A few stalls down the street, Linda again stopped to watch a vendor work with one of his large reptilian specimens. “Hey Sam, come quick check out.” she said excitedly.

I was not feeling up to another Darwinian exhibition, but she insisted, so I readied myself for more macabre.

The merchant grabbed the front section of a long thick snake, raised its head several feet above a steel table then smashed it down with all his might against the edge, stunning it. He then skinned it alive and cut it into small pieces that’d be used to prepare various dishes for the evening rush.

That ghastly demonstration totally put me off, and I vowed never to try snake meat regardless of how many times my in-laws insisted, “Taste like chicken.” To which I'd reply, “In that case, I'll just stick to KFC." Lucky for me I've never seen a steer or lamb slaughtered, or I'd have nothing to pair with my red wine collection.

Speaking of red wine, I found it interesting that many of these vendors use the snake blood to make some very potent alcoholic beverages. One of the most popular is Cobra Sake, which is made from the blood of the venomous cobra and brings new meaning to the term "dead drunk".

Linda once double dared me in front of my young nephews: "C'mon Sam! Why you big pussy? Every week, Ma drink two shots."

"I thought only men use it—to increase their sex drive," I countered. "Why is your mom drinking it?"

"She like taste," Linda shrugged. "You man or mouse?"

I put my hands up to my ears, palms out. "Squeak, squeak, squeak."

The minute after we'd arrived at the Hua Xi night market, a foul odor had begun attacking my olfactory receptors. As we continued through the market, it became apparent we were heading toward the source. With each step the stench intensified.

I thought I'd figured out where it was coming from and said to Linda, "Holy crap, do you smell that? The sewer must've backed up."

She turned to me and said, "Really? I no smell anything."

I suspected that her allergies were acting up, clogging her nasal passages. However, I didn't hear her doing the usual sniffing, and she didn't appear to be breathing through her mouth.

There was something so familiar about the offensive fetor. I flashed back to our recent Tower Air flight, remembering when I complained to the Chinese stewardess about the strange smells coming from the passengers' carry-on items. She had offered up the same response as Linda: "What smell, sir?"

Asian people, in general, have much smaller noses. Maybe sensitivity to odor is somehow related to the size of your nostrils, I concluded. *Therefore, my larger Jewish schnoz will pick up a much greater volume of smells than Linda's petite nose.*

To make sure I'm being politically correct and not coming off anti-Semitic, I'd like to state for the record that not all Jewish men have a large proboscis like me. To further clarify, mine's not really that big, but compared to Linda's it's like Mt. Rushmore.

In any event, I've always been overly sensitive to strong scents. I'm viciously repulsed by the smell of vinegar, limburger cheese, curdled milk, garlic breath and body odor to name just a few. However, the offensive reek coming from somewhere down the street was far worse than anything I'd ever experienced. The smell had grown so strong it caused my eyes to tear up and my head to start throbbing. I had no doubt we'd reached the source of the fetid, rotting smell. I looked down at my feet to see if we were standing in a pool of raw sewage. I thought there might've been an overflow into the streets, but below me was only dry pavement. I whirled my head left and right, surveying my surroundings. I saw food vendors everywhere with open carts cooking their food to sell to the evening crowd. I wondered how soon the city's health department would show up to shut down the market.

I was a little wobbly and grabbed ahold of Linda. “I'm starting to feel nauseated. How about we head back to Sister Four's apartment?” We hadn't eaten dinner yet, and I could tell Linda was getting hungry by the second.

She asked, “You can wait? Want buy something eat.”

I was about ready to hurl, but I knew from experience, when Linda gets hungry, she must be fed quickly before Dr. Banning turns into The Hulk.

Linda gave me a non-compromising look. ""No worry. Be quick. I want buy over there." She pointed to a vendor, three carts away, who was frying something in a large wok.

With each step closer the feted rotting odor assaulted my nostrils and amplified the throbbing in my head. Raw sewage wasn't bubbling up under the merchant's station, so the strange contents cooking in the wok had to be the source of the rancid miasma.

Linda became oblivious to my agony; her face lit up like a child at Christmas when she pointed to the bile the vendor was preparing and exclaimed, “This all-time favorite snack...chou4 dou4 fu5!” (Translation: “stinky tofu.”)

My stomach was doing somersaults and my head was jackhammering as Linda skipped up to the ancient looking metal cooking vessel. I, on the other hand—or foot—took a few steps backward.

Clearly, Linda either had masochistic tendencies or suffered from an acute case of anosmia, for she pointed to the sewage-like substance that was floating in a dark brown bubbling liquid, and said to the vendor, “Qing3 gei3 wo3 da4 fen4 de5.” (Translation: “Please give me a large serving.”) The dish was ladled into a plastic bowl. Linda handed him 10 yuan (about 25 cents U.S.) then spun around and headed back toward me.

Every horror flick where the monster approaches the trapped victim flashed before my eyes. I dared not let her get any closer, there was a serious chance I might projectile vomit all over her. “Honey, you go on ahead. I want to check out a couple other vendors. I’ll be along soon.”

"I see you back home,” she replied in a trance-like state, spooning down her beloved swill.

Wouldn’t you know it? The wind would be blowing in my direction. I decided to wait until Linda was a full block ahead of me before following her back to Sister Four’s apartment. It may have been all in my head, but I could still smell it and detoured down another street. Once the nasty funk of the smelly tofu disappeared, *bada bing bada boom*, my stomach settled down and my headache vanished. I proceeded at a crippled snail’s pace to give Linda plenty of time to finish eating.

When I arrived at the apartment, probably around midnight, Linda conceded, "That batch more stronger." Then added, "But still delish! Wish have second helping."

I distinctly remember Mom telling me, "Don't eat anything that smells like it's spoiled." Even after Linda professed it was a cherished fave of hers, I could never summon up the courage to try even a tiny bite.

I did some research on the subject and found that stinky tofu is indeed rotten. Many Asian people fully admit the aroma of this highly prized Chinese dish resembles that of decaying garbage or a dollop of fresh manure. Some compare the smell to a cross between rotten meat and real bad body odor. But despite this tofu's stench, most claim the flavor is surprisingly mild. And many enthusiasts swear that the worse it smells, the better it tastes. How that logic works will baffle me to my grave.

The traditional method for producing this nasty substance is to prepare a brine made from fermented vegetables and meat; it can also include dried shrimp, amaranth greens, mustard greens, bamboo shoots, and miscellaneous pungent Chinese herbs. The brine fermentation can go as long as several months. While stinky or smelly tofu is scary popular in East and Southeast Asia, very few Chinese Americans prepare stinky tofu brine in their homes due to its wall-penetrating odor, especially in metro-residential areas. I assume that if someone did try to make it in the middle of a large city, riots would ensue.

It's still widely practiced in many U.S. metropolitan Chinatowns, but only within the confines of an enclosed kitchen. And I read that a more modern method is being employed in American factories where faster aging techniques have been mastered, allowing for mass production. To quote John McEnroe, "You cannot be serious!" *Mass production* of this so-called *edible* sewage? Now that's a bloodcurdling thought! On the order of hearing they're now mass-producing anthrax.

The nature of the production process makes it extremely difficult to pass government food regulation, even in Asia. The diversity and lack of specific formulated methods makes it nearly impossible for any government to inspect or regulate. In Asia no stinky tofu factories are ever officially licensed nor are they constantly monitored; in most instances, government inspection can only focus on the cooking procedure and ventilation.

In North America, it's often "homemade" in cities with significant numbers of Asian immigrants. For example, some Asian tofu factories in Vancouver, Canada produce the offensive slop "underground" as a side-business to avoid government inspections.

There are many different types. The one the vendor prepared for Linda that day was a spicy soft version in a gelatinous base. The most common type found in Taiwan comes in the form of deep-fried cubes garnished with sweet and sour pickled vegetables, which help to reduce the greasiness of the dish. The fried type puts out a slightly stronger stench. Contrasting the fried version with the spiced up soft type Linda consumed is like comparing the difference between being shot in the head with a .45 caliber pistol versus a .38.

A recent introduction to the street food scene in Taipei are vendors selling stinky tofu “french fries”. The putrid tofu is cut into thin strips, deep fried then doused with grated cheddar cheese. French fries, as we know them today, were invented in the 1700s in Belgium. They soon became a popular food staple throughout the Western world. While the preparation varied, the key ingredient to this day remains the same—*potatoes*.

There's no doubt in my mind now that I'll pass the next time a Taipei vendor hands me my order and asks, "You want fries with that?"

28. Lifestyles of the Rich and Frugal

After a solid year, including most weekends, working my butt off, I paid down a sizeable chunk of the consumer debt we'd accumulated from settling my in-laws. Linda monitored our bank and credit card balances like a hawk. She realized our economic load was beginning to lighten and decided to open the floodgates a crack. "Sam always so tired. Need work break. Some fun in sun."

"A vacation? Surely you jest," I laughed and launched into an arm's length list of objections and obstacles, including, "Samantha's only a year old. It'll be too difficult traveling with her…"

"No worry," she cut me off, "I talk my family. All coming—surprise!"

"H-Huh? *A-All* of them? And we're going w-where?" I blubbered, readying myself for the other shoe to drop.

"Last week, call Sam secretary. She know vacation schedule. Help set whole thing up. Already buy tickets." Linda said brimming with excitement. "This much fun. No need worry 'bout Samantha. Ma coming too."

Somebody pinch me to wake me from this nightmare, I wanted to explode. But I saw how juiced up Linda was, and tweaked my words: "Hao3 bang4," (Translation: "That's so great,") please pinch me so I know I'm not dreaming." I asked, "Where are we going? Can we really afford this now? How much were the tickets?" and braced for her response.

"Get good deal. Buy in bulk. Ocean front suite. Four bedrooms. Palms resort on Providenciales at Turks and Caicos," she provided, turning away without revealing the exorbitant cost of an exotic vacation with the posse of Ma, Big Sister, Sister Four, Sister Five and her boyfriend.

The morning of our flight I packed two small suitcases, one for us and one loaded with baby supplies, then hailed a cab to JFK.

Vacations in the Caribbean don't require much in the way of clothes. Shorts and T-shirts were regulation attire for a short week of sun, water and relaxation. Linda and I had been there once before. The Regent Palms was situated on the white sandy beaches of Grace Bay. The hotel had a spectacular pool, waterside bar and two upscale restaurants. There were numerous beachside dining options within just a minute's walk.

The grand accommodations Linda booked came with a fully equipped kitchen, which to me was a huge waste. Daily breakfast was discounted with our package, inexpensive lunches were available by the pool, and romantic dinners by torch light on the beach were the most desirable option. The purpose of the trip was to relax and recharge my batteries. I figured the only work-related activity for me would be removing the little umbrellas from the glasses for the unobstructed flow of a fresh fruit drink mixed with vodka or rum.

I loved the vibe of the place and the notion that you could hop a morning flight and be sitting on the beach by noon, basking in the sun at 80+ degrees with a margarita in hand. Actually, I'd be the only one basking, because while Linda loved warm weather, she hated the sun. To get ready for the beach, she'd put on her sexy two-piece swimsuit then laminate her entire body with 1000 spf sunscreen, don a pair of oversized dark sunglasses and an enormous straw hat; one beach towel to sit on and another to use as a blanket covering any remaining exposed lily-white skin.

"You know, it'd be a lot easier," I told her, "to just wear a burka."

The morning of departure, our taxi pulled up to the terminal. I grabbed our two diminutive carry-on bags from the trunk; Linda scooped up Samantha and placed her in our Baby-Flex car seat/carrier. We approached the American Airline's counter, and I spotted my in-laws waiting in front of check-in. It was a very early flight, and there was no one else in line. I spied a mountain of luggage piled up against the wall, and a feeling of dread came over me. Sister Four's new boyfriend, Lorenzo, a middle-aged, burly Italian who favored loud, flower-splattered shirts, was off to the side keeping an eye on the suitcase Mt. Everest.

I approached Big Sister. "There's no way those are all yours," I said, looking for a sign that read "Luggage Lost and Found".

"Yes ours," she replied cheerily.

"Did you know we are staying there only five days?" From the sheer volume it looked like they planned to make this a permanent move.

"Yes, Mr. Sam. Me know. Two bag clothes. Eight bag food."

My brain went numb for a second trying to make sense of what she'd just uttered. I held back a primordial scream, turned to Linda and said, "Your family is trying to bring luggage stuffed with food into a foreign country. Did you know about this?"

"Yes, Sam. Don't be worry wart," Linda pooh-poohed my concerns, as usual. "They want eat Chinese home cooking."

"Linda, do you know it's *illegal* to bring food across international borders?"

"Of course. But who follow silly rule." She flicked her wrist. "Family *always* take food when travel."

I couldn't believe Linda knew about the grocery store her family was trying to smuggle in, but never said a word to me.

Relaxing vacation goodbye! Now I'd be stressed the entire plane ride over being searched, fined, not allowed into the country, or worse yet jailed by the local authorities.

I helped Lorenzo carry the luggage over to the airline counter. Each piece felt like a bag of bowling balls. The airline had a 50 lb. per bag weight limit with a surcharge of $50 up to 71 lbs., $100 for 72-99 lbs., anything over 100 lbs. would not be allowed on the plane. Lorenzo and I heaved each one up onto the scale to verify the weight. Without exception, every piece was over the limit by at least 20 lbs.

"Lorenzo, keep your mouth shut about the added baggage charges. I don't want to upset Ma," I whispered.

"No problemo, Sam. I'm not paying for it anyway," he shot back gleefully.

At least this was a one-time charge. Coming back most of the suitcases would be empty. I cut a deal with the agent who kept the added charges at $50 per bag, even though at least four were a pound or two over the 100 lb. mark. However, one weighed in at 123 lbs., and the agent insisted she could not accept it.

"What the hell is in this one—a set of weights?" I asked Lorenzo.

"Sorry Sam, after I zipped up her suitcase, Ma gave Tina a big bag of rice to take," he shrugged helplessly.

"How big?" I inquired.

"A twenty-five pounder," he grimaced.

"Linda, we can't take the rice with us. Maybe we can buy some Uncle Ben's on the island. They sell it everywhere," I offered.

"Sam, you nuts?" She shook her head emphatically. "That premium Chinese rice. Ma no use process brand. Must take on plane."

"Hey, I didn't put twenty-five pounds of starch in *my* suitcase," I said with accusation. "Lorenzo, you have the honors."

Lorenzo was embarrassed at the thought of carrying the unsightly bag of rice onto the airplane. Linda came to his rescue and offered one of Samantha's baby blankets to wrap around it. I paid the $500 additional baggage charge then our group headed to security.

I had to laugh when Lorenzo gently laid the swaddled rice onto the conveyor as if it were a real baby. The second it passed through the machine, I saw an expression of bewilderment cross the TSA agent's face. He looked up at Lorenzo, who was now surrounded by four Chinese women all giving him instructions in Mandarin. The security officer's demeanor changed to a look of sympathy, and probably out of pity, Lorenzo was allowed to proceed without questioning. Fortunately, this was before 9/11 when security was way more lax.

We boarded the American Airlines Boeing 727-200; Linda and I found our seats, eight rows forward from the rest of the family in an exit row. Samantha rested comfortably between Ma and Big Sister.

Linda took the window as usual. Before taking my aisle seat, I looked back and saw Lorenzo struggling to hoist up the bundled rice and secure it in the overhead bin. I settled in and began working on excuses to clear our next hurtle, the Turks and Caicos Department of Agriculture.

Three and a half hours later we landed at Providenciales International Airport, and the passengers started filing out. Linda and I decided to wait for the family to catch up and go ahead of us. Lorenzo popped open the overhead compartment. He was having trouble pulling out the rice. It was a full flight and the bin was crammed with carry-ons.

Linda's sisters were all nauseous from the flight and anxious to get off the plane. Tina yelled at Lorenzo in Mandarin, "Kuai4 dian3, wo3 xiang3 tu4!" ("Hurry up, I think I'm going to hurl!") With the pressure from the agitated tribe of Chinese women and the blocked rear passengers, Lorenzo decided it was now or never. He grabbed the blanket and pulled. It did not budge, apparently caught on something.

An impatient passenger behind him yelled out, "Come on, buddy, move it, I ain't got all day."

In a slight panic, Lorenzo grabbed the end of the bag itself and gave a hard yank. It came halfway out, then tore open creating a Niagara Falls of rice, showering nearby passengers, spilling over the seats and piling up on the floor. "Holy shit!" he screamed, desperately trying to stop the flow by folding up the corners of the bag.

The girls had already hustled out the exit door, completely unaware of the problem precipitated by their relentless quest to save a buck.

Two stewardesses rushed over to assist but ended up just standing there with no clue how to deal with this bizarre incident. I'm sure there was nothing in the airline training manual to cover a rice avalanche. Half the passengers were still lined up behind Lorenzo, shaking their heads in astonishment, waiting for him to get a move on so they could deplane.

Lorenzo quickly gathered up the lightened load and hotfooted it from the plane like it was on fire, keeping his head down, not wanting to lock eyes with anyone, including me and Linda. As he sped by, I couldn't help myself and blurted out, "Welcome to the family."

Unbelievably we made it through customs without a hitch. Lucky for us there were no luggage scanners. The airline stewardesses also hadn't blown the whistle. They were probably too busy pulling KP duty in preparation for the next flight.

Immediately after checking into our luxurious four-bedroom suite, we zipped open the suitcases and unloaded the Asian food products into the refrigerator, freezer and pantry. There were boxes and bags of frozen meats and fish, parcels of dried Asian snacks, glass bottles full of spices, zha4 cai4—pickled mustard tuber, lu3 rou4 (pot stewed meat), cha2 ye4 dan4 (eggs stewed in tea), boxes of tofu and countless bags of green vegetables that can only be found at the Chinese markets in Flushing, Queens.

Lorenzo carried in what remained of the rice, substantially reduced to less than half. I saw the look of grave concern on Ma's face and tried to read her lips as she grumbled under her breath, “Ai1 ya1! Zen3 me5 zhe4 me5 bai2 chi1!” *Loosely* translated: *"Damn it all to hell! What a bonehead!*

The moment the food items were stored, the cooking began and didn’t let up until a few minutes before the taxi ferried us back to the airport. Breakfast, lunch and dinner were all prepared in the hotel suite. My in-laws were determined not to spend a penny, which meant no dinners at the beautiful ocean side restaurants, no relaxing lunches by the pool and no snacks in my private cabana on the beach.

By the third day, I yearned for some fine dining. Parallel 23, the hotel’s upscale restaurant, offered a thick juicy Porterhouse and a succulent Caribbean lobster.

I said to Sister Four, “You guys should take a break from eating in the room and have dinner at the hotel restaurant. There’s always a cool tropical breeze and a spectacular sunset.”

“Shi4 de5, Shan1 Mu3 Xian1 sheng5,” (“Yes, Mr. Sam,”) Sister Four nodded her head in agreement then darted into the kitchen; I assumed to alert the family of my great idea.

I knew this was going to be a very expensive meal, but I needed to satisfy my cravings, and it’d be impolite not to invite everyone. Besides, this was *my* vacation, not the time to stress over money. The entire trip was going on my credit card. I’d have thirty days to figure it out.

Around 5:30 PM, while sipping brews on the balcony of our suite, Lorenzo and I saw Sister Four walk onto the ocean side restaurant patio lugging two bulging plastic bags. She stopped at a large round table set for eight, opened the bags, and began removing an array of cooked Chinese dishes, which she placed in the center.

“What the hell is she doing?” I smacked my forehead.

“Looks like she’s setting up,” Lorenzo said in amazement.

"Linda!" I yelled. "I need you to come here right now!"

“Why you so grouchy?” she said casually, walking out onto the balcony with Ma and the girls.

“Look down there.” I jabbed an angry forefinger toward Four.

From our perch two floors above, we observed numerous hotel guests at the restaurant and around the pool turn their heads in Sister Four’s direction. Some were just curious, while those downwind were reacting to the strange smells.

There must’ve been a complaint because a staffer hurried over to investigate. The employee talked until he was blue in the face, trying to explain the rules and regulations of the hotel, but Sister Four could barely understand a word of English. He was getting nowhere, and marched away, throwing his hands up in frustration.

A minute later, the restaurant manager approached to take a crack at the uncooperative guest. When he too realized she didn’t speak his language, he gestured with his hands like a mime; apparently doing his impression of “This is not a picnic area.” Sister Four just sat there smiling unwittingly and rattling Mandarin at the agitated stranger. He too saw the futility of playing Charades with a China woman and stomped away annoyed.

With no one else showing up to toss her out, Sister Four turned and gave us the "Soup's on" sign, and the family went down to eat.

Lorenzo and I stayed cowering on the terrace waiting for the call from management, which never came. At least Sis Four didn't bring down the large container of the family's beloved fetid tofu sludge. A whiff of that would've gotten us thrown off the hotel property; or equally possible, given us the place to ourselves after all the staff and guests fled the island.

Two weeks after our return to New York, I received my American Express bill. I almost went ballistic when I saw the hotel had hit me with a $5,000+ drink charge. Linda had no idea where it came from until she spoke with Big Sister who said, and I quote: "What? Drinks no free? Ask sign name. No pay money."

I told Linda, "Please…the next time you think I need to bask in the sun, just book me a session at the tanning salon."

SECTION THREE-AND-A-HALF

Return to Asia

29. Lost in Translation

I’ve been married to the lovely Linda Liu for more than 30 years. The moment I knew I’d be spending the rest of my life with her, I decided it was important for me to learn her language. That decision was reinforced when I met her family. Other than being able to read some Hebrew, which was a necessity for my Bar Mitzvah, I'd never taken a language class. I went to a technical high school where the language requirement was auto shop lingo: “Dig the fab big block 426 Hemi with cylinder walls enlarged and crankshaft throw modified, lengthened channel rods, plus exhaust manifolds to reduce back pressure! Sweet ride, huh?”

From the moment my brother-in-law gave me that basic Chinese language book, I was hooked like a junkie. At first, Linda was very excited when I told her I wanted to learn Mandarin. However, I soon became a pest. When I’d constantly ask her what this or that word meant, she’d default reply, “Hao3 wu2 liao2” Translation: “Very boring.” And so, I studied on my own, trying to learn one of the most difficult and complex languages in the world.

Where's My Alphabet?

A snap lesson in Chinese: In Taiwan they speak Mandarin, which recently became the national language of Mainland China and Hong Kong. In English and almost every other language you have an alphabet, but in Chinese there is none. With English, once you master those 26 letters, you can create, sound out, and read and speak thousands of words.

In lieu of an alphabet, the Chinese use thousands of characters. Each character is essentially a word with its own meaning. Sometimes you need multiple characters to create a word. For example, "lei4 si3 le5". Translation: exhausted or literally "tired to death".

The question of how many characters there are is still the subject of debate. However, to achieve basic literacy in the language you need to be able to read approximately 4,000 characters. A high school graduate usually knows somewhere between 5,000 and 6,000 characters. An average Chinese dictionary will have anywhere from 10,000 to 20,000, and some academicians estimate that there are well over 100,000 characters in one form or another.

After almost three decades of struggling with the language, I know maybe 1,200 which puts me roughly in the second or third grade. Bummer! Now in my late 50s, I can barely remember where I put my car keys, what I had for lunch; and on some days, who's that person in the mirror? I often forget to turn off the lights when I leave my apartment, and rarely remember special events such as birthdays or anniversaries. Thank God for my smart phone which helps me out with many of these lapses. With home systems such as Crestron, Lutron or Control4, I can use my phone to turn things on and off through an app. That same device also holds all my contact numbers, calendar, photos, emails, texts and yes, I still use it to call people. However, most kids rarely use it as a telephone. They say that's "old school".

Technology has also helped me learn the language. The app called Pleco has made it possible for me to continue my uphill battle with Mandarin. With this amazing tool, and a lot of hard work, one day I hope to make it to the fourth grade. The Pleco software also uses the phone's camera to capture characters then translate them to English. Now I don't have to bother Linda with my boring pursuit of her difficult language...well, not as often.

Without an alphabet, there's only one way to learn Chinese. That method is called "memorization", and it gets more difficult the older you get. To complicate things, many of the characters look very similar. Each one is made up of small lines called strokes. For example, in English the letter F has three strokes, one vertical and two horizontals. Chinese characters can have an insane number of strokes. Their word for turtle, "gui1", has 16: 龜.

Writing the characters is so difficult that several years ago the government of Mainland China decided to simplify them to improve the country's literacy rate. Isn't that mindboggling? The people of China struggled so much with their own language, that even after using it for several thousand years, the masses still found it too difficult to learn!

Taiwan still uses the traditional, more complex characters. Since my wife and her family hail from there, I needed to learn the complicated version. For me, learning to speak the language was an extremely challenging endeavor, but still possible. Being able to read Chinese is a lifelong pursuit. On the plus side, all that memorization may help prevent Alzheimer's, which runs in my family. At my age, expecting to one day be capable of writing the intricate Chinese characters is pure folly. But as much as I feel sorry for myself, I feel even sorrier for Chinese kids. Unlike me, growing up they don't ever get to enjoy a bowl of alphabet soup.

From the beginning, I truly felt that being able to converse with my in-laws and my wife's Asian friends was important for the long-term health of our marriage. Having the ability to read Chinese at even a grade school level would also dramatically improve the Taipei experience. It's not much fun being a tourist in a town with so much to offer if you can't find your way around. All the shop signs in Taiwan are written in traditional Chinese characters. If Linda was preoccupied, and I went out alone for lunch, a hair wash, or just to find a café to sit down for a Bubble Tea, I'd need some basic reading skills. In addition, the menus at most of the restaurants were written only in Mandarin.

One day, during a brisk morning walk by myself, I decided to grab a bite at a neighborhood eatery. I'd been there once before with Linda who'd ordered for me. Their specialty was roast pork. The waiter provided a typical menu—no English. I knew what the character for pig looked like and was confident I could locate the dish. I scrolled down and *Bingo!* an entire section that began with "pig". However, I was lost as to the characters that followed. But assuming they all had the delicious roasted pork in the mix, I selected the top one.

Five minutes later, he returned with a bowl containing gelatinous reddish-brown rectangles floating in what looked like a base of gruel. The pale colored mystery blocks reminded me somewhat of week-old chocolate pudding.

I asked the waiter, “What is this?”

He replied, “Solly, no Yinglis.”

I stabbed an alien cube with my chopstick; took my first and last bite. It had a rubbery texture with a nasty metallic aftertaste. I took a picture with my phone, pushed the bowl aside, paid the tab, and left hungry and disappointed; my first unescorted dining endeavor a flop.

When I met up with Linda at Sister Four’s apartment, I showed her the photo. “What the heck did I order?”

“Wow, Sam! Not know so adventurous," she marveled. "You eat Pig Blood Curd.”

"Please tell me you're joking," I winced.

"No, love it!" Linda enthused. "Also, like duck, chicken, cow, sheep and yak blood curd. All delish! You should try!"

"Yeah, right," I recoiled, "maybe in another life...if someday I become a vampire."

Ding-Dong … The Five Tones

To speak Mandarin there are several layers of difficulty to overcome. Each character has its own *tone,* which also must be memorized. There are five possible tones, or intonations. The first tone is high and level; the second is rising; the third is falling then rising; the fourth is falling, and the fifth tone is neutral and soft. Are you confused? Don't feel bad, after 30 years I still regularly mess up.

The tones are very subtle and often impossible to differentiate by the language challenged ear. When I first started learning, Linda often corrected me by first pronouncing the word then telling me I was using the wrong intonation. I'd ask her, "Why are you correcting me? That's exactly what I said!" It took me quite some time to develop the ability to hear the difference between the tones. The only way to really get a handle on them is to listen as much as you can to native speakers. There's no substitute for actually hearing the tones.

I kept asking Linda to speak to me at home in Mandarin. She'd agree to do so, but as soon as I said, "I don't understand," the switch in her brain clicked back to English and that was the end of that. She'd say, "Tai4 ma2 fan5" meaning "Too much trouble." That I understood. This went back and forth until eventually I just gave up and spoke to her in English.

Sometimes, when we were out somewhere surrounded by the non-Asian public, like on a subway train or in a restaurant, and she wanted to say something private, she'd switch to

Mandarin. If I understood I'd respond in kind. If I didn't, I'd just nod my head up and down like a ninny.

Several years later, on a return trip to Taipei we were invited out to dinner with some of my wife's college friends. There were four couples, all of whom were extremely accomplished and affluent. We met at a fancy restaurant famous for its Kobe beef, and all sat together at a large round table. My Mandarin was slowly improving. At the time I knew close to 1,000 words and my confidence level was rising.

As I'd soon learn (the hard way); due to air pollution in Taipei many citizens wear masks to filter out contaminants. A breathing or surgical mask is pronounced "kou3 zhao4" with the numbers after the letters giving you the intonation. To show off my language skills, I asked the group, in Mandarin, why so many people in Taipei wear the masks. Right after the words escaped my lips, Linda cringed while the whole table erupted in laughter.

My wife shook her head and informed me, "Last word wrong. Not say kou3 zhao4. You say kou3 jiao1."

If you do not speak Mandarin, and I said the two words back to back, I'd bet you wouldn't hear the difference—but believe me there's a big difference. The first word "kou3" means "mouth" and second word "jiao1" means "to pay money". I'd just asked some of the most powerful people in Taipei, "Why do so many of your fellow citizens get blow jobs?"

The Idiom versus the Idiot

The final layer of complexity is the Chinese Idiom (cheng2 yu3). Linda graduated from both the top high school and college in Taiwan, and most of her friends were well educated. Therefore, their vocabulary was by far larger than the average person. In addition, they often used idioms to express themselves. In Chinese, an idiom is a phrase made up of four or more characters. Most were derived from stories in ancient literature. Often the characters reflect the moral behind the story rather than the story itself. Similar to idioms are proverbs which have a connotation that's greater than the meaning of the individual words when put together. However, the literal meaning of an idiom usually doesn't make sense, and they are almost impossible to understand unless you know the derivation.

For example, a Chinese idiom for clumsy, "ben4 shou3 ben4 jiao3," literally translates to "stupid hands, stupid feet." An example of an idiom in the English language would be: "The cat's out of the bag" which of course means "The secret was given away." A famous English proverb is: "An apple a day keeps the doctor away." In this case the phrase gives you a good idea of the meaning.

Even after my many years of studying the language, I still felt like a moron when we were out with her college friends in Taipei. With so many complex words mixed with multiple idioms, I wondered how the hell they were all able to understand each other. Would you understand what the speaker was talking about if he said in English, "The army marched forward to attack—followed by the idiom: *guard a tree-stump, wait for a rabbit, and climb a tree to catch a fish.*" This idiom: "shou3 zhu1 dai4 tu4, yuan2 mu4 qiu2 yu2," translates to: "without any practical course of action."

Often, I'd be able to pick up on what they were discussing and then four or five words would flow into the conversation that made no sense to me. You guessed it, some obscure idiom had been thrown into the mix. By the time I'd figured it out, or didn't, they were already on to a new topic. I just sat there hopelessly lost. However, I never gave up, constantly using my Pleco phone app, asking questions and writing down the meaning of new words which I reviewed every night before bed.

I focused so hard on my language studies, my brain often protested with nasty headaches. There is of course a Chinese idiom that could be used to describe my persistence at learning the language. It loosely translates to: "If you dedicate yourself to the job at hand, success will not be far away." Another way of saying it is: "Hard work pays off." That idiom: "xuan2 liang2 ci4 gu3" literally means xuan2—*to hang or suspend*, liang2—*beam of a roof*, ci4—*to prick, pierce or stab*, gu3—*the thigh.* The literal meaning is impossible to understand. However, you can comprehend how it was derived in the following ancient stories:

During the Warring States Period of Chinese history (380-284 B.C.), there was a political strategist named Su Qin. Although his family was very poor, he dreamt of being successful, even at a very young age. He studied from dawn to dark and would become very tired after such long hours. He discovered he could keep himself awake by stabbing his thigh with an awl. The sharp pain kept him up, so he could continue studying on into the night. At long last, Su Qin became highly respected because of his knowledge. He eventually was elevated to the position of ruler of the six kingdoms of ancient China: Qi (齊), Chu (楚), Yan (燕), Han (韓), Zhao (趙) and Wei (魏) as well as his own country, the State of Qin.

Another inspiring story, related to the same idiom, takes place during the Han Dynasty. A young man, Sun Jing, was also very hardworking. He rarely left his house, preferring instead to stay home and read. On the few occasions he did leave to buy food at the market, people called him, "Mr. Door Shut" behind his back. Unwaveringly, Sun Jing studied late into the night. He too was always worried about dozing off. To stay awake, he tied one end of a rope to his hair and the other end to the beam of the roof. When he started to fall asleep at his desk, his head drooped downwards, and the rope tugged at his hair. The pain served to wake him up so that he could continue studying. After years of continuous hard work, he eventually became a highly revered scholar—albeit a bald one.

Grammar...Schmammar

English can be one of the hardest languages in the world to master. Why? Because its rules of grammar are numerous, confusing and sometimes contradictory. We Americans spend untold hours in the classroom learning to navigate through this difficult structure. Chinese grammar is really an oxymoron. It's almost nonexistent. You may think an absence of grammar would make it easier for an English-speaking person to learn Chinese, but quite the opposite. When you try to form a sentence in Chinese using your own language's grammar structure it makes you sound mentally challenged. Whenever we met up with the elite group from the illustrious Taiwan University, I half expected Linda to gesture at me and say, "Please excuse husband, the retarded egg."

Even though I loved Taipei, I often found myself in situations where I felt left out, unable to follow the ongoing complex and probably interesting discussions that my wife had with her friends from college. Sometimes, completely lost and abandoned, I just sat there like a moron with a goofy smile on my face. Thank God for Taiwan beer!

But I'll never give up. All the embarrassing moments where the stupid egg shows up, and all the times I'm lost in translation only drive me to work harder to gain fluency. Sometimes you need to strive for the unreachable goal to make it to the next level. A person never really knows what they can accomplish until they commit themselves to obtaining it. Remember the moral of the stories: Whether you hang by your hair from a roof beam, or jab yourself in the thigh—"Hard work always pays off."

The exception to this rule is if you stand to inherit great wealth, and your toughest decision is, *Do I buy the classy Rolls, or the sporty Lamborghini?*

30. The Invisible Man

I was becoming more comfortable hanging out with Chinese people. I'm not talking about ABCs (American Born Chinese) but the real McCoys, natives of Taiwan, Hong Kong or Mainland China including Asian transplants to the U.S. To modify a previous quote, "When a man marries a woman, he also marries her family—AND all her close friends." Except for a few Caucasian coworkers, who she met during her career at the bank, Linda's clique was almost 100% Chinese-Chinese. Most ABCs look like the real deal on the surface. However, if you could zip open the outer layer of skin, you'd find a typical Caucasian lurking inside.

Immediately after we were married, I moved to New York not knowing a soul. Linda's Asian friends, who were for the most part all girls, became my friends, which had both advantages and disadvantages. Linda only spoke to me in English because she had no patience for my butchery of her mother tongue. However, when we hung out with her family or friends, Mandarin was predominant.

ADVANTAGE: Without hearing spoken Chinese, you can study all you want, but you'll never master the sounds of the characters along with their corresponding intonations. This was my main method of practice, albeit a slow and inefficient process when compared to working with a professional language tutor.

DISADVANTAGE: Most of the time I didn't know what the hell the clique was talking about. They all spoke way too fast. To my ear the sounds of the characters melded together into a continuous hum of highs and lows. I was only able to pick out a few of the more familiar words including: ben4 dan4—stupid egg; da4 bi2 zi1—big nose (yes, I was the Jewish stereotype—then again, compared to most Asians, everyone has a big nose. Maybe this was slang for Caucasian?); and tu1 tou2—bald head (unfortunately, the men on both my mother's and father's side were all bald and it looked like I'd soon follow suit). Chinese women can be very blunt.

A week after we arrived in Taipei, (my third trip), Linda's friend Lulu and her husband invited us to their apartment for dinner. It was on the top floor of a new hi-rise condominium. From our experience, we'd found that most buildings in Taipei were far inferior in terms of luxury, service and finish to their NYC counterparts. We arrived by taxi and were pleasantly surprised. This truly was a full-service white glove address. There was a parking valet waiting in the driveway that ran from the street to the building's regal main entry. The staff also included both a doorman and separate concierge.

We stepped through a huge 10' tall wood and bronze door into the lobby where we were greeted by the cool refreshing air provided by a state-of-the-art HVAC system. The attendants appeared to be well trained. They were dressed in new, matching, crisply pressed uniforms, all extremely polite and professional.

The building had a spectacular marble and glass lobby with an interior waterfall feature that cascaded down from an opening in the ceiling into a stone and metal channel running the length of the building to an outside rear courtyard. For Chinese people, running water is a positive Feng Shui feature. In this case it created a calm and relaxing atmosphere for arriving residents and guests. It also signified wealth going out and flowing back in. I looked into the trough and noticed the crystal-clear water was full of goldfish.

"Clean water mean fresh opportunity," Linda explained. "Goldfish increase prosperity. Mean big money."

At the rear was a well-designed waiting area backed by a floor to ceiling glass wall that framed a private stone patio with outside seating; all surrounded by a landscaped garden with mature palm trees and multiple flower beds.

Her friend Lulu, who I'd met twice before, was also a graduate of Taiwan University. She was a sweet, and elegant lady. Like most of my wife's college friends, she had long silky jet-black hair, usually tied up in a ponytail, dark brown eyes, white smooth skin, a thin body—and always dressed in whatever was the current *Vogue* style. Also, just like Linda, she looked years younger than her actual age.

I assumed Lulu led a charmed life. She had her own private car and driver to ferry her around the city, and she always seemed to be in a good mood.

Linda once said, "Lulu most happy, positive person."

This would be my first time seeing her apartment and meeting Friederich, her husband, who'd also attended the renowned Taiwan University.

Friederich was only two years his wife's senior. However, he appeared much older than her. He was casually dressed in loose white linen slacks and a black short sleeve polo knit shirt with a red stripe in the collar; but the rest of him screamed ultra-conservative and deeply serious. He was extremely thin, which initially gave me the impression that he might be suffering from an illness. His hairline had already started to recede, and through the superior vantage point provided by my above average height, I had a clear view of his balding crown. To my eye, this was a person with a lot on his plate. He was quiet with a solemn, slightly troubled look on his face. Throughout the entire evening I rarely heard him laugh or saw him smile. However, he was considerate and socially savvy, constantly making an effort to keep me engaged.

I later learned from Linda that Friederich's father had made a fortune in residential construction, which now included numerous large-scale projects in Mainland China. He was the oldest of three siblings and was in charge of the family business which employed over 10,000 people. In addition to Friederich's wealth, Lulu's mom and dad had also made a fortune manufacturing clothing for several large retailers including the Gap, Banana Republic, Adidas and Kmart.

Linda had informed me in the elevator, "I hear family sell business. Price $550 million. Buyer most biggest clothing maker, MAS Holdings."

But you'd never know that either were born with a sliver spoon in their mouth. Both were gracious down-to-earth people.

The couple times I'd gotten together over lunch with Lulu and Linda, the conversation was always in Chinese. Lulu knew I was still struggling with my Mandarin and would periodically reestablish eye contact with me, switching back to English to make sure I wasn't left out. She'd obviously briefed Friederich on my limited language skills. During the early part of the evening he made a concerted effort to keep the conversation running in English. However, things would change soon after the other unexpected guests arrived.

Lulu and Friederich's apartment was huge, slightly over 117 ping (approximately 4,100 square feet), and stunning. It was one of three penthouse units. At 39 stories, or 420 feet above the ground, it offered spectacular vista views of Taipei and the surrounding mountains. The interior finishes were exquisite, combining exotic woods and local Dragon Bone stone to create a Zen-like atmosphere. I noticed that the apartment had absolutely no base or crown moldings and no door casings. In fact, there was no trim of any kind. The ceiling height throughout the space was 12 feet and the walls appeared to be floating with one-inch reveals at the top and bottom. The door frames disappeared into the walls with no sign of connection. Hinges were recessed, and all hardware was slight, clean and functional. A finely applied low luster Venetian finish, with virtually no movement, covered most of the interior walls.

The furniture was eclectic with many pieces appearing to be custom made to fit the various nuances of the space. Everything blended together creating a masterpiece of form, function and design accented by the perfect color palette.

Upon Linda's request, our friends gave us the complete tour. Without having even one materialistic bone in my body, it was hard not to be impressed. Their apartment blew ours away. They could have used both flats to film a new reality show entitled "Rags vs. Riches". I was personally not an object-oriented person and therefore, not the least bit envious. However, under the proper scientific lighting, assuming it did exist, Linda would probably have shown up in a dark green hue.

When it came down to the clique from Taiwan University, she was extremely competitive. After seeing this space, and a few of her other friends' high-end luxury apartments, I knew for sure, immediately upon my return to New York, I'd be spending a lot more time at my job to provide the means by which my sweet, beautiful, sometimes tender, usually aggressive and always competitive Taiwan University graduate, could rise up to the level that was the crème de la crème of Taipei's social elite.

While walking through the space, I was constantly filing away the details into my memory for future projects of my own. I took numerous pictures. But not wanting to be blatantly open about it, revealing my sole purpose to capture images of their interior, I asked Linda and her friends to pose in key areas of the space. Unfortunately, photography is not a strong suit; most of my pictures missed the target, just showing people at odd angles with partially cutoff faces or limbs.

At the end of our tour Linda openly discussed all the details of the construction with Lulu, and even asked how much each element cost. While some Americans would be offended by this type of behavior, in Chinese society it's fairly standard. Linda also asked Friederich how much they paid for the apartment ($9,989,000… yikes!). I was waiting to see if she'd next pry into his personal finances, quizzing him on how much money he made that year and their family's total net worth.

The apartment had a fabulous terrace that faced east toward the Four Beasts Mountains, which included Elephant, Tiger, Lion and Leopard. With the intense heat beating down on the building, our viewing lasted only about 10 seconds before we all fled back into the centrally air-conditioned interior.

Lulu then announced, "Appetizer ready. All please come."

This was not the norm in Taiwan, but our hosts were both well-traveled and liked the leisure aspects of this type of Western style entertaining. Lulu set things up in the living room, which still offered spectacular views through a set of floor-to-ceiling windows. While our hosts could clearly afford to keep a full-time staff, for this evening, they were doing things in a more casual and domesticated manner. I was not sure if this was how they normally lived, or if they nixed the help to avoid the perception that they were dangling their incredible wealth in front of clearly less affluent guests. If that were indeed the case, then their entire attempt at camouflage was negated by the $1 million Harry Winston watch that Lulu was wearing. How do I know how much it cost? Linda asked, of course.

Tonight, the setting was an informal one, much more comfortable and relaxing with all of us working together to prepare and consume a simple home cooked meal. There's a special bonding that goes on when friends cook together that I always find makes the evening more memorable. When Linda and I entered the kitchen, we saw several trays of food lined up on the counter. One had a small bowl of black caviar with an accompaniment of chopped egg whites, yolks, red onion, crème fraiche and toast points. Another tray had scallops wrapped in bacon, and a third had deviled eggs, each topped with a dollop of crème fraiche and a neon orange salmon roe.

When I first met Linda, the thought of eating fish grossed me out—and the only way you could get me to eat fish EGGS was at gunpoint. However, once I tasted the delicious pop of those salty bits of delight, I became a BIG FAN, always on the edge of my seat, excited with the thought of once again savoring that rare and luxurious decadent black roe. The only thing missing was the face paint and a Styrofoam finger emblazoned with "#1".

Tonight, the experience would take me to a higher level. We were eating one of the world's most premium caviars, Caspian Osetra. It was paired with a primo bottle of 1982 Cristal Brut. Back in New York, if we invited friends over for caviar and champagne it was usually paddlefish or American hackleback washed down with a domestic sparkling wine. From our experience that evening, I can tell you to beware: Once you've tasted the really good stuff you're ruined for life.

Soon after we placed our trays on the table, the apartment's intercom rang. Lulu said, "Other guests here. They join us, eat dinner."

Linda of course knew about the other couple but never said a word to me (Once again I was excluded from the need-to-know list). With my growing but still limited vocabulary, I was always a bit nervous when meeting new people in Taipei. Slightly uncomfortable, yes, but still willing to be a participant in Linda's always busy social calendar. Meeting with people who only spoke Mandarin forced me to practice. Each time I met with a new group of Linda's friends, it was like starting a new chapter in a Chinese textbook. If I was having difficulty understanding the conversation, most of her college friends spoke enough English to make things work. Therefore, based on my previous experiences, I really had no reason to be concerned about tonight's festivities—or did I?

The new additions to our little soiree were Hwai-Min and Chun Hua Chen. A husband and wife team, Chun Hua was the interior designer and Hwai-Min was the architect who assisted Lulu and Friederich with the build-out of their amazing apartment.

When the doorbell chimed, Lulu went to the front door, led the couple to the living room, and made the introductions.

Hwai-Min and Chun Hua were both tall, thin and attractive. Hwai-Min looked much older than his wife. His advanced age was betrayed by the wrinkles in his neck and hands. I surmised that he was in his mid to late 60s. I consistently found it difficult guessing the age of an Asian person. They always ended up being much older than I expected.

Hwai-Min still had a full head of black hair, though it was lightly streaked with grey and white. His body looked lean and strong which, in my mind, was the sign of an older person who was still motivated enough to include regular exercise as part of his daily regimen. With a much younger wife it might also have been a necessity to avoid a stroke.

Hwai-Min wore stylish rimless eyeglasses with dense lenses, another possible sign of his dotage. He had on a pair of designer dark grey pants that were cut way too short exposing the top of his dress socks and upper ankle. On the other end, they currently rode up almost to where his belly button would be located. He modeled a very chic white linen shirt, which Linda later told me was made by TSE, a designer clothing company. The final accoutrement was a pair of turquoise Ferragamo loafers, which were now in a closet by the front door replaced by white slippers provided by our gracious hosts. Hard and fast rule in Asia: "Always remove your shoes before entering someone's home."

Chun Hua looked closer to mid-30s in a red sleeveless dress that accented her slender figure. I could tell from her watch and jewelry that they were well-to-do, but not in the same league as our hosts. Her face had a delicate appearance with a perfectly shaped nose, dark brown eyes, and not a wrinkle in sight. Her skin tone was close to that of a porcelain doll, flawless and lily white. She wore her hair up in a partial bun with medium length bangs that blanketed her forehead. While I still got weak in the knees from staring at my own version of Aphrodite, Ms. Linda Liu, there was no doubt that Chun Hua was a stunning woman. Her much older husband would need to keep a watchful eye on her.

Even though the conversation started out in English, with Hwai-Min doing quite a bit of the talking, it was not easy for me to understand his words. His English-speaking skills were probably just a tad better than my Mandarin. I was able to follow along since the other participants' English were all far superior, with the exception of Chun Hua, who hardly spoke a word and was clearly lost. She constantly tried to switch the conversation back to Chinese.

Hwai-Min appeared to be quite the chatter box. He loved to grandstand, blurting out his affiliation with some of the wealthiest and influential people in Taiwan, who all just happened to be close friends, travel companions, clients, etc. He told story after story of how he wined and dined with this person who was the Chairman of the Board at some global behemoth and was related to that person who'd just brought his company public making millions on the transaction. He made sure to inform us that his driver was waiting outside in a brand-new black stretch Mercedes sedan he'd just bought. Hwai-min was the personification of Foghorn Leghorn as he roostered on and on about how fast his business was growing, and that he was contemplating expanding internationally, with plans to open an office in the States.

This went on for quite some time. After his seventh or eighth name drop, I tuned him out. I can't stand pretentious people. It usually stems from a lack of confidence which I believe Sigmund Freud or Howard Stern said was compensation for having a small penis. By the way, after eight years of marriage, they didn't have any children. Coincidence?

Most of the super-rich in Taiwan had graduated from Taipei University, so Linda, in one way or another, knew them all. Later that evening, when we were in a taxi heading back to our modest apartment, Linda said under her breath, "Hwai-Min full of shit."

"Even with my limited understanding of the general conversation tonight," I chuckled, "I'd already arrived at that conclusion."

We finished our appetizers and champagne, then Friederich said, "All please come dining room. Dinner soon served."

I instinctively picked up my plate and Linda's and carried them both back to the kitchen. No one followed suit. I went back a second and third time to pile up and remove all the remaining dishes, utensils and glasses, carefully transporting them to the kitchen and depositing them in the oversized double sink.

Lulu returned to the living room to find out what had happened to me. She really didn't know what to say about my efforts to clean up the leftover mess; appearing somewhat flabbergasted that a guest would ever pick up after themselves, let alone others.

Maybe, I wondered, *in her charmed life, she never saw anyone, other than a staff person, clean.* She must have said "thank you" at least four times.

Linda also returned to see where I'd disappeared to, and finally Friederich showed up at the kitchen to investigate why there was a decreasing number of people at the dining table.

I told them, "This is how my parents raised me—which was further reinforced by my new master—Wonder Woman." They didn't get the last part, so I asked Linda to translate. Everyone erupted in laughter. Even Friederich got a kick out of it and used up his once-a-week smile quota.

While it was apparent that Lulu and Friederich had never cleaned anything in their lives, it was obvious they both enjoyed cooking and knew their way around the kitchen. For the next thirty minutes we all worked together to prepare dinner which included: a roasted rack of lamb, Chinese broccoli woked in oil and garlic and steamed white rice mixed with bok choy then packed into a tiny round bowl. The bowl was then turned over and removed with the outcome being a rice/vegetable mixture formed into a perfect circle. You learn something new every day. This dish was added to my ever-growing list of recipes—delicious, easy and elegant.

Working together, the three items were all quickly plated, then carried out to the dining room. When we arrived, the other couple was still sitting at the table sipping champagne. The full magnum that Lulu had earlier placed there was now half empty. When I looked over at Linda, I knew exactly what she was thinking: These two social climbers, with their private car and driver, both felt they were too rich and too special to get their hands dirty. During the rest of the evening they never rose from their chairs. They were invited as guests and expected to be waited on hand and foot.

After all the plates were served, I went back to the kitchen to fetch two bottles of wine, returned to the dining room, and circled the table, filling everyone's glass before sitting down to enjoy the bounty of our labor. Hwai-Min's skinny ass remained glued to his seat, and he also enjoyed the bounty of our labor, the pretentious prick!

As the night wore on, the conversation about-faced from English to Chinese. Friederich was very interested in Ancient

Calligraphy. He'd taken several classes and spent numerous hours each week practicing to improve his skill. Hwai-Min was also interested in the same topic which, over the course of the evening, flowed into Asian art, culture, politics, business and other complicated subject matter. With Hwai-Min not comfortable speaking English and his wife only knowing a few words, once the switch flipped to Mandarin, it never flicked back.

With the wine flowing and our hosts both locked into what looked to be an in-depth intellectual discussion, everyone forgot about the sole American simpleton who had no idea what the hell anyone was saying. I decided to stop drinking wine to avoid dulling my senses. I was going to need every available brain cell working at its full potential tonight. I tried to listen as intently as possible, but I still couldn't make heads nor tails of anything. I couldn't even follow what Linda was saying. In addition to speaking at a speed that made everything sound like gibberish, I assumed they were using high level vocabulary mixed with those abstruse Chinese idioms, making any chance I had to understand anything nil. Occasionally I caught a word that I knew. But understanding one word in a sentence of 7 to 10 means you don't have the foggiest notion of what's being said. They could've been talking about me behind my back directly in front of me and I wouldn't have known it.

When we were out with Linda's Asian friends, she normally kept close tabs on me. Tonight, I was sitting right across from her, but she was so engrossed in a chat with Lulu that she seemed to forget I was there. Chun Hua, who sat next to her, was constantly interrupting. Even without being able to follow the conversation it was apparent that she was in competition with Linda for the hostess's attention.

I tried several times to interject some English into the conversation. This was difficult to do without being rude since I had no idea when to jump in. Finally, I decided it'd be best to wait until there was a lag. So, I waited and waited and waited, but it was as if it was one interminable sentence without a period. Everyone was so engaged with their neighbor that no one seemed to notice or acknowledge my presence. Even with no breaks in the conversation, somehow the participants at the table found a way to eat their meal and drink their wine.

I was always a very fast eater in contrast to Linda. Normally by the time I started on dessert, she was just finishing up her appetizer. But tonight would be different. I'd take my time and ever so slowly savor each bite. To the others at the table, I hoped it'd look as if I was too busy eating my dinner to engage in discussion. That was if they even realized I still existed.

I cut off a small piece of lamb and popped it into my mouth. It was pink, juicy, perfectly cooked and seasoned with just the right amount of salt, pepper, rosemary and crushed garlic. It occurred to me that the lamb would be far better if paired with the excellent bottle of 1961 Chateau Figeac that was sitting on the table right in front of me.

To hell with it! I thought and poured myself a glass. *Maybe the wine will relax me, and the Chinese words will start making some sense.* Who was I kidding? The more I drank the less information my already overtaxed brain cells could process. Between sips of wine and nibbles of the various items on my plate, I'd somehow stretched the meal to over two hours. During that time, I spoke to no one and no one spoke to me. That evening I became the invisible man.

So, what's the big deal? I rationalized. *I went to someone's house and methodically enjoyed, by myself, a great meal and a legendary wine?* Well, that would've been okay by me if immediately after I finished, we stood up, thanked our hosts, said our goodbyes and headed home for the evening. That would've been a reasonable ending to a mediocre evening, but it was a far cry from what transpired. The exclusionary conversations continued for three more hours. During the first two of those hours, I remained sitting at the dining room table. Most everyone had long past forgotten that they had the ability to speak English. I wondered if Linda even remembered that she brought me.

With the chatter not abating, no more food on my plate and the two bottles of wine now empty, I needed something to keep me busy. Lucky for me, I'd brought my cell phone. Unlucky for me, this was back before the advent of the iPhone or android software when "smart phones" were more accurately called “simpleton phones”. For tonight my hi-tech distraction was limited to a boring game of Tetris. Within a fairly short time, I realized there was not much battery power left on my phone. At best I had 20 minutes of game time remaining. The power indicator was a series of bars in a tiny box at the right-hand corner of the display screen. As I played the game the power bars slowly faded away one at a time. I watched in distress as the last one disappeared, and my screen faded to black. Having nothing else to eat or play with I could only sit there like Rodin’s *Thinker*.

I noted the conversation between Friederick and Hwai-Min had slowed with the latter hitting the alcohol more frequently. I waited until the next time he took a pull, then jumped in and asked Friederick a question in English. But Hwai-Min immediately interrupted to ask his own question in Mandarin, diverting the attention back to him. The s.o.b. did this three times before I gave up.

At long last, everyone was standing up, bowing and saying a beloved word I did recognize: "zai4 jian4"..."Goodbye." Then we four guests donned our street shoes and exited in single file. Linda went out the door first and was in the hallway. I hesitated at the threshold when Hwai-Min addressed me (of course, he took the lead, making his wife follow behind him).

"Excuse me?" I said, looking over my shoulder.

Hwai-Min had the audacity to ask, "Enjoy evening, Sam Lowe?"

"My American mouth doesn't always get the Chinese intonations right," I replied, "so let me put it this way..." and I squeezed off a rip-roaring fart.

Not wishing to be crude, or draw unwanted attention, I'd been holding it in for the past half hour. But what better way to have the last word than the universal ass-blast that speaks volumes in any language?

31. The Agony of De-Feet

During my second trip to Taiwan, Linda took me to a spa to indulge in a full body massage. She accompanied me into the treatment room to circumvent the “happy ending”. I’d heard about this erotic bonus from one of Linda’s male college friends at a party. He was discreet, making sure he wasn’t in earshot of any women before giving me the scoop. Probably the reason I hadn’t heard about it before: Linda and her group of female Taiwan University graduates seemed to control everything around them, including their male counterparts. I wondered if one day Taiwan would evolve into some type of matriarchal society similar to the Amazons. I guess I could adapt to being dominated by a Chinese Amazonian. Come to think of it, I already was.

On my third trip to Taipei, my bro-in-law, "Stevie Nicks-Wonder" became my Taiwanese buddy. As pretty as Linda was, that's how handsome was Stevie. Though small in size, he lifted weights regularly resulting in quite the Adonis physique. In America he'd be Arnold Schwarzenegger's Mini-Me.

Stevie was a happy-go-lucky guy with a perennial cheerful disposition and a heart almost bigger than him. Whenever he smiled or laughed, his eyes turned into two tiny slits that made me wonder how he could possibly see. Just to be on the safe side, I made a point never to crack a joke while he was driving.

Stevie always had spending money but worked only sporadically during the day. Doing what was never clear. When asked, his and everyone else's response was "Zi4 you2 ye4" ("This and that.") Wild guesses: male model, movie star stand-in, or gigolo? Random nights he worked security at a trendy club that Linda never suggested we visit—which made me wonder what really went on in there. So, you can imagine my trepidation the day Stevie invited me to join him for a massage at *his* favorite spa. But I'm getting ahead of myself...

When I was in Taiwan, Stevie always took time off from—whatever—to be my personal tour guide. My pretty little social butterfly was frequently out and about. I was dead weight for her. If I tagged along, Linda always had to stop and explain to me what was said. Thus, she and her gal pals couldn't engage in their usual 100 mph chick-chat.

Close family that they were, Stevie always knew Linda's schedule and would show up at my door offering to take me to one of Taipei's renowned tourist spots. At first, I thought my wife had bribed him to alleviate her guilt for leaving me alone. I later realized two things:

(1) My wife never felt guilty about anything, and

(2) Stevie actually enjoyed my company.

On this particular day, Linda was running late for lunch with friends at a restaurant called Xiu Lan, and hurriedly informed me, "Make very special dish—shi1 zi5 tou2."

"English please."

"Lion head," she said and shot out the door.

Did I hear her correctly? I wondered. I'd heard about Chinese people eating monkey brains, but seriously…is boiled, baked or barbecued *lion* even legal?

Not two minutes after Linda had departed, Stevie was knocking on the door. When I told him what she'd said, he burst out laughing. I wasn't sure if my reaction amused him or I'd said something offensive again in Chinese.

"Shan Mu," (Shan1 mu3 da4 shu1: "Uncle Sam,") his new pet name for me, "they no eat real lion head."

"Then what is it?"

"Big-good pork meatballs."

"Meatballs?" I echoed. "So why do they call it lion's head?"

"Meatballs on shredded cabbage," he explained. "Meatball like head. Cabbage like mane."

A week later I tried that very dish. Now, if someone asks me if I ever ate monkey brains, I'll have a killer comeback.

Chinese often name dishes according to their appearance. Some of the names are not too appetizing. Another one you may see on a menu: "ma3 yi3 shang4 shu4", translates to "ants climbing a tree". The name of this Sichuanese recipe describes the way the ground pork clings to the strands of glass noodles. I can immediately think of one courageous American who'd read this on the menu, take it literally, then eagerly order it: Celebrity Chef Andrew Zimmerman, star of the Travel Channel's *Bizarre Foods*.

Here's when Stevie dropped the bomb. “You lucky day, Shan Mu. I take you special Chinese Massagy.” He presented me with two eye slits and an ear-to-ear grin.

“Did you tell Linda about this?” I asked, hoping he’d kept quiet. If Linda found out where I went, the constant digging for details would last till my dying day.

The first week of this trip she'd already treated me to a couple’s massage at the famous Takinoyu Spa at the Beitou Hot Springs. Linda made sure our treatments took place in the same room, so she could keep her eye on the gorgeous Asian girl who was doing me—er, massaging me.

“You crazy? No tell female man’s business,” he said with a wink.

“Are we going to Takinoyu?”

"No, this better. You see. Chop-chop," and he bounded out the door.

At least I think that’s what he said. His English was awful, and I struggled with his Mandarin. When he did speak it, his accent was so heavy I often found it easier to understand the Chinese. For a sense of what I had to deal with, imagine someone is talking to you over a cell phone with a bad connection and every other word is dropped. To factor in his regional accent, there’s also annoying static on the line. Good luck trying to follow along.

With Linda out and about doing her gal-pal thing, I was looking forward to some male bonding with my Asian bud. But, at the same time, I had mixed feelings. What if the place offered the bawdy bonus package? While that possibility added some excitement, it also opened the door to serious repercussions, including the possibility of divorce, should Linda ever catch wind of any sexual exploits. We hopped into a taxi and five minutes later arrived at the spa.

"Shan Mu, today you get treat," he gushed with delight.

There's that 'treat' word again, and my uneasiness ratcheted up another notch.

I reflected on the last Asian spa experience I'd had with Linda. The interior was soothing and Zen-like; the air scented with the light sweet fragrance of flowers; and the restful background music put you in a tranquil, almost meditative state. All the female masseuses were attractive, petite, young and soft spoken. The treatment was performed with firm pressure, but I still found it to be quite relaxing. I even fell asleep during the process. Afterwards we were both gently woken, bathed and given a few quiet minutes to put on our robes before being served a wonderful flavored tea.

Today I looked forward to the same level of pampering, but I was nervous about the distinct possibility of a happy ending. *When the time comes, if I decline, will that be the ultimate insult to the massage girl? I could try and preempt the dirty deed, but at what point in the process do I inform her I don't want it? What if I send the wrong signal and give her the impression I'm up for full-on intercourse?*

Stevie flung open the front door and ushered me in. I looked left and right for the young, nubile receptionist waiting to greet us in a beautiful entry hall with silk curtains and lotus flowers. Instead, this place was one big open room with no privacy, zero atmosphere, and the smell of a men's locker room. Twenty or so massage tables were stationed on the open floor, each one just a few feet from the other. No flower aroma, just the odor of body sweat and Taiwan's version of Ben Gay called Tiger Balm. No enchanting Asian women dressed in colorful silk robes—instead, slightly plump middle-aged masseurs and masseuses clothed in drab t-shirts and sweat pants. All of them looked like they'd lived a long hard life. No soothing background music. All I heard was a cacophony of grunts issuing from the all-male clientele, who appeared to be in some distress as they got worked over.

My first thought: *Stevie has made a serious mistake!* Second thought: *This austere hospital therapy center is a front. At the rear is a hidden door to a den of iniquity!*

But almost every attendant in the room started waving and greeting him. I couldn't understand what they were saying, but it was apparent he was a regular and they were expecting us. A man dressed in slacks and a stained white dress shirt approached and spoke to Stevie in rapid-fire Mandarin. I was once again lost in translation, but no matter, Stevie was taking care of business and the man, who turned out to be the manager, kept nodding his head. The specifics of the services to be provided were set. We were led over to two side-by-side tables in the center of the room then told to take off our clothes and lay face down. I followed Stevie's lead, quickly stripped down to nothing and hopped on the table, pulling the large towel over my butt.

A minute later someone showed up to start my treatment. Since I was now facing down, my only view through the donut hole was the ceramic tile floor. I was curious to see who'd be working on me and rolled over slightly to take a peek. Standing next to me was a very short, slightly plump woman, possibly 50 or 60 years old. I was still confused and found myself at a loss for words, so I just smiled at her. She was looking right at me, but there was absolutely no facial expression or return gesture. I smiled once more, this time showing teeth but again no response. I thought, *Have I somehow offended her? Maybe she doesn't like massaging Americans because we're larger—too much real estate?* I looked over at Stevie who was smiling like the boy who got a pony for his birthday.

He said, "Ta1 yi4 chu1 sheng1 jiu4 shi1 ming2 le5."

I understood the first part, something like "from birth", but I didn't catch the last few words.

He saw the puzzled look on my face and said in English, "She blind."

A blind masseuse, really? No wonder she didn't respond.

Stevie spoke to her in Chinese. I assumed he was giving instructions.

She started at my feet and worked her way up. In lieu of the relaxing and soothing long firm strokes from a sweet petite Asian girl with soft hands, I was getting very painful short thrusts and finger probes that felt like karate chops with nothing held back. Her strong rough and calloused hands searched for muscles and tendons. Forget working slowly and gingerly to loosen up the tight areas, she jabbed her fingers deep into the tissues with all her might.

Now I understood why I was hearing all the sonorous grunting. I didn't want this diminutive Chinese woman to laugh at the big strong American, who turned out to be an even bigger pussy, so I didn't complain. I was determined to lay there and take whatever she dished out.

After 45 minutes the assault stopped. Relieved my misery was over, I started to raise my aching body off the table, but a hand on my back pushed me down—a much stronger hand.

Did Stevie finish first and he's screwing with me?

Next thing I knew, my masseuse had climbed on the table and stepped onto my back. I twisted my head slightly and saw that Stevie was still lying on the table next to me. Likewise, there was a woman standing on the mountain of muscles that was his back. But contrary to me, the look on Stevie's face was pure ecstasy.

Okay, this should be interesting.

While walking on my back, my masseuse periodically stopped at selected points to dig her toes into the various joints, muscle groups and the numerous vertebrae. *Yee-ouch!* Simultaneously, a second male masseur was working on my neck and shoulders. His hands were much more forceful than the blind lady's. In just a few minutes, his vigorous technique had pushed me well past my threshold for pain.

I'd been worked over for almost an hour, completely stressed out, trying my best not to scream out in agony. It was finally over…*Or is it?* I remembered Stevie had also ordered me a famous Chinese foot massage. I was not too happy seeing that the man with the vice-grip hands would be the one to rub my feet.

Stevie saw my expression, flashed a thumbs-up and said, "This guy really good!"

All right, I made it through the body beating, how bad can this be?

He dug his fingers deep into the tissues of my sole and a keg-of-dynamite pain exploded in my foot. This time a grunt would not suffice. I let out a muffled scream. He didn't even look up.

Maybe he's deaf? Does this place systematically hire the handicapped?

I tensed up so much that I wrenched a muscle in my neck. He seemed oblivious to my suffering and continued his assault using both thumbs to manipulate every joint and muscle in my foot. If the Chinese had used this method to extract information from their Japanese prisoners, they might not have been defeated in WWII.

Linda once told me about the health benefits of a foot massage. She added, "You no experience pain if organs all healthy."

I figured my body must be in such bad shape I could keel over dead any moment; in fact, I was already having visions of the afterlife.

There are 33 joints, 36 muscles, 56 ligaments and over 7,000 nerve endings in each foot. I had no doubt that my masseur had hit them all. When he finally stopped the torment, it was about as close to a religious experience as I'd ever had.

Please God, is he done? Of course not.

I was about to swing my feet off the table and hobble for the exit when he started on my ankles. He rubbed them so hard I thought he'd pull the skin off. His hands felt like an iron vice. He worked from the top of my ankles down to the heels. The pressure was so great I was concerned he'd crush some of the bones in my feet.

After 15 minutes of pure agony, he finished; this time for good. I had tears running down my cheeks. *Will I be able to walk? Or will they have to gurney me out to an ambulance?*

But the strangest thing happened: I stood up, got dressed, and headed toward the front door...*Wow! Feels like I'm walking on a cloud.* My feet had never felt so good! And you can damn well bet they'll never feel that good again. I'm not a masochist and not that brave.

I reached for my wallet to pay the manager, but Stevie stepped in front of me with a fistful of yuan.

"No, no, no, Shan Mu. Like I say, I *treat*." He giggled like a mental patient.

So that's what he meant, I thought, feeling buffoonish. I didn't know if I should thank him or punch him in the face.

During lunch, at the restaurant next door, as I mulled over in my mind the spa torture chamber, something occurred to me: *Was this all set up by Linda, with unsuspecting Stevie acting as her accomplice? Was she trying to circumvent any unsupervised visits to a sex spa?*

All I knew for sure was I'd never again go for a Chinese massage without her. So, either way, I guess you could say that Linda had the happy ending.

32. The Mountain of Youth

At 7:00 AM, on a typical hot and sweltering summer day in Taipei, I was awakened by the sound of the shower; opened one eye a crack; saw steam billowing out the bathroom entrance. I was still groggy from our late-night romp through the Raohe night market where we shopped for souvenirs and finished up the evening with candied strawberries on a stick, purchased from a street vendor.

I sat up, leaned forward, and peeked into the bathroom. Through a dense fog I caught the faint outline of Linda's naked and inviting frame. She took two or three seemingly endless hot showers a day. On a monthly basis she probably used more water than a small town.

"Honey, why are you up so early? We didn't get in until after 2:00 AM. Come back to bed," I begged, hoping she too was in the mood.

She flicked on the hair dryer and said, "Ben4 dan4 (Stupid egg), you forget? This morning meet three girlfriends. Go Dim Sum eat."

"I don't think they'll mind if you're a few minutes late," I pleaded, watching her reflection in the mirror from the angle I had, perfect breasts jiggling with each movement.

"No can be late. Yao Yao just find out she pregnant. I still need buy her celebrate gift."

"How about a 'quickie gift' for your husband?" I inquired, awash in desire.

"You go sleep. Tonight, need much energy. Satisfy wife," she teased.

Linda threw on a white linen sleeveless dress that exposed her shoulders and accentuated every curve of her lithe body, tormenting me some more.

At the door, she turned and tapped her forehead with her knuckles. "Oh…Sam, almost forget. Today Stevie take you hike. Better get ass in gear. He come soon. Have fun. Remember tiger, no make too tired for hot date."

Great, I shook my head. *Only four hours of sleep, and now I'll be punished in 100-degree heat by my gung-ho brother-in-law.*

Still aroused, thanks to my steamy wife, I turned the shower to its coldest setting and jumped in. Ten minutes later I was dressed.

There was a loud knock at the door. Stevie opened it himself and called out, "Shan Mu ready?"

I could see he was euphoric at the prospect of pushing his muscular body to its limit.

In preparation for the taxing climb, we stopped at the corner vendor where I devoured three breakfast sandwiches with a glass of bing1 dou4 jiang1 (cold soybean milk). Stevie, I think showing off, just had a cup of tea. "Shan Mu, we walk to mountain now."

"How long will it take to get there?" I asked.

"Thirty minutes. Okay to go, my man?"

I wanted to suggest a taxi but knew mucho macho Stevie wouldn't go for it.

"Lead the way bro," I conceded.

It was only 8:00 AM, and the air was already thick with humidity. Soon the heat would start to build, amplified by the activation of millions of air-conditioning units spitting out hot air, turning the city into a huge urban blast furnace.

Our route took us past the Taipei 101 skyscraper and through several old neighborhoods to a small side street that dead ended at a set of stairs cut into the vertical stone of the Four Beasts Mountains.

"OK, I lead, you follow. Try keep up, Captain America," Stevie joked. Given his daily workouts at the gym, Stevie fancied himself a sort of Asian Superman.

"Piece of cake," I replied, slightly worried he might leave me in his dust.

Then he asked, "Shan Mu, if you Captain America, who me?"

I took in his five-foot-even stature and said, "Mighty Mouse."

The look on his face told me Stevie wasn't thrilled with my super-hero selection, and he bounded up the steps picking up speed as he went.

Probably should've told him "Rambo"—my bad.

There was a man about 30 steps ahead. He seemed to sense Stevie and me closing the gap, and he began moving at a faster clip, pulling away from us. Stevie accelerated his pace, as if he'd been sent a challenge. We were only 10 minutes into the ascent, and I was already huffing and puffing. With the temperature rising, beads of perspiration were turning into a torrent of sweat. I kept all my focus on each step trying to avoid tripping and falling onto the stone path, splitting open my knee—or worse yet, tumbling back down the mountain. I could also hear Stevie breathing hard. Linda had informed me that her super jock brother made this trek at least twice a week. From the sounds coming out of his mouth, it was evident his normal weekly climbs were not this intense.

I increased my tempo, eyes fixated on my feet, completely oblivious to my surroundings. We were now twenty minutes into the climb, both gasping for air, trying to stay close to the front runner. I looked up to catch a glimpse of the fearless leader, who was still ascending like a bat out of hell and saw a pair of sun-tanned legs dominated by massive calf muscles that bulged with every step.

Continuing up the mountain we passed three rest stops, but the speed demon zipped right on by them. If he didn't rest, we'd follow suit, surging toward the summit at breakneck speed.

The competition was heating up. Stevie was clearly intent on not only catching but passing. And that's when Iron Man found an even higher gear. As if he'd been toying with us, he pulled away like we were standing still.

A half hour later we reached the summit. Stevie and I were both bent over, gasping for air. My heart was beating like a race horse in the home stretch at Belmont. Bro and I plotzed on the ground, completely spent.

Except for the stone path itself, I hadn't seen squat all the way up. When I caught my breath, curiosity drove me to stand up and survey my surroundings. The view was stunning. The Taipei 101 tower took center stage with the entire city virtually sitting at my feet. I turned to the right and saw an old man sitting on a boulder, eyes closed in a meditative posture. He looked as if he'd been up here for some time. I wondered how a person of his advanced age could've made it to the top without the help of his children, grandchildren, or great-grandchildren to assist him. I looked 360 trying to spot the marathon man, but he was nowhere, as if having disappeared into thin air. There was only one way back down: same as up. My attention turned back to the ancient on the rock when he stood up and stretched. I scanned the old geezer head to toe: White scraggly hair; wizened face with deep crevices; 8-inch wispy beard; skinny arms; no chest to speak of; pencil thin torso, supported by—and there they were—massive calf muscles. "That's the guy we couldn't catch?" I said to Stevie, who by this time had figured it out as well and was shaking his head in wonderment.

Stevie went to converse with the old man. A minute later he waived me over to fill me in. Turned out the old boy lived in a neighborhood next to the mountain. After his retirement, 24 years ago, fresh air and daily exercise was his ticket to staying healthy. “He climb five time every week.” Stevie informed me.

Our leader, who I nicknamed “The Flash”, was 89 years old. He nudged Stevie and said, “Mei3 guo2 chao1 ji2 ying1 hong2 bu2 shi4 na4 me chao1.” They both burst out laughing.

“What’s so funny?” I asked.

“He say, 'American super hero not so super."

“Hey, Mighty Mouse,” I retorted, “you weren’t able to catch him either.”

Stevie and I were starving and grabbed something to eat as soon as we got down the mountain. I called the wife on my cell and told her to go ahead and have dinner on her own—which by now ever-hungry Linda had already done. One thing that hadn’t cooled off throughout the long, strenuous day was my libido, and I reminded Linda of her promise.

When I got home, she’d already negligeed up, and was smokin’ hot ready for our X-rated date. Alas, it was not meant to be. My attempt to consummate was bushwhacked by severe cramps in—you guessed it—my Captain America calves.

33. The Hatfields vs. The McCoys

Other than Samantha's birthday, Thanksgiving was the only day of the year I insisted the family get together to celebrate a slice of Americana. For my Chinese in-laws, it was a welcomed excuse to have another multi-course feast. This year, however, I had serious misgivings since the Lowe and Liu families would be dining together for *the first time*. In fact, this would be my parents' introduction to Linda's family, and vice versa.

We'd just returned home from our third trip to Taiwan. The holiday was three days away. Mom and Dad would arrive tomorrow morning and spend a week with us. My sister Gail and her husband Alex were also flying in from San Francisco.

Dad called me the night before to chat and confirm their itinerary, then turned the phone over to Mom.

She opened with, "I'm terrified about this trip. With the language barrier and cultural differences, how the hell are your dad and I supposed to communicate with *those* people? There should be a law: Immigrants must pass an English proficiency test before they're allowed to step foot on U.S. soil."

"Mom, don't worry, except for Linda's mother, they all speak passable English. But if you have any problem understanding, Linda and I will translate. Actually, my Mandarin's getting pretty darn good," I replied, hoping to impress.

She let out a sigh of exasperation. "We expected you to marry a nice Jewish girl. Instead of learning that China-gibberish, your second language should've been Hebrew, and we'd have our *own kind* to kibbutz with."

My parents, Sydney and Beatrice, were shell-shocked when I told them I was going to marry not only a gentile but an Asian one, to boot. Nothing I said could change Mom's opinion that Linda was an illegal alien using her son to snag a U.S. residency.

When I first told them about Linda, Mom said, "Sam, this Chinese thing is just a phase. You'll quickly outgrow it, like at fifteen when you up and stopped playing with your collection of Marvel action figures."

But smitten to the end, I refused to give up my China doll.

After Linda and I tied the knot, my parents summarily declined all my invitations to visit us at the Manhattan apartment. We'd since moved to a house in Roslyn, Long Island that had a big backyard, equipped with a swing set, for our little girl to play with friends.

Mom's long-standing shibboleth went: "I've tried, God knows I've tried, but I just can't forgive you for marrying a non-Jew, let alone a non-white."

I didn't get the last part, since Linda is much whiter than me. As for Dad, he was smart enough to Switzerland it, stay out of the fray, refusing to take sides.

But Mom did a 360 after Samantha was born. My mother couldn't resist lavishing (read: spoiling) baby Samantha with copious amounts of grandparental affection. And at the same time, allowing just a smidgen of love in her heart for the woman who co-produced Gramma's new obsession.

I picked up my parents at LaGuardia Airport in the early morning, two days before the big event. Driving back, Dad kept mostly silent while Mom rambled on and on about the preparation of her favorite holiday recipes.

“Sam, how many of them are coming?” she inquired in a deprecating manner.

“Well, we’re 2.5 with Samantha, then there’s you and Dad, Gail and Alex and six more from Linda’s family. So, it looks like there’ll be twelve mouths to feed,” I informed her.

“How much does a Chinese person eat?" Mother worried. "Do they even know what a turkey is? I heard they only eat rice and noodles. Maybe we should order in some Egg Foo Young and Chicken Chow Mein just in case?”

“Please, relax Mom. I’m sure they’ll like whatever you make. And yes, they have turkeys in Taiwan. They also have electricity and indoor plumbing.” I shook my head, stupefied by her questions.

When we arrived at the house, Linda was waiting to greet my parents. But when Mom saw Samantha, she brushed right past her as if my wife was invisible.

Gail and Alex landed two hours later, and I returned to LaGuardia, hitting heavy traffic all the way home.

We entered the house through the garage, and I found Mom in the kitchen pacing back and forth in a frenzied manner, clearly anxious about meeting her new in-laws.

"What took you so long?" she said, annoyed by the delay.

"Mom cool your jets. Linda's family won't be here for another forty-eight hours."

"Okay, let's move on," she said, taking up her role as Supreme Commander. "We need to set the Thanksgiving dinner plans. Alex will be my second in charge, and I'll assign everyone their individual tasks. Lots to do—not a lot of time."

When it came to cooking, my brother-in-law was by far the best in the family—and he was not the least bit modest about it. He'd never cooked professionally, but still fancied himself the next Jean Georges. When Alex was in the kitchen, it was his way or the highway. Overall, we got along fine—except for those times he became Analman. Less than a minute after arriving, I caught him staring, transfixed, out a back window, at my brand-new professional series Viking gas grill. It was built into an outside kitchen and stood proudly atop a bluestone patio.

"Pretty sweet, huh?" I asked, expecting some love.

"I can't cook the turkey on that commercialized hunk of metal!" He threw his hands up in utter frustration. "Sam, you have to go out, right now, and buy a *real* grill. If you want the bird cooked properly, I need a thirty-two-inch Komodo Kamado!"

I swallowed my pride and called BBQ Hut. They had just one left in the store. But I went from relief to almost shitting my shorts—it was their most expensive model.

"Do you know how much one of those friggin' things costs?" I squawked after hanging up. "If you can't cook on my Viking, or in the oven, why don't *you* pay for it?"

"*Me* pay for it?" he said, shocked at my request. "All those times you came to our house for Thanksgiving, did I ever ask you to reimburse me the out-of-pocket for *my* Kamado?"

Linda sensed I was about to explode. She pulled me aside and laid down the law: "This first Thanksgiving together. Buy the damn grill, Sam!"

An hour later my credit card choked down the $4,995 purchase. I did the mental math: Estimating we'd need somewhere around a 20 lb. turkey, that's $250 per pound. Dividing that further by 16 ounces, then subtracting the bones…*E-gad! That's about $25 dollars per bite. We're eating Dom Perignon meat!*

When I returned to the house, Mom was waiting in the kitchen, ready to talk turkey, literally. "Okay Sam, with twelve people at one and a half pounds per person, and planning for leftovers, we'll need at least a twenty-four-pound bird. Now, Alex can cook it on that exorbitantly priced oriental toy you bought yourself. I assume that's what *those people* cook on, wherever it is they come from."

"Mom, the Kamado is a *Japanese* grill," I corrected her. "Linda's family is from Taiwan. They are *Chinese*."

"Chinese, Japanese, Pekingese…What's the difference? They all look the same to me," she said with a dismissive shrug.

Oh-boy, this is going to be some fun, I winced inwardly.

Alex's fuel preference was a combination of coals and Jack Daniels Whiskey Barrel Smoking Chips. The finished product had a crispy golden-brown crust with a smoky-juicy interior. He was indeed a grill master, especially when cooking on the Kamado. Over the past several Thanksgivings at Alex and Gail's home, the turkey was always as tender as butter.

Mom would prepare her famous carrot ring; a green bean casserole with a fried onion topping; homemade mushroom, sausage and bread stuffing to be cooked in the bird; and mashed potatoes with gravy. And lest we forget: the hallowed jelly cranberry sauce (made by Ocean Spray and comes in a can).

This would be her first Thanksgiving cooking for her Asian in-laws, and it was crucial that she made a superb American presentation. My constant raving about Chinese cuisine had clearly set up a challenge to prove her United States of America food was just as good—if not better. This year everything had to be spot-on.

The next morning, Linda, Mom, Gail and Alex went shopping to pick up the ingredients for the traditional holiday feast, including the pre-ordered free-range organic heritage turkey. I stayed behind with Dad. Sydney was craving some bonding time with his granddaughter, since Mom generally hogged all of Samantha's attention.

I was well aware there'd be far too much food, and after polishing off the last piece of pumpkin or pecan pie, everyone would regret how much they ate. The over-consumption would last for several days starting with the initial grand slam dinner followed by countless meals where the remaining turkey was recycled into a seemingly endless succession of sub-entrees including: sandwiches, pot pies, burgers, meat loaf, meat balls, hash, chili, etc. I imagined that Linda's family would call dibs on the bones, as a base for their beloved Swamp Soup.

At 2:30 PM, I heard the garage door open. Linda pulled in with our SUV grocery-bagged to the ceiling. She had already stocked the pantry with snacks, appetizers, hors d'oeuvres, munchies, etc., in anticipation of my family's arrival. Everything purchased today were "must have items" needed by Mom for her Thanksgiving recipes. The enormous pile of foodstuffs stacked on the kitchen counter triggered a childhood flash back…

I was sitting with my sister at the kitchen table when Dad chastised us for not finishing the food on our plates: "You two are spoiled rotten. Did you know millions of children are starving to death in Africa?"

Of course those kids were starving. We gluttonous Americans were hoarding all the food!

At 7:00 AM, the following morning, ye old caffeine junkie, headed downstairs for my morning fix. When I entered the kitchen, I was surprised to find Mom, Gail and Alex already hard at work prepping for tonight's edacious event. Moments later Linda popped in to join the prep crew. Alex was seasoning his turkey, Gail was peeling potatoes, and Mom was grating carrots for her signature carrot ring. Linda started on her assignment, washing and slicing the French green beans for the casserole.

Having mastered the toaster, they now trusted me with my second recently developed culinary skill: operating the electric can opener. I deftly removed the lids to two cans of Ocean Spray jellied cranberry sauce, exclaiming with mock-pride, “Hey, where's my tall white hat?” As it slid out of its metal container, I heard that classic sucking sound. Mom directed me to slice it along the rings formed by the ribbed interior to reduce its industrial appearance.

Alex refused to eat processed food. All the dishes he prepared were made from scratch using only fresh ingredients. In general, I'd agree that fresh is the better choice, but when it comes to cranberry sauce…Bravo! Ocean Spray, you truly got it right. The sweet and tart flavors coupled with a melt-in-your-mouth texture provide the perfect pairing with all the Thanksgiving trimmings.

I'm pretty sure I inherited my culinary ineptitude from Dad. His explicit job was "staying out of the way". But Syd wasn't complaining about the kitchen being no dad's land, since it afforded him more baby-holding time.

Just before returning the seasoned turkey back to the refrigerator, Alex stuffed it half full with Mom's special filling, leaving space for the smoky flavor from the BBQ to penetrate its interior cavity. He'd later mix the delicious contents with stuffing prepared on the stovetop, spreading out and softening the intense flavors into a greater volume.

By noon, all the prep work was completed. The only thing left was the final assembly and cooking of the side dishes in the oven; and the turkey in the Kamado.

Everyone was near-death exhausted, and with a long day of cooking, eating and cleaning still ahead of us, we all decided to go upstairs for a short siesta.

Prior to our nap, Linda called Big Sister Sarah and said in Chinese—translated as follows: "Hi Sis, everything's ready to go, but Sam's family is spent. We need to catch a few winks before dinner. Please bring the family over at 5:00 PM sharp."

My in-laws apparently couldn't tell time; Ma & Co. arrived at 2:00 PM. They had a spare key, (standard Chinese protocol—*your casa, mi casa*), walked into my abode as if it was their own, and headed straight for the kitchen.

Sarah opened the refrigerator and saw the turkey, grated carrots, sliced green beans and peeled potatoes we'd prepared. She first pulled out the big bird not knowing it'd been seasoned by Alex with his secret sauce coating.

Ma and Sarah had prepared various items for the feast even though Linda specifically told them we'd have plenty and not to bring anything.

The exact translation of her words: "Listen to me, Ma and Sarah, Sam's mother is cooking a traditional Thanksgiving dinner. Please do not bring *any* Chinese food!" Which, in hindsight, would be like telling Wyatt Earp and Doc Holiday not to bring any shotguns and six-shooters to the OK Corral.

So naturally they brought a feast of dark green Chinese vegetables, three roast ducks, jars of spices and fermented vegetables; and for dessert, Ma made a pot of her famous 'hong2 dou4 tang1' (red bean soup) with chunks of sweet yam added for a festive twist. Just like Mom, my mother-in-law wanted to make a good impression on her Caucasian relatives—and the duel was on.

Ma opened a jar of a dark rich marinade she'd prepared by mixing together soy sauce, Chinese five spice powder, black pepper and enough garlic to wipe out Transylvania's entire vampire population, then spread the mixture over the exterior of the turkey. She also lifted the skin in various places to cram in more garlic. After the marinade was applied, she looked inside the turkey and saw there was still some empty space. Ma pulled out another large jar containing her own homemade Asian stuffing. The mixture included dried black mushrooms and shrimp, thinly sliced Chinese sausage, minced garlic, green onions, water chestnuts, chopped cilantro, oyster sauce, soy sauce, white pepper and cooked white rice. She spooned out Mom's traditional stuffing and packed hers in until every crevice was filled. Afterwards, Sarah and Tina hoisted the heavy bird back into the refrigerator.

Next, Ma took out the carrots, green beans and potatoes and carried them to the reconfigured Chinese kitchen to be included as ingredients in some of her dishes.

It was already 3:30 PM and none of her sleeping in-laws had stirred. With all the ingredients surrounding her, the urge to cook was overpowering. She could no longer wait. Ma opened a large plastic bag filled with several live crustaceans and began making her specialty, Cantonese lobster.

Her cold and cruel killing technique, the preferred Chinese method, was to shove a chopstick up the lobster's anus through the intestines, heart and brain and out the head. She brutally executed them one by one, oblivious to their frantic squirming. What a ghastly way to go. Even the horrific beheadings by Muslim fundamentalists seems more humane. I do lobster American-style: Drop them into a pot of boiling water, slam the lid on, then run from the kitchen so I don't have to listen to the high-pitched whine I assume is the lobsters' death throes.

Ma used a meat cleaver to chop the still-writhing crustaceans into large chunks; coated them with an egg wash, then dragged each piece through a mix of flour, salt and pepper. They were then dropped into the wok and removed partially cooked. The final step: Chopped garlic…*of course;* plus, ginger, oyster sauce and scallions were plopped into fresh hot oil, and the lobster's tossed back in.

Strong smells were drifting upstairs. I snapped awake, instantly knowing that Linda's mom, against orders, was busy doing her thing. I woke everyone else, and my entire clan hurried downstairs to meet the Asians.

The Liu's were lined up in the living room facing the Lowes. Linda acted as the Master of Ceremonies and introduced each person, zigzagging from one side to the other. For her family, she gave both their Chinese name and my English nickname. Big Sister (Sarah) was at the end of the line, next to Ma, whispering the translation into her ear. The final introduction was Mom and Ma who were facing each other.

Mom, thinking she was paying a compliment, popped off with, "What lovely names you Orientals have."

A sea of frowns crossed my in-law's faces. And Ma's darkened severely after hearing the translation.

Mom looked at me guilelessly. "What? What'd I say? What's wrong?"

"Mother," I said kindly, "they don't like being called 'Orientals'."

"Why? They're from the Orient," Mom insisted, "that's what they are."

"No," I explained. "Their rugs are oriental; the people are *Asian*. It's like calling us Himeys, Kikes, Yidiots, Hooknoses, Jew Yorkers..."

"Enough already," Mom huffed. "I got the picture."

"Okay, but I think, in good faith, you should apologize to Linda's mom."

Beatrice was incensed by this suggestion and shot Ma a hard look. "I shall do no such thing. It was an honest mistake."

"WHAT THE FUCK!" issued from the kitchen, shattering the tension, then raising it to a new high. Alex had been anxious to get started and had drifted over to the fridge.

Everyone turned to see him holding the aluminum pan that bore his prized bird.

"Who the goddamn hell tampered with my turkey?" he demanded to know, emphatically kicking the refrigerator door shut behind him with his heel.

I swear, the look on his face was as if he were holding a dead baby. His *piece de resistance* was now nothing more than a big hunk of garlic-reeking meat.

Alex set down the foul fowl (How could I resist that one?) and jabbed a finger at Ma and her girls. "*They* did this! Damn it, they ruined my turkey, ruined our dinner, and ruined the holiday!" He turned to me and growled, "Sam, I demand an apology from that Mongol horde you invited!"

"Ta1 shuo1 shen2 me5?" ("What did he say?") Ma asked Sarah.

After she got the translation her face turned red with rage. "Dao4 qian4? Men2 dou1 mei2 you3!" ("Apologize? Not a chance in hell!")

Mom went directly to the refrigerator and flung the door open to discover all her prepped vegetables had also disappeared. The only thing still standing was a plate with the cranberry sauce, jiggling by itself on an otherwise empty shelf.

"Where the hell are my carrots and green beans?" she shrieked, realizing they too fell victim to the Asian in-law interference. "Who do you people think you are?"

Ma, Sarah, Tina and Joan were receiving fierce, hateful stares from Mom and Alex. My mother-in-law shot back her infamous evil eye, which I could see unnerved my family. Fortunately, her lobster cleaver was out of reach or I'm sure she would've been brandishing it.

Linda jumped into the middle of the war zone and pleaded to the group, "Please. Now all one family. This no big problem."

Ma rattled off in Chinese and Big Sister, equally angry, translated: "White devil family insult us. We no stay unless get apology."

KABOOM! Mom gave them her own Jewish version of the evil eye and shot back, "No way am I apologizing to this family of heathens." She turned to Dad and said, "Sydney, get on the phone right now and book the next flight out. We're outta here unless *we* get an apology!"

The gauntlets were thrown down and utter chaos ensued. The Liu's began pointing fingers and jabbering in Mandarin at my family, who took up the challenge and shouted accusations and insults back. The verbal shootout raised in tempo until it reached a fever pitch that threatened to break the sound barrier.

I was heartsick at my failure to bring the two families together, and was just about to yell, "Screw it all!" and leave myself, when Linda, still in the eye of the hurricane, screamed above everybody else, "I pregnant!"

It was like a neutron bomb, silencing the room. The look of shock on everyone's face was priceless. But let me tell you, nobody was more surprised than me. Still, I was the first to speak.

"When were you planning to tell me?"

"I want surprise all family at dinner," she said with the saddest puppy dog eyes that melted everybody's heart.

What followed looked like a rugby scrum with each person, all at the same time, struggling to hug Linda and extend their loving congratulations.

While this was going on, I spotted a gallon jar sitting on a table by the back door, filled with a clear liquid. "This calls for a toast," I announced.

I brought out 12 shot glasses and filled them to the brim. "Linda and I are truly blessed to have both our families here today to celebrate this wonderful news." I held up my glass and the others followed suit. "Here's to the new addition," I said, patting Linda's tummy.

And with that, all in attendance downed their shot. For the Liu's it was like drinking Kool-Aid; whereas every member of the Lowe clan, me included, coughed and gagged on the "oriental" moonshine.

I realized my mistake and grabbed Linda's arm a second before she was about to down her shot of the nasty. "Honey, you can't drink that! Who knows what kind of deformities that rotgut will cause?"

"Oh...uh…yes...you so right, I no think," she said with a look of sheer disappointment.

What happened next would have brought tears to your eyes. The kitchen became a blur as both families, like the staff of a five-star restaurant, pitched in and worked together to prepare the feast.

More Gaoliang was consumed while we waited on the bird. Fortunately, the Komado did its job in half the time, or we would've all been too drunk to eat it.

At last, Alex made the announcement: "It's turkey time!" He put it on a cutting board and started carving.

Ma, Sarah, Joan and Tina filed out of the Chinese-American kitchen, each carrying a different dish: four kinds of green vegetables, a mixture of shredded pork and sliced bamboo, fried cubes of tofu breaded in a Japanese panko and smothered in a sweet tangy sauce; and finally, a large plate piled high with slices of roast duck that Sydney practically polished off all by himself.

My brother-in-law seemed to have forgotten that my mother-in-law had sabotaged his turkey. He had three helpings that evening. Alex was too arrogant to come right out and admit how much he liked Ma's doctoring. But the following year, we learned through the family scuttlebutt, he used Ma's special marinade to prepare a turkey for his brother's annual BBQ party back in San Francisco.

And Mom? Well, I spied her sneaking seconds on the lobster.

We had a rocky start, but Linda saved the day. Our disparate families buried the cleaver and came together in peace and harmony to share an East meets West Thanksgiving smorgasbord.

On the way out the door, Ma paused to give Beatrice a goodbye bear hug, causing Mom's eyes to pop out of her head cartoon style. Love and affection? Or could it have been the residual effects from the booze?

“Time to hit the sack,” I said, faking a yawn. I was anxious to celebrate one-on-one with my wife and the second heir to the Lowe family name.

Linda disappeared upstairs after a very brief goodnight to my parents. I though it slightly rude, but she was with child and raging hormones often lead to abrupt mood swings. From now until the baby arrived, she'd always be given special treatment.

When I walked into our room, Linda, appearing lost in thought, was sitting on the edge of the bed. She seemed a bit nervous, fidgeting with her wedding band.

“Sweetie, close door. Need say something,” she said with a slight quiver in her voice.

“Sweetheart, I wish you’d told me earlier about the baby,” I gushed, “but no matter, I’m absolutely thrilled. And your timing couldn’t have been better. I just want to say how much I…

“Sam, stop!" She put a hand to my mouth. “I no pregnant!”

My jaw dropped, hit the floor, and bounced back up. “What do you mean, *not* pregnant? You just told both families you *were*. Are you *sure*?”

“You think I not know, ben4 dan4!” She rolled her eyes.

That set me off. “How could you blatantly lie like that to my parents? They’ll never understand this. And what about Ma? She’ll go ballistic when she finds out. Not to mention…”

“Put a sock in it, Sam!” She stomped a foot down. “Family all want abandon ship. Someone need step up to plate.”

“So how the hell do we get ourselves out of this mess?” I demanded, still upset about the nonexistence of Little Lowe II.

"Sam’s turn at bat. Must hit home run," Linda said, stripping naked. "Now, come here slugger, put baby in me!”

EPILOGUE

In case you're wondering, I hit that home run with another player on base. Three months after our chaotic family gathering, Linda dropped the good news bomb. For real this time she was pregnant, with twins.

My transformation from Lowenstein (Jewish) to Lowe (Agnostic) to Lo (Buddhist) was now complete, altering my life for the better and sometimes the worse...

TOP 11 SIGNS THAT SAM'S CHINESE CONVERSION IS NOW COMPLETE

#11 Alcoholic tolerance exponentially elevated by exposure to Ma's homemade rocket fuel. Other uses include paint & tar remover, oven cleaner, and truth serum.

#10 Finally accustomed to home functioning like legendary Roach Hotel: Chinese in-laws check in, but they don't check out.

#9 No more indigestion having abandoned my American food shovel (i.e., the fork) for Chinese chopsticks.

#8 Tranquil weekend drives to the Hamptons replaced by densely packed carpool rides to Queens for Asian grocery restock.

#7 Instead of a domineering Jewish wife guilt-driven husband training program, I'm in the domineering Chinese wife guilt-driven husband training program. (Oops, my bad...no change.)

#6 Former boring haircuts are now salon-spa ecstasy—only downside: the creampuff hairdo.

#5 Chinese health food regimen heralds a sad goodbye to my dear old friend, the #3 Big Mac, Coca-Cola, and supersize fries.

#3 ½ Some things you just can't shake: My reading and speaking Chinese is up to 2500 characters—in-laws still tag me ben4 dan4 (stupid egg).

#3 Hooked on Mahjong—play three times a week—in the hole to Ma the equivalent of $10K in Dim Sum.

#2 Have finally developed a tolerance for foul-tasting Swamp Soup. Now just need to develop a tolerance for Ptomaine, Salmonella, and E. coli.

And the #1 sign...

To paraphrase an old Chinese proverb, if you want to be happy, do what you love. I gleefully told my Stealthanator boss, "Take this bank and shove it." Now, most evenings, yours truly is welcoming diners at NYC's new Asian fusion restaurant, Siam Sam's.

ACKNOWLEDGEMENTS

To my loving wife, Janice, for her indefatigable assistance with the Mandarin translations, but mostly for adding depth and richness to my life.

I also want to thank my dad, Seymour, for his love and support; and for taking the time to review the book to correct all my spelling and punctuation errors. The master grammarian is alive and kicking.

A big shout out to my adopted Chinese family in New York and Taipei for providing me with a treasure trove of material. You all have a special place in my heart.

To my dear friend, Harry, who nudged me to write this story; and for always telling me I was funny. When you've heard something enough times you start to believe.

Finally, I want to thank my incredible editor, Cliff Carle, for always being brutally honest when critiquing my work. Any author would be lucky to have you on board.

ABOUT THE AUTHOR

Ross Nodell was born and raised in Chicago. He relocated to New York City in the late 80s to pursue the affection of a Chinese woman. Ross worked on Wall Street before starting his own real estate investment firm. He now follows his passion as a novelist.

Ross draws material from a wealth of life experience. He has traveled extensively in Asia, hiking the Great Wall, the Peak in Hong Kong, and Yang Ming Shan National Park in Taiwan. He's a true adventure-seeker having climbed Mount Rainer in Washington State, and The Grand Teton in Wyoming; scuba dived with hammerhead sharks off the North Wall in Grand Cayman; walked Kruger National Park searching for water buffalo; biked through the South of France; windsurfed thc Maldives; and skied the black diamond runs at Jackson Hole, Wyoming, although more time was spent on his ass than his skis.

Ross has a love affair with food and wine, always seeking out new and exotic cuisines, no matter how peculiar or offensive. He brings all these experiences to his readers through the lens of a comical microscope.

Made in the USA
Columbia, SC
16 January 2019